La Belle
Communauté

DEBORAH R. PROCOPIO

In memory of Lou and Joan Procopio, who lost the unwinnable war.

In honor of Mom and Dad. You guys did a great job raising a stubborn child!

Dedication: This book is dedicated to all those who have cared for family members living with dementia. No one knows the difficulties, pain, heartbreak, and frustration you witness each day as you watch your loved one slowly slip away. It is also dedicated to the staff of memory care and nursing home facilities everywhere who care for our families when it is no longer possible for us to do so.

And of course to Tom, the other half of Team Procopio, who has made this crazy life one of love and laughter.

Special thanks to Mary Koenig, Malgorzata (Margaret) Swieton, aka "Goof Ball," Brian Williams, and the entire staff at The Heritage in Syracuse, New York, who have done more than feed and clothe our parents. They laugh with them when they are happy, hug them when they cry in the midst of confusion and homesickness, and visit them at the nursing home on their own time. You guys are our rock stars!

Thank You, Lord, for the creative ideas in the night season!

Chapter 1

It was a beautiful late spring day in the small upstate New York village of Avion, its quaint Main Street evidence of days gone by. The village was one of many across New York that sprung up in the 1800s along the Erie Canal. Interconnected three-and-four-story red brick buildings still line the street with all their early settler charm. What were once mercantiles, cobblers, ironmongers, and milliner stores are now trendy coffee shops, chocolatiers, boutiques, florists, and bistros. The merchants do an impressive job making sure their first floor storefronts are beautifully painted and adorned with flowers. Across the street sits Crystal Spring Pond. I pulled the car into the south parking area. I'd been by the pond numerous times in my life, but never stopped.

"Do you think the swans are here today?" Mom asked.

"I don't know," I said, "let's go have a look."

Mom and I stepped up to the black wrought iron fence. Sure enough, a pair of mute swans with three cygnets were gently paddling their way around the pond. The little feathered family glided along the perimeter hoping those gathered on the railing would release the next air drop of pellets.

The pond itself was an oval that stretched half a block. In the midst of the aquatic landscape was a plume tree fountain. Its narrow, round spray giving the appearance of a tree as it rises and falls, hence the name.

Mom was well acquainted with the place, so she headed up the sidewalk to get feed. As my eyes followed her path along the railing, I couldn't help but notice the inconsistencies in the fencing. Two sections looked like old medieval style fence with level spears set atop the posts that would be best used for impaling Dracula. Other sections of fencing were a simple spearless flat top, but the faded, peeling black paint led me to believe some sections were older than others. Perhaps it was age? Or maybe it was winter salt spray from the road maintenance that forced sections to be replaced? Then again, maybe the village planning board had recognized that no one could safely feed the water fowl with the spears in the way.

The sun glimmering off the water created flashes of light that swayed in sync with the rhythm of the fountain ripples. Spectators squinted as flares ricocheted off the cement and bounced around the pool. Spires of emerald green vegetation sprouted upward from the stony bottom, giving the illusion that the pond was rather shallow, but as I strolled along toward the fountain, the seaweed cleared out and the pond deepened.

I caught up to Mom at the feed machines situated in front of the fountain. She was now giving me the shake down for quarters.

"Honey, I didn't bring my purse. Do you have any quarters?"

I scrounged around in my pocket and dropped two into her awaiting hand. I leaned on the flat rail and watched the fountain.

Stones terraced upward from the depths of the pond with four tiers rising above the water line.

Within the top tier sat the fountain halo that released several small streams of water ten feet into the air. I watched as the halo ejected the water upward until the streams became a cloud of spray at the apex. A warm southerly breeze dispersed the cloud into a fine mist, creating a faint rainbow before the whole thing came crashing down into the moat. The water made its way through two small valleys in the rocks and back to the pond creating a constant rhythm of aquatic sight and sound.

Metal clinked on metal as Mom slid the quarters into the feed dispenser. As she twisted the handle, I heard the familiar sounds of a gumball machine and turned my focus back to her. With her hands full of feed, she headed up the pond. I decided to drop another quarter in and get a handful for myself.

I watched Mom as she threw a few nuggets out to the swans. She now had their undivided attention. I couldn't deny it, the babies were cute. Their hopeful little black eyes were peering up from their fuzzy silver-gray feathers, beckoning Mom to drop the next round. Judging by their diminutive size, I guessed they hadn't been in the world long, and this was likely one of their early swims. I released a few pellets and watched as they dropped downward while Mom continued her walk along the fence, cooing to the little family as she went.

They were happily floating along following her. I decided to have a seat on one of the worn wooden benches that lined the sidewalk. When she got to the end of the pond, she stopped again to feed them and converse with mom and dad swan.

"Your little babies are beautiful," she told them. "You're doing such a good job. Keep it up. They grow up so fast, and will be as beautiful as you before long."

Mom. The voice of continual encouragement.

On the ride over she informed me that she probably wouldn't be able to go too far. Mom was in her early eighties and had struggled with lupus for decades. The disease caused inflammation in her joints and left her extremely sensitive to sunlight. This combination sometimes meant an outside jaunt was limited. I assured her that she would be the pace-setter, making it her call for when she'd had enough. And yet, in typical "mom fashion," she kept walking with the swans in tow until she got to the opposite side of the pond.

I left the bench and passed the newly planted "Easy Wave" pink petunias, jogging to catch up to her. As I rounded the north end of the pond, the concrete sidewalks gave way to a gray stone dust path. I followed the path and crossed a small wooden plank bridge. The footbridge was suspended over the tiny creek that helped feed the pond. When I caught up to her, she insisted I accompany her to the lower pond. I didn't know there was a lower pond.

The path guided us to a second worn wooden plank footbridge. This bridge carried us over a second small creek that was created by the overflow from the upper pond which rushed down an embankment with a border made of stones set in place like castle keeps. The cloudy gray fortified towers were framed together, escorting the waters to their assigned position in the lower pond.

As we followed the path past the brushy overgrowth, a canopy of trees rose above us to form a shady archway. It was obvious that the space was once intentionally planted, but a lack of maintenance led to a host of volunteer crops that now called the space home. Box elder and buckthorn trees were the most prominent invaders creating disorder within the landscape. Wild grapevines slithered their way across the ground overtaking irises like a thick morning fog. The vine continued its horizontal journey until it reached the spruce trees. Using its tendrils, the grapevine grasped the branches and hoisted itself skyward, weaving a tapestry through the boughs. The vine had clearly celebrated many birthdays on the trees. The canes wrapped their arms around the spruce and embraced it with a giant bear hug which caused the beauty of the spruce tree to fade into obscurity.

Surprisingly, there were sweet gum trees along the path. They are considered marginal in our area by the USDA's hardiness zone and yet, they seemed to be thriving.

Our straight stone dust path came to a fork.

"To the right," Mom said.

We went right.

She stopped and pointed through the trees. "You can park over there as well. When I come with Francesca, we park there sometimes."

Francesca is Mom's older sister. The two could pass for twins in spite of their two year age difference.

"I didn't know there was parking there, Mom."

The area has several streets that intertwine to make their way behind the pond. We walked a short distance, the lower pond now in view.

Mom stopped again and pointed across the pond and stated, "You can park over there too! Francesca parks there sometimes."

"Really? I didn't know there was parking there."

We made our way past two benches and stopped along the path to gaze at the lower pond. I spotted a wooden dock and stepped onto it. I was leaning on the well-worn rails, checking out the little island that mimicked a brushy volcano in the center of the pond when Mom spoke again.

"Honey, there's parking over there," she said pointing across the pond. "Francesca parks there sometimes."

"Maybe we'll check that out the next time we come, Mom."

And there it was. Alzheimer's.

***

Lupus produces what the medical profession call lupus fog. As a family, we had been dealing with Mom's forgetfulness for years. It was not uncommon for her to ask the same question twice. My father, brother, and I just simply answered her a second time. For us, it was the norm.

In those days, we knew nothing about lupus or the brain fog it produced. The advent of the Internet afforded us more information than we cared to know, and back then ignorance was bliss.

When Mom started exhibiting signs of dementia, I Googled lupus. I learned about the fog as well as other issues that had gone unexplained and were simply knitted into life with Mom.

This autoimmune disease had spent six decades forging its way through Mom's body. Her body was attacking itself, especially her internal organs. Medicines can only do so much and often "kick the can down the road," so to speak. It helps her feel better in the short term, but the long term effects are anybody's guess.

Shortly after Dad died, I noticed slight, intermittent hand tremors. That's when I read that the last stop for the disease was the central nervous system. The shakiness didn't worsen and for the most part, it was just an annoying reminder of a chronic illness.

According to the experts, dementia is almost a given with lupus. Mom had been telling me for a few years that she was getting bad. I kept my eye on her and her driving. The house was still neat and clean, her memory was fairly normal (for her), and the bills were paid on time. Balancing the checkbook became a challenge, but she never overdrew her account. She was having some problems adjusting to change. Things like a new TV remote or cell phone would confound her no matter how many times it was explained. And then it happened. A car accident that resulted in her old car being totaled.

I got a call on a Sunday afternoon last year in March. A man on the other end of the phone told me Mom was in an accident, but was okay. The police and ambulance were already there, and they were taking her to the hospital to be checked out. I met the EMT in the ER, who said neither Mom nor the other man, who was also in his eighties, could tell them what happened. I was hoping it wasn't Mom's fault, but my gut said otherwise. Cameras mounted outside a local business captured the entire episode. As it turned out, Mom was turning left into a shopping plaza on a busy four-lane highway. The light to go straight was green, but she had an advanced arrow which was red. Mom ran the light and was hit by oncoming traffic, resulting in a broken collar bone.

Of course she wanted another car, but I said no. I didn't want her to feel bad and tried to avoid telling her what happened. She argued, and was insistent that the accident wasn't her fault. I finally had to fess up. She didn't believe me, and the next round of arguments began.

When she finally seemed to understand that she ran the light, her reply was an angry, "Well! That didn't give him the right to hit me!"

And that ended her driving days for good. I also grasped just how bad she was getting, but I had no idea the toll that the constant running would take on me.

***

We made our way back around to the top of the pond where the car was. Mom was enjoying the beautiful day and the swans. We discussed how the swans were mates for life, and Mom decided to name them—Freddie and Frieda it was! I sat down on a bench in the sun as Mom continued her stroll along the pond, gently calling to Freddie and Frieda by name as she went. They were happy to follow her now that she had gotten another quarter's worth of pellets out of the machine.

As she continued conversing and feeding the swans, I took notice of the white golf hat she was wearing. She had the brim pulled down to shade her eyes and face. It reminded me of a similar one I had when I was four. Mine had two different colored eyeholes that I guess were supposed to be sunglasses. Pictures of me in that hat at a game farm flooded my mind. I could see me and Mom resting on a bench when a goat wandered up to us. We didn't have any food, and Mom tried to shoo it along. The goat was having none of that. Mom was sitting with her legs crossed, and the goat went for the next best thing—Mom's shoelaces! The goat grabbed the end of a lace and pulled until he untied it. My four-year-old self thought it was hysterical. Mom tied her laces only to have the goat untie it again. This little game went on a number of times with me laughing uncontrollably each time. Much to my dismay, Mom finally managed to get rid of the goat. She scooped me up into her lap, and we laughed along at the silliness.

"Look!" Mom exclaimed, pulling me out of my memory. "There's a rainbow in the fountain spray!"

"I see that!"

"You know what God says about them. He promised Noah he wouldn't flood the earth again. It was given as a sign of God's promise."

"Nice, right, Mom?" I thought to myself, *She's been telling me that my entire life. I could use a promise. Or a sign. Or both would be nice right now. Dementia is such a miserable disease.*

On that note, we decided it was time for lunch. We headed across the street to the local pizza shop which is owned by Italian immigrants. Mom left "the Old Country" when she was twelve, spending most of her life in the States. She has long since been a citizen and managed to lose her accent. She doesn't have the Mediterranean complexion and never really looked all that Italian to me, but the guy running the pizza shop took one look at her and said something in Italian.

"No," was her reply.

"Yeah right," he said. Then he looked at me and asked, "What part of Italy is she from?"

"A tiny mountain village in Campobasso," I answered as he handed me our pizza to go.

***

Mom's small three-bedroom ranch was the house I spent most of my younger years in. It was situated on over a half-acre in the middle of the suburbs, which was the selling point for my father. An avid golfer, he liked the idea of being able to whack golf balls back there.

I watched as Mom dug paper plates and drinking glasses out of the old wooden cupboards. She was a tiny thing, barely weighing a hundred pounds soaking wet. Her short, once thick, curly, jet-black hair was now thin, but still retained most of its wave and black color. For a woman of her age, she was still agile and looked younger than her years.

A deeply devout Christian, she had always spent a lot of time praying for others. In fact, praying for people was one of her favorite pastimes, and she was happy to take requests. It was not unusual for her to tell stories of what she prayed for, how God answered, and what God said.

Listening to Mom tell stories of her conversations with God made it difficult for me to sit in a church where the order of worship was the same every week: candle lighting procession, opening hymn, welcoming and announcement, another hymn, a reading from the Old Testament, a reading from the New Testament, a reading from the Gospels, a fifteen-minute message from the pastor, ending with a congregational hymn with several verses cut out for the sake of time.

No one in church ever heard anything from God that I was aware of, and I always thought that was odd. Mom never understood her impact, but she gave me a front-row seat to a God who was real, alive, and talked. There wasn't a church around that could top Mom. She really wanted us to be a churchgoing family, but the fight to get us there was too tiring, so she gave up on church—but not on God.

***

We were chatting about family and friends when Mom asked about my in-laws, Joe and Barb Preston.

Joe. Salt of the Earth is how he is often described. A natural people-person, he loved to hear other people's stories. He was attentive, kind, and gentle, and people loved him. Joe attended a local business school and eventually become a regional manager for Protection Plus Insurance Company. He was a natural who could sell ice to an Eskimo.

Barb was a horticulturist. She freelanced for wealthy people in the community and was known for her magnificent garden designs; she did everything: fountains, ponds, arbors, English gardens, topiary gardens, annuals and perennials. You name it, and she could do it. Need some interior plantscapes? She did that as well. She was highly sought after, and as a result, could name her price.

Joe and Barb had moved to La Belle Communaute' at the age of eighty. It wasn't officially a retirement community, but most of the residents were sixty-five and over. La Belle, as they call it, was a place Barb and Joe couldn't agree on. She explained that while she liked the all-inclusive resort living, which included meals served in the dining room, laundry service, cleaning service, a salon, activities and trips, she wasn't thrilled with the gated-community aspect of it. Barb admitted the building was beautiful with its stately Greek columns, Brazilian mahogany flooring, and crystal chandeliers adorning the common areas. However, she hated the drab courtyard, complaining of its lack of "appropriate gardens."

Barb loves to tell the story of how Joe finally persuaded her to move. The last stop on the tour of La Belle was at the Grande Ball Room. As they entered the room, a small, formally dressed orchestra was just finishing set up. The tour guide was completing her spiel when the orchestra began to play Strauss's "The Blue Danube." Joe gently took Barb's hand and kissed it. "Dance, Barbara Jean?" She couldn't resist—and she couldn't say no to Joe.

Each spring La Belle hosts an outdoor party to which family and friends are invited. Barb was particularly excited about this one. She gushed to us that La Belle had done extensive remodeling indoors and out. The courtyard was being transformed into an exquisite garden space. As usual, she was the guiding force and ecstatic to show off the end results.

"Well, Mom," I said, "off to another garden party."

"Wow. I'm surprised Barb is still at it. How does she do it with her arthritis as bad as it is?"

"Oh, I'm sure she managed just fine. She always does. I'll be glad when these parties are finally over with. I hate the stupid things."

"Honey, if it wasn't for Barb and her gardens, you would never have met Jim."

Jim, my husband, is the youngest of Joe and Barb's three sons.

"Yeah, you're right. I'm not sure if I should love him or hate him right now!" I said jokingly to Mom.

With a laugh she replied, "He's just like his father. A very nice man and my favorite son-in-law!" she finished with the running quip between them.

He's her favorite son-in-law, and she's his favorite mother-in-law.

I threw out my cup and plate, hugged Mom good-bye, and headed home.

Chapter 2

Mom is correct. *If it wasn't for the gardens, I would never have met Barb. If I didn't meet Barb, I wouldn't have met Jim,* I mused to myself as I drove along. I can't believe I've reached an age where I think in terms of thirty years ago, but it's been thirty-three years since I applied for a job at Sapphire Stone and Gardens.

Why the idea of hardscapes intrigued me, I'll never know, but it did. I loved the notion of building decorative brick and natural-stone walkways that would lead those who strolled on them to entryways, gardens, and patios. I loved patios that created a quiet space for people to enjoy the weather and visit with friends and family over food and drinks. I also loved retaining walls that stopped the earth in its tracks and allowed for interesting garden terraces.

At ten years old, I was mesmerized by the short, flat rock walls that surrounded an old farmhouse we passed on the way to visit my grandparents. On one particular ride, I wondered aloud, "Who dragged all those rocks to their spot and how far did they drag them?" My father explained that they were a farmer's nuisance at plowing time. The farmer simply made lemonade out of the lemons. Or an amazing wall out of fieldstones.

My brain immediately went to an episode of a dearly loved show about a family in the pioneering west that I'd watched. I could see the dad plowing with horses calling for his two girls to come pick up the rocks. In that moment, I wished I was one of them. I vowed to build that wall at my house someday.

When I got older, I loved to wander through the oldest sections of the city and gaze upon stately old homes on the tree-lined streets. Their fieldstone retaining walls showed off the styles of last century, and surrounded many of the houses in the University and Sheffield areas. More than one wall towered over my head as I walked by.

My favorite was an old, red-brick mansion that sat on a hill. It was one of several large houses that spanned both sides of the street and covered two city blocks. The homes stared at each other across a park shaded by gingko, locust, and maple trees. Today, it wouldn't fit our definition of a park, but a hundred years ago, that's what the residents called it.

"Old Red," as I called the mansion, had elongated windows placed like two rows of dominoes, one row on the bottom and one row on the top. I was sure that peering through them delivered a beautiful view of the city. The hill it sat on terraced toward the street until it was stopped by a wall running along two sides of the property. The walls connected at the corner with one wall being constructed of decorative concrete block that matched the mansion's foundation blocks. The house was built somewhere around 1910, and I often wondered if the blocks had come from Sears, Roebuck & Co. Sounds strange, but Sears sold building materials at that time.

The second wall was made of flat fieldstones that ran the width of the mansion's property. I often walked along it, noticing the color patterns. Light grays, mimicking overcast skies, were the dominant color with the charcoal grays and slate blues mixed into the fray.

The wall that started above my head met the adjacent property where it began its descent. I would follow the wall along the hillside as its slope ended at level ground. The mansion had the flat-rock wall repaired, while the wall of the neighboring property dropped its stones onto the sidewalk. The gaping holes that were left behind had small trees taking root and reaching for the sun. The house that occupied the land was gorgeous and most likely a frat house.

An article in the Sunday paper years ago featured Old Red. Photographs showed the construction of the house and its surrounding walls. Small sugar maples, held in place by stakes, were planted along the side of the finished abode. Those little trees have grown for over a century and now preside over the clay tile roof.

The photos revealed an intriguing set of stone stairs that were once on the property which gave access to the park across from the flat stone wall. Both sets of stairs had hand-hewn stone arches that matched like identical twins.

During my next trip by the house, I looked for the spot where the stairs once were. I crossed the street into the greenspace and stared at Old Red. My mind's eye could still see the stairs leading down from the house and onto the sidewalk. I could see the keystones carefully resting at the peak of the arches, holding everything in its correct place.

I pictured a husband and wife, the owners of Old Red, making their way down the stairs to the park for a picnic. I imagined the man dressed in a gray, English tweed Edwardian sack suit, the cuffed pants hanging slightly above black laced dress boots. A white high-collared shirt was held snuggly in place with a flashy red tie. The gold chain for his pocket watch matched the gold monocle set on his right eye.

The wife accompanied her husband, wearing a tailored coat and skirt. The cranberry cloth with its onyx lines formed a lattice that stretched down her long pleated skirt, just resting on the tops of her black boots. Her long, dark hair was pulled into a bun and pinned to the posterior of her head.

The neighbors were all spilling out onto the green. Ladies with parasols, men with top hats and walking canes—just another Sunday afternoon in a bygone era taking place in the spot where I was standing. How I would love to reset those stone walls, stairs, and archways to their former glory.

***

When I turned nineteen, I applied for a job on the hardscape crew at Sapphire Stone and Gardens. I broke the news over dinner.

Mom didn't love the idea of that kind of work but Dad interrupted and said, "Stop worrying. I've seen Abby drive a golf ball as far as a lot of guys, and she hits a softball over their heads as well. She'll be fine."

"That's not my concern," Mom answered, "it's the hard physical work that she will be doing."

My brother Jeff, two years my senior, sat across the table from me. We sucked in our spaghetti while the ping-pong game went on.

"Mother Hen, if it's too hard, she'll find that out too," Dad said in his tongue-in-cheek fashion.

"Honestly, Mom. I only applied for the job. Who knows if they'll even call? Maybe they don't want a girl on the crew. Plus, it's my choice anyway," I said as I took my dishes to the sink.

"Well, I just don't like the idea."

Jeff got up and tucked his hands under his armpits, arched his back, cocked his knees, jerked his head forward and back, and began circling Mom and clucking like a hen. The conversation ended in laughter.

***

Sapphire did call and ask me to interview. They were a new company that had only been in operation for about two years. It was one of the reasons I chose them. I honestly didn't think the bigger companies would give me a chance.

My interview was early while the crew prepared for the day. I pulled through the black-and-rust colored gate and made my way to a parking spot, waiting a second for the dust from the unpaved lot to settle before I got out. I scanned the yard, looking at pallets of paver bricks, cages of fieldstone, limestone boulders, and mounds of aggregates that were scattered around with no sense of order. Piles of colored mulch, topsoil, and plant materials were in the mix as well.

As I walked to the small building I checked out the ten-by-ten foot squares of paver designs that were set along the entryway. Each display had a number that corresponded to a nearby poster that gave the specs and prices.

I entered the dusty building to see displays for decorative walls and retaining walls adorning the place. The floors were filthy from guys in muddy boots tracking through. Muddy footprints had dried and now left a dusty powder in their wake. There was an equally dusty counter with an old cash register sitting on it. A credit card imprinter sat beside it along with a grimy telephone. Behind the counter was a back wall with an open door. I guessed it was the owner's office. Bob Marley's "Jamming" was cranked and blared from the office.

I looked around but saw no one. Finally, a guy wearing untied yellow work boots, dusty jeans, and a blue shirt that read "Sapphire Stone & Gardens" on the upper left entered from a creaky side door. He seemed about twenty years old and was pulling up the bottom of his shirt to wipe the sweat off his face.

"Can I help you?"

"Yeah. I have a seven a.m. with Steve Gallus," I replied.

He tilted his head back and yelled into the air, "HEY STEVE! THAT CHICK YER INTERVIEWING IS HERE TA SEE YOU!"

Nice, I thought to myself, *this place already has a lot of class.*

Bob Marley quieted down and a voice from a back room yelled out, "DUDE! SHUT YOUR STUPID MOUTH!" and out stepped Steve Gallus.

***

Steve was a well-built guy who stood six feet tall and was all muscle. His dirty blond hair was pulled back into a ponytail, minus a few wavy pieces on the side that weren't long enough to get caught in his black hair tie. He was sporting a pair of Original

Jams, yellow Timberland boots, a Sapphire T-Shirt, and a sapphire earring in his left ear.

I had always loved Jams with their loud, bold colors. His were red and black checkerboards running from the waist to the bottom of the shorts. The checkerboards were encompassed by purple stripes on each side. On each side of the purple lines were horizontal columns of red rectangles with bright yellow in the middle.

"Hi," he said as he extended his hand, "I'm Steve Gallus. You must be Abby."

"I am," I replied as I shook his hand.

"Come on back, Abby." He hesitated for a minute, staring at his worker, who had now decided to lace his boots at a snail's pace all while staring up at the two of us.

"Jay, what are you doing? Why are you dressing yourself on my time? And why are you staring at us?" He fired off at him in quick succession. "Never seen a young woman before?" he said, needling Jay. "That explains a lot." Before Jay could answer, Steve continued, "Do you have nothing to do? Is the dump truck loaded with crush? Are the baskets loaded and ready to go?"

"No."

"So, again I'll ask, what are you doing in here?"

"I was headed to the bathroom, Steve. Geez."

As we entered his office, Steve turned to Jay and yelled, "And don't take a newspaper with you!"

Jay rolled his eyes at Steve as he pulled the bathroom door open.

***

The office was small, semi-disorganized and, like everything else, it was dusty. Steve's desk sat dead center with a taupe, metal bench-style filing cabinet set against the back wall. I guessed it wasn't used much, judging by the stacks of papers piled on top of the cabinet, on the desk, and set in stacks on the floor. I scanned the walls that were covered with posters: Prince, The Police, Lou Reed, Springsteen, R.E.M., Depeche Mode, The Pretenders, Metallica, and the infamous Johnny Cash middle finger shot. They did make a nice wallpaper that covered the old, dark 1970s paneling.

"Have a seat," Steve said, turning the boom box off. He shuffled papers around until he managed to find my resume on his desk.

I sat in a grimy, black upholstered chair that was likely retrieved from the side of the road. Probably in front of a frat house, no less.

"Don't mind the mess," he said. "Trying to do sales, bids, interviews, and manage the crew has proved to be a bit daunting." He paused for a second, "I tried to get my mom to help," a smile emerged, "but she said it's worse than cleaning my teenaged room."

I chuckled.

"Okay, so, first question. You want to work in hardscapes and not landscapes, is that correct?" Steve said, half in disbelief.

"Yes."

"You do know it's a physically demanding job, right?"

"I do," I answered as his blue eyes stared at me with some skepticism.

"Sooooo…I have to ask why. I do understand why women like landscaping, although it can be hard work, but hardscapes? What's the attraction?"

"Kind of similar to landscaping. I love the look of stones. Old walls and their restoration, modern walls, retaining walls, stone dust paths, flagstone paths, brick patios…I've always thought they were cool and I'd love to learn how to install them. I may hate the whole process and only do it for one season. Who knows?"

"Most of my guys quit after a couple jobs."

"Maybe you hire wusses."

That comment caused a smirk to form as he continued, "Think you can do the job?"

Again, he doubts me.

Feeling a mix between being challenged and being demeaned over my gender, I answered, "Don't let this Cindy Crawford body and Lady Diana haircut fool you. I will make it through the season…which is apparently more than most of the guys you hire can do."

The smirk on his face turned into a grin. "Yeah, but can you drink them under the table at happy hour on Friday?"

"Since I'm nineteen and the drinking age just went to twenty-one, probably not. Plus, I suck at drinking, so I go with my strengths."

"Strengths?"

"Yeah. Strengths. Foosball. They will all get beat by a girl," I said as I flashed a fake cheesy smile.

"Okay," Steve said, "any questions for me?"

"Yes. When and why did you start Sapphire?"

"This is my third season, and I started it because I wanted to be my own boss and take my own chances. What else do you want to know?"

"What else do I need to know about you? What's with the earring, and are those Jams an option?" I asked, grinning as I indicated his choice of attire.

Now Steve started to laugh. "Well, I graduated in '83 from SUNY Cobleskill with an AAS in landscape design. In high school I spent summers working for a landscaper. On spring break of my final year I applied for my DBA and legal paperwork to form Sapphire, which I started that summer. We're doing a pretty decent job of growing. I like physical work and I don't care what people think of me. The earring is my birthstone and how I named the company. When I look in the mirror, it reminds me to keep pushing my business ventures and personal goals. I know your next question will be, 'what are my personal goals,' so I'll answer it now. I'd like to finish climbing all the Adirondack High Peaks, visit Yellowstone National Park for two weeks, and white water raft the Colorado River in the Grand Canyon for starters. Jams are optional but highly encouraged. Now it's my turn," he stated as he leaned back in his black office chair with his fingers clasped behind his head.

"What do I need to know about *you*?"

"Hmm," I thought for a second, then leaned toward the desk with my hands folded in my lap, and in a smug tone answered, "I used to like to wear dresses. And then the great, 'I see London, I see France' Kindergarten Incident of the fall of 1972 happened during recess, and that ended that. I once ate two flies on a third grade dare, my favorite album is The Who's *Quadrophenia*, and while in high school I worked a job where I was told I lacked tact and diplomacy on two successive job reviews. I am both blunt and honest, and I'll own my mistakes, even if it costs you millions." As I finished, I sat back in my smelly roadside chair.

"Wow!" said Steve in the voice of a cartoon duck. "You may be the craziest person I'll ever hire!"

"Oh, I doubt I'll be the craziest person you'll hire. I saw some of your crew outside. Obviously they are former paste eaters… and a duck? Seriously?"

The duck voice continued, "I'm not a fan of the pig voice. That dumb pork chop does nothing but stutter. The duck took a little more finesse to perfect. Especially the laugh."

"Well, we all have our strengths. When do I start, what are you paying me, and can I count on you not to lose my time sheets in this mess?"

The duck answered, "Monday. Four dollars and fifty cents an hour, plus overtime, and I'm smart enough to hire a payroll company."

"Fair enough," I said as we left the office and headed back into the customer area.

As I got to the front door, Jay was entering the side door to ask Steve a question when I heard him say, "So, do I work with a girl now?"

"Yup. And I bet she not only out-works you, but I bet she spanks you at foosball."

"HA! Doubtful on both counts!" Jay retorted standing with his hands on his hips and a sly smirk on his face.

I was standing on the threshold holding the screen door that was just as grubby as the rest of the place when I turned back and answered, "Jay, Jay, Jay," shaking my head back and forth. "Don't make me do to you what I did to my fifth grade boys kickball team."

"Yeah? What happened to them?"

"Have you *seen* them?"

"Huh? No," he answered, running his fingers through his collar length brown feathered hair.

"That's my point—you haven't seen them or Jimmy Hoffa's body," I said with raised eyebrows and a soft vocal tone that I hoped sounded like a serial killer. I turned around and headed to my car.

Jay rolled his eyes, Steve laughed and yelled after me, "Foosball Friday. The crew often heads to The Greatest for food and drinks…or soda and Shirley Temples for you teeny-boppers. Jay is an awesome foosball player and this I gotta see this!"

"Monday, Gentlemen, I'll see you Monday," I said over my shoulder as I walked to my car.

***

The following week came, and I'd be lying if I didn't say it was hard. Boot camp hard. I was basically a stone laborer. It was an unusually hot spring, or maybe it wasn't and it just felt that way to me. By the end of Tuesday, I was looking for Friday, and by Friday every muscle in my body hurt—including the ones I didn't know I had.

My hamstrings took the brunt of it. The constant bending over reminded me of how inflexible the backs of my legs were. My forearms hurt, my elbows hurt, my biceps and triceps hurt, my shoulders hurt. I was amazed at the muscular structure of my hands—every fiber in them ached, and my fingertips were killing me from prying up the bricks. I was reminded of the posters in biology class that showed muscle structure and fiber. I was pretty sure I was now intimately acquainted with each of those groups.

Friday finally came and I couldn't have been happier. I forced myself out to The Greatest, short for The Greatest Grill in Town, where I ordered a burger and fries and plopped down in a booth. The booths were the generic red vinyl ones, which of course had red tape covering the tears. The place ranked somewhere between a quaint tavern and a dive bar. But for right now it was dinner and cold drinks.

Steve ordered at the bar and then slid in across from me and asked how I liked my first week. I had spent the week at one house constructing a new paver brick patio. We excavated sod, dumped crush, tamped the crush, installed the edging, spread the sand, laid the bricks, and brushed sand in the seams. It did look sweet when we were done. I told him that I enjoyed watching the space transform from a boring backyard to a beautiful brick patio.

"Now," Steve said, smiling as he sipped out of the clear plastic cup holding his draft beer, "be honest with me. After your first sixty-five-hour week, every muscle in your body hurts, you're completely exhausted, and you just want to eat, shower, and chill."

I was sipping my soda out of a cup that had more crushed ice than beverage. I put the cup down on the wooden table that displayed years of graffiti, and with a giant grin and squinting eyes I replied, "Now, Steve…why would you *ever* think that?"

Steve had a knowing smile and said, "Why do you think the turnover is so high?"

"And again I'll say, because you hire wusses."

At that moment, our waitress, wearing a red apron with "The Greatest" printed in white, served our food.

As we put ketchup on our burgers and fries, Steve continued, "See the boys?" he asked, pointing with the ketchup toward the bar. There in a semi-circle stood about a dozen of my crewmates who were waiting for their beers and sodas. The wooden high-backed bar stools had been pushed aside as they huddled along the bar.

"Do you know what they're doing?"

I had a mouth full of French fries, so I shook my head no.

"They're settling their bets. They had a pool going as to what day you would quit. All were expecting you would be a no-show by Wednesday. Thursday at the latest."

"Gee, not one of them thought I would make it through the week, let alone the season?" I said in a mockingly snide tone while reaching for a napkin from the holder at the side of the table. I thought it was pretty funny.

"Only one guy was positive you'd make it through the week. The same guy is the only one who is sure you'll make it through the season," Steve said as Jay walked over to our table.

"Here you go Steve. You won," Jay informed him as he dropped sixty dollars next to Steve's plate.

"SUCK-AHS!" I said to Jay in between French fries. "Tsk, tsk, you've all underestimated me. Ain't found Jimmy Hoffa yet have ya?"

As usual, Jay rolled his eyes, shook his head, and headed back over to the boys where dinner was waiting on the bar for him.

Steve was counting his money when he said, "You know you're not going to get out of foosball right?"

"I know."

I finished dinner and felt all those sore muscles stiffening. My hands were starting to feel like claws that were curling up and freezing in place. My forearms were just plain tired, but I had run my mouth, so it was time to pay the piper.

I stopped at the foosball table. Two guys were finishing up, so I dropped my dollars' worth of quarters on the corner of the table, securing my place in line for the next game. From there I headed to the boys at the bar.

"Foosball, Jay? We're up next."

"Hell yeah! You're goin' down!" he said with a teasing smile.

The game ahead of us was finishing up and I said, "C'mon, tough guy, let's go!"

The crew gathered around and I assumed there was another bet in place. Jay won the first game with a score of 5-2. By the second game my muscles had loosened back up and I won, 5-4. My hands and arms were toast by game three, and I lost the tie breaker 5-3. Jay did concede that I was a pretty good player.

***

I made it through the season, and once I got used to the physical labor I really loved the job. I got along well with the guys, and I believe I earned their respect as a coworker. I wasn't as physically strong as them, but they were always willing to give me a hand with the really heavy stuff that they knew I couldn't possibly pick up without injury.

Jay and I went back and forth with our foosball victories when we decided to call a truce and become a team. We were unstoppable, and being too young to play for drink chips, we decided to play for a dozen chicken wings. When we tired of wings, we decided the loser paid for the game. We became legendary—even if it was only in our own minds!

I met and became friends with several of the crew's girlfriends, who ended up joining us at The Greatest on Fridays. Steve's girlfriend, Vicki, was awesome. Also in her early twenties, she was a five foot four inch, gorgeous spunky brunette. She and Steve complemented each other well. Vicki encouraged him to build his business, get organized, clean the hole he called a showroom and office, and called him to the carpet when his ideas were a little crazier than normal. She was a bank teller, and Steve was always encouraging her as she embarked on new things in order to advance her career. I figured they'd marry one day.

The season flew by and ended with a more limber and muscular me—with a great tan to match!

Chapter 3

Winter came and went, and I returned to Sapphire the following spring. Steve offered me a position as a hardscapes crew leader, which I accepted. Two years later I became the supervisor of hardscapes which provided year-round, full-time work and allowed Steve to continue the growth of Sapphire.

Meanwhile, Jay moved out of hardscapes and into landscapes. He ended up loving it and became a crew leader. He had planned on doing a self-study of plant material identification, but with Steve's encouragement, he enrolled in a local Ag & Tech college. Two years later, we watched Jay, who was all smiles, proudly walk the stage. He shook hands with the dean and the president, and moved his tassel from the right side of his cap to the left. Jay was an official college graduate. We never were sure who was the most surprised—Jay or his parents, or maybe it was Steve? A nice picture from that day of Steve, Vicki, Jay, and Jay's parents still hangs on the wall of Steve's office.

Unsurprisingly, Steve and Vicki married. She became the office manager, and, being very organized, she did a great job at keeping our scheduling straight. When Jay graduated, Steve promoted him from crew leader to supervisor over the landscaping side of Sapphire. Steve was good to Jay and me. He paid us well and threw in a bunch of benefits. With the two of us running the day-to-day end of things, Steve continued growing Sapphire. He added aquatics, ponds and fish, along with perennial garden installations to his growing list of services.

***

Enter Mrs. Barbara J. Preston, owner of Preston's Garden Designs and perennial garden designer extraordinaire. She had been in business for over thirty years, and was renown by both her peers in the industry and the upper class of the city. Her talent in design and expertise of plant knowledge resulted in her being in high demand. At one time she had her own crew and did her own installs, but demand allowed her to move solely into design while subcontracting to landscapers.

Residing in Syracuse guarantees winters of unpredictable lengths and springs that are often rainy. Landscapers run on a seasonal basis, which makes finding reliable help an issue. Every year new people arrive and need to be trained in the basics. It's not only a frustration to business owners, but also an annoyance that Barb Preston was determined to get around.

Word around the local nursery yards was that she had difficulty finding subcontractors. She demanded excellence and basically took over and ran someone's crew while on her jobsites. She was not particularly mindful of the business owner's time or their deadlines with other customers.

It was the dead of January when Steve called a Friday lunch meeting. Steve, Vicki, Jay, and myself slid into the booth at The Greatest and ordered lunch.

The duck voice opened with, "I'm sure you're wondering why I called you all here today," an old generic line from God only knows where.

Jay looked at me and rolled his eyes as Steve continued, "We've all heard the rumors that Barb Preston is having a hard time getting what she wants out of her 'subcontracted' garden installers. I have an idea. Vicki and I have been discussing it, and we're curious what you guys think."

Just as the waitress was setting our drinks down, Jay answered, a grin beginning to form, "Oh, thank *God* Vicki was involved in this…it must be a pretty good idea."

Steve tore the paper off the end of his straw and carefully pulled the wrapper from the opposite end until he had about an inch of overhang. He put the straw to his lips and blew the wrapper at Jay, hitting him in the forehead. Jay tilted his head and raised his eyebrows at Steve.

"You can't say it's not true, Steve," Jay said as he sipped his Pepsi.

In Jay's defense, Steve came up with some strange ideas.

In Steve's defense, I liked that he was always looking for ways to grow, and that he trusted us enough to take our opinions into consideration.

Steve and Vicki believed a connection with Preston's would be valuable to Sapphire in a number of ways. In the short term, it would be the perfect way to expand Sapphire's reach to the upper class and build new connections. Steve had vision and he figured that in the long term, it could set us up for Barb's eventual retirement. Jay and I were all of twenty one, and Steve and Vicki were twenty-six and twenty-five respectively. We guessed

Barb was somewhere in her mid-fifties and postulated that retirement would come in the next five to ten years when the four of us would be in our prime.

Vicki and Steve were such a great match. When she came on board with us not only did she get everything cleaned up and organized, but one of her biggest assets, by far, was goal-setting. She managed to harness Steve's energy and ideas through a plan which ultimately extended to the entire crew of Sapphire. Vicki posted an "idea board." The rules were simple:

- Write your idea on the idea board
- No idea is a dumb idea; even if it really is dumb, it gets others thinking and tweaking the original idea into a workable idea
- Details: Anything else the writer felt was important

The crew loved it. Steve, initially a skeptic, came to realize it was a valuable tool. His crew came up with ideas for being more productive, which in turn saved money. We came up with things like streamlining scheduling, splitting the crew into one or two tasks—mowing crews mowed and moved on with the trimming, and clean-up crews following behind. An above-ground fuel tank was installed in the yard so we didn't have to visit the local gas station, which wasted time and created another step for accounting.

When the ideas saved money, Steve handed out a one-hundred-and-fifty-dollar bonus. The crew had an investment in the company, and it really did help with retention rates. From there, he and Vicki decided to do profit-sharing for the season, which they hoped would allow them to have their pick of good, reliable help. Some of it was so new that they were waiting to see if it really worked.

"None of us know Barb, but I'm guessing the woman likes a plan," I said. "Did you guys do the idea board yet?"

"That's where you all come in," Vicki said. "Steve and I did a basic one, but now we're at the 'count-the-cost' part. We need to really run the numbers but we don't want to miss anything that will be an expense."

We did the best we could to guesstimate the number of jobs Barb did each year and the number of extra crew that would be needed. We figured we would have a crew dedicated to her projects and her projects alone. The crew needed knowledge of perennials and hardscapes. She was known to put paths around a yard and occasionally short, flat rock walls.

"I think you need to put one of us on the initial crew," Jay added as he finished his fries. "From what we've all heard, Barb's a stickler. I think if she had you or Abby onsite for at least the first year, she would have a go-to person who's always the same. From there, we can see who has the personality, organization, and aptitude to handle the jobsite and Barb. Then we can hand it off to them."

"Agreed," Steve answered. "Abby, how do you feel about taking this on? I know you love hardscapes, but maybe for this year you can deal with Barb while Jay and I can float to cover sales and estimates for you?"

"Fine by me," I answered. "You know perennials and garden construction are my next favorite thing to do anyway."

By the following Friday we had a business plan in place. Vicki did a great job typing up the proposal and purchasing a professional glossy blue folder with silver lettering that read, "Sapphire Stone & Gardens LLC," in standard type with the tagline, "Where

Excellence Resides," in cursive underneath. The interior of the folder had a slot that held Steve's business card along with a detailed proposal.

We decided we were as ready as we'd ever be when Jay asked, "What are you going to do? Just give her a call?"

The duck answered, "I'm going to let my fingers do the flipping," followed by the cartoon character's laugh.

He pulled out the phone book and thumbed through the business section until he found Preston's. He took a deep breath and called. We were all surprised when she answered the phone. We thought for sure she'd be escaping the winter snow in Florida. Before we knew it, we had a nine a.m. sharp Monday morning meeting.

***

The four of us met in the parking lot of the Sheffield Building where Preston's Garden Designs was located. It was a smart looking old red brick building in the upper class Sheffield section of the city. We entered the building and headed for Suite 110. When we arrived we found construction going on and a sign that directed us to a general conference room down the hall.

"Reserved: 9-10 a.m. Preston's Designs" read the board to the right of the door.

It was 8:59. Steve lightly knocked on the door, and a voice from the interior invited us in.

Barbara Preston glanced at the four of us and then at her watch. "Punctual. So far you are all off to an acceptable start."

La Belle Communauté

She put the palms of her hands flat on the table to give herself a push up out of her chair. We had been correct; Barb was in her mid-fifties and very stylish. She examined us from behind her Yves St. Laurent wire framed glasses. Giant glasses were in style then, but hers were much smaller with what appeared to be two frames. The thin frame holding the glass was a chocolate-colored tortoise shell. A second decorative frame of golden brushed-metal extended above the tortoise shell and rested just at her soft-angled eyebrows. The side pieces were held onto the frame with a small, matching gold rectangular piece. The frames, no doubt made in Italy, complemented her short brunette hair that fell at the midpoint of her ears, exposing small pearl stud earrings. The back of her hair was clipped short and tight to her neck. Her makeup and lipstick were perfect. Generally, she carried a professional elegance. Dressed in a brown fitted pantsuit with a peach-colored blouse and a flowered pastel scarf tied neatly around her neck, she limped her way around the conference table to greet us. About forty pounds overweight, she extended her hand to Steve.

"Barbara Preston. You would be Stephen Gallus, I assume?"

"Yes ma'am. Please, call me Steve," he said, reaching out his hand to shake hers. Not counting his wedding day, it was the first time in the three years I'd know Steve that he was dressed up. His navy cotton pants were without wrinkle. The long-sleeved, pale blue button-down was surely pressed at a local dry cleaner, and his hair was very meticulously pulled into a ponytail with his earring in its usual place.

"This is my wife, Vicki Gallus. She is our office manager."

"Wonderful to meet you. I am quite sure you are the backbone of the organization," Barb said as she grasped Vicki's hand with a knowing smile and respect for her position.

Vicki smiled warmly and replied, "I am. It does get a bit crazy during the peak season."

"This is Jay Williams, he is the landscape supervisor. Jay has been with us for four years. He started as a laborer and recently graduated with his associates degree in landscape design, and is currently studying for the certified nursery and landscape professional exam."

Jay, dressed in black pants and a light yellow button down, beamed when Steve introduced him with his education.

"Very nice Jay," Barb said, smiling as she shook his hand. "Education and professional certifications are excellent resume-builders."

"Lastly, we have Abby Field." She has worked at Sapphire for three years in our hardscapes department. She also started as a laborer, became a crew leader, and now supervises the department. She has a love for perennial gardening, although she hasn't had the chance to focus on that as much as she'd like!"

Just my height at five foot eight inches, Barb looked me in the eye and said, "Abby, you just may be a young woman after my own heart! Wonderful to meet you."

"Thank you. It's nice to meet you as well. Your reputation precedes you."

"Thank you. You are quite a young bunch of entrepreneurs. Sapphire is beginning to build a reputation of its own within the city," Barb said as she invited everyone to remove their winter coats and have seats. Her administrative assistant, Diane, offered us coffee and tea, but we all politely refused. Honestly, I think we were all afraid of inadvertently knocking it over on the conference table.

"Please, cast your vision with me. I am quite interested in your proposal."

Steve did a great job presenting. He gave a brief overview of his personal story of starting Sapphire and explained that he was always looking to grow his business. He opened the blue folder and pulled out the proposal that we hoped would meet Barb's expectations and secure our position with her. She seemed to be impressed. Steve ended by asking Barb if there was anything we missed that she would need to accomplish her goals.

Barb explained that she averaged seven to ten large projects each season, and while that may not seem like much, it was often a complete renovation. Occasionally it was an easy green space without much in it. Most times it was a complete overhaul, beginning with the removal of old, worn-out plantings. Once the general preparations were done, she worked with a local company that mixed soil to her specifications. Her choice of perennials was often varied and not always found in area nurseries. Nurseries tend to carry the twenty most popular perennials and not much else.

She was a perfectionist, so the soil and plant materials were responsibilities that she personally dealt with and had delivered to the site. Sapphire would be doing the installs and gathering any hardscapes and mulch. She had a reputation for excellence, and considered the projects her babies which she watched over from conception to delivery.

"Employee retention is a notorious problem in our area. What plan do you have in place to guarantee me a crew of excellence?"

"As an organization," answered Steve, "Sapphire has been working on its own retention issues for the last two seasons. Obviously we hire college students to fill in a lot of our laborer spots, but we are working with the state agriculture schools to find employees who already know that it's hard work. We surveyed our workers and asked for ideas on how we could improve Sapphire. From there, we began implementing several things. We start with a higher wage than our competitors so we can glean the top performers. We also do extensive background checks instead of hiring any warm body. We provide a lot of training with new employees and take suggestions from them for improvement, which gives them a say in their workplace. Those who save the company money receive a bonus. Next year we plan on adding snow removal to our business in order to offer more full-time, year-round positions."

"I see. Do you believe progress is being made?" Barb queried.

"Last summer we saw a definite drop in employee losses," Vicki answered. "The number of employees who stayed for the entire season was up twenty-five percent over the previous year."

"It appears you are headed in the appropriate direction for marked improvements. If I agree to your proposal, with whom will I have the pleasure of collaborating with onsite?"

Steve answered, "Abby will be taking that spot. We feel she has the most insight to both hardscapes and plantings. The crew works well with her, and she's a hard worker."

"One final question for you, Steve. Do you have the skill and ability needed for aquatics? I do receive occasional requests for small ponds and fountains. I have not found a business entity that I am confident in retaining for aquatic installation and mainte-nance. Therefore, I have denied my customers what they would prefer, not wanting to tarnish my personal reputation."

"We began pond installations last summer, which includes the care of fish, if needed. To date, we have only installed five, but we are expecting to grow that area. Jay is currently in charge of that. The four of us went to a weeklong seminar last February to learn the ins-and-outs of it. This February we are headed to a class that teaches pergola, arbor, and deck construction."

"I do use a general contractor for installations of pergolas and arbors…" she trailed off. We could see her thinking, "It would be advantageous to acquire one company that is able to handle all aspects…then I would not be detained by the schedule of the construction company…"

Her blue eyes had wandered off to a distant place in her mind. She realized that and snapped back to the conference room. "Thank you all for your time. It was a pleasure meeting with you. I shall take your proposal into sincere consideration. I will give you some manner of reply by Friday."

We all stood up, exchanged pleasantries, and exited the Sheffield Building. We held a quick parking lot meeting, all believing it went well. Jay was right; the woman sounded like she majored in English and ate a thesaurus for breakfast. Her diction contained no slang, no contractions, and no slurring of things like "going to" into "gonna." Bet she never said the word *ain't* in her entire life.

We sweated it out all week, and finally at four forty-five Friday afternoon she called Steve and agreed to give Sapphire a shot. They committed to a one-year deal where either party could back out after the first season. The two of them ironed out the details, and we became co-laborers with Preston's.

Chapter 4

During the first season we teamed up with Preston's, we did seven installs. Barb was right, it was a long way from start to finish, and I had to admit, she was an amazing designer. Her use of color, form, and structure put her miles ahead of any competitor.

Our first project was at Judge Cleary's house in the Sheffield section of the city. Several of the city leaders lived in this area; judges, lawyers, city servants such as police officers and firefighters, along with city school principals called Sheffield home. Many were required to live within the city limits, while others thought it best to live there since they were on the city payroll.

The judge and his wife, Lynn, recently purchased their home on Suffolk Drive. They decided to turn their entire backyard into a garden area. Lynn loved to paint and write, and she was looking for a peaceful place to enjoy her hobbies.

Barb asked if I would meet her at the Cleary's. She wanted me to experience her entire process, beginning with planning meetings and ending with the completed install. I was ten minutes early for the initial meeting and waited in my car parked across the street from the judge's house.

La Belle Communauté

The house was a pretty bungalow built in the 1920s with extensive renovations to the residence already complete. Ancient cedar shake siding had been replaced with beveled wooden siding painted charcoal gray. Two sets of double-hung windows were positioned side-by-side and framed the small front porch. The window frames were painted black while the surrounding moldings were white. I loved how the black roofing shingles, railings, and windows pulled the look together against the gray background.

To the left of the windows another section jutted out, relieving the house of its symmetry. It was set three feet back from the front and appeared to be an addition complete with matching windows.

A sidewalk led to four newly poured concrete steps that ended its journey at a flagstone porch. Two white columns held the front of the gabled roof above the landing. The gable's hypotenuse stretched downward to the right and left of the hazelnut colored front door. Black iron rails connected the columns to the house, creating a small shelter for guests to wait.

A dormer with two small windows in the middle and two standard sized double-hung on either end peeked over the top of the porch roof like a set of sleepy eyes adjusting to the light.

Two small landscape beds used round stones to create the border that united the front walk to the front of the house. A third matching bed settled itself in front of the addition.

Barb pulled up and parked behind me. We greeted each other and made our way up the walk. She leaned hard on the black railing, using it as a crutch to give relief to her bad left knee. I rang the bell, and the two of us scoped out the front beds while waiting for Lynn to answer.

The beds were home to Annabelle hydrangeas that were waiting to peek their heads up from a long winter's nap. It was the first week of March, and the snow was beginning its slow glacial retreat.

Lynn answered the door and invited us in. She seemed to be a pleasant woman whom I guessed was in her late forties, although her fashion sense made her seem ten years younger. She wore a fitted pink button-down blouse that hung over her indigo acid-washed jeans. The cuffed three-quarter sleeves displayed multiple gold bracelets. She completed the look with a flipped up collar and a simple, gold rope necklace. Her highlighted hair was tapered at the collar and ears, with long layers that swept down from the crown of her head. Burgundy fingernails brushed her bangs off to one side as she offered us tea.

Barb began working with the Clearys last year but didn't have time in her schedule to do the install. In order to catch me up, we decided a quick look at the backyard would be best.

We made our way to a narrow, screened-in back porch that was lined on either side with two white wicker rocking chairs. Between the two chairs sat a small matching table. I gazed through the screens to see an ancient red-brick patio two steps down.

Like most urban yards, there was a wooden fence surrounding it. At Barb's insistence, the Clearys had replaced the rotting and broken boards last year. It was understandable. No one wants to put the gardens in and then have to deal with fence companies and painters shortly after, and since they were wait-listed until this year, it made perfect sense. Barb suggested three different colors she felt would be the right backdrop for her plans. Having a penchant for the look of weathered wood, the Clearys decided on washed gray.

The rest of the yard was mostly a worn-out lawn that had more weeds than grass with a tired, old mountain ash struggling in the middle of the space. It was surrounded with one of my most hated landscape techniques—black plastic edging. Not only is it ugly, it quickly becomes the victim of frost heave in this climate. Snowdrops, the first that sign spring was on its way, encompassed the tree with its marshmallow heads drooping over the irregular border.

***

The three of us sat down at the dining room table to discuss the plans. Barb reached into her large, black leather bag and pulled out three neatly folded drawings. I opened mine and began reviewing it. It was fairly standard in terms of design. A scalloped bed followed the fence around three sides. The ash tree, along with the snowdrops and edging, were slated for removal with a small fountain being put in its place.

"Abby," Barb began, "Lynn and I discussed this last year. We are reviewing for clarity and to be certain that the Clearys are content with the choice of plant materials. Please ask any questions you may have."

Although Barb was pleasant, she could also be intimidating, and wanting to make sure we could keep her as a customer, I was initially on pins and needles. I had a couple questions, but was too scared to ask them. They were more of a suggestion, and I was afraid I would step on Barb's design toes. I kept my mouth shut, but Barb read my quizzical expressions.

"Do you have any questions, Abby?" Barb asked.

"No. I'm good."

"The expression on your face seems to suggest otherwise."

I mustered up my courage and turned to Lynn, "Do you like the Annabelles out front?"

I held my breath, waiting for Barb to give me a disapproving look.

"I love them!" she replied. "Don't you?"

I tried to read Barb before I answered, but I was met with a poker face so I continued, "I love the plant, just not the placement."

"What do you mean?" Lynn asked.

"It is a great choice for long-blooming summer flowers, but from a design point of view, it overwhelms the beauty of your house and entryway."

Lynn was pondering when Barb said, "What would be your suggestion to correct the issue, Abby?"

Her tone and gaze were steady, and I couldn't tell if she was angry or testing me, but I had no other choice than to continue.

"Well," I said, thinking on my feet, "we have a couple options. We could get rid of them, which I don't suggest, or we could move them to a different location, and Barb could redesign your front beds."

I intentionally mentioned Barb to reassure her that she was still in control.

"Hmmm, maybe we could move them..." Lynn trailed off, obviously in thought.

Barb was sketching something onto her design. She didn't bother to look up to ask me if I had any other thoughts. Feeling like I had already stuck my neck out like a Thanksgiving turkey, I figured I might as well finish.

"The front beds have round stones that are being used as a border...do you love them or would you be open to suggestions?" I knew Barb had great disdain for them along with the red-brick patio.

"They were there when we moved in," Lynn said as she sipped her tea, "we just kept them. What are you thinking?"

"We could get rid of them all together and just cut an edge on the bed." I really wanted to use the stones elsewhere but didn't want to intrude on Barb's design more than I already had. "Or we could build a small fieldstone wall as an edge. It would only be about eight inches high."

"I like that idea. Barb, what do you think?" Lynn asked as she turned in her direction.

Barb slid her sketch in front of Lynn.

"May I present to you a rough sketch of Abby's suggestions? I have included a resetting of the Annabelle hydrangea along the posterior of the house."

Barb had already drafted a quick front view, complete with the fieldstone edge. The two of them chatted away about color and form, but I didn't really hear them. Honestly, I was still concerned about my neck.

I rejoined them when Lynn said with a smile, "I know you hate the red-brick patio, Barb. But that's staying!"

Barb pleasantly replied, "This is your piece of serenity, Lynn. If you enjoy the patio, I cannot say otherwise. It is simply an old structural style that I personally do not care for. I am quite certain that Abby will side with you. She seems to be enthralled with the design and architecture of stones."

At least Barb was smiling at me when she made that remark.

"Lynn," Barb continued, "we could reset your beloved patio."

"What do you mean?"

"Abby would carefully remove the bricks and level the foundation. When that is satisfactory, the bricks would be returned to their original position. It would correct the peaks and valleys caused by decades of settling."

I swear Barb knew I was thinking that and I had been dying to suggest it, but I decided I'd best keep my mouth shut.

"That's a great idea!" Lynn said with excitement. "I love to sit out there to write and paint."

"I believe we are completely settled on the project. Do either of you have any other areas of concern?" Barb asked us.

"No, I'm all set," I answered.

Lynn followed on my heels. "I'm ready for nice weather and a new backyard!"

Barb and I picked up our belongings and headed out the front door. I was sure she was going to say something to me about my suggestions, I just didn't know what.

She was silent.

We got to our vehicles when I spoke, "We'll begin the destruction phase as soon as the weather improves." Both of us already knew that, but I was trying to break the silence and get a feel for Barb.

"Yes, Abby. You will," she said, her voice lacking any emotion as she opened her car door.

I got in my car while trying not to slam my door in frustration. "What is with this woman? If you don't want my opinion then DON'T ASK!" I grumbled as I pulled away.

***

The weather finally broke, and we began. It was still too muddy to easily strip the sod, so I decided to pull the patio up first. Lynn was right; it gave their home a charm from days gone by. Of course, my mind's eye could visualize people in the Roaring Twenties. Women dressed as flappers and men in their double-breasted gangster suits. Everyone seated on the patio in clunky metal furniture secretly sipping prohibition cocktails—The Bee's Knees, Grasshoppers, or maybe a Hanky Panky? Ah, if only the patio could talk! I'm sure it would be something right out of *The Great Gatsby*!

While we finished the patio and removed the old ash tree, the early spring sunshine did its job of drying up the lawn. I called Barb the day before to inform her we were ready to build the beds. She had an early morning appointment and insisted we wait until she arrived before making any marks.

This is why other landscapers refused to work with her. The standard scallop that ebbed and flowed around the perimeter of the yard was an easy design. Anyone with experience would have it marked in an hour or less, but she played the "control-freak card" that bogged the crew down. She expected to be there by ten, but crews generally arrive on-site at eight, leaving a two-hour gap, and with a crew of six, that's twelve hours wasted.

I tried not to be aggravated as we had accounted for all this in our initial plan, and yet I still was. I could have marked the bed and had the crew begin cutting the sod along the fence until she arrived, but nope, we had to wait for her before we could pull out string and spray paint.

I decided to have my crew help the other guys with the morning loading rituals before we left. We arrived at nine-thirty, and with measuring wheels, twine, rebar, and spray paint sitting at our feet, we waited.

Barb showed at ten-ten and tottered up to us.

"Good morning, everyone!" she said with her usual pleasant demeanor before turning to me. "Abby, the arcs are to be symmetrical. No flat portions and none will present themselves as lopsided."

"No problem Barb."

I motioned for Amy, a newbie, to give me a hand. Knowing Barb was watching me like a hawk about to swoop down on her prey at any sign of weakness, I took the plans, double-checked the bed, and began to measure. I had Amy, a December horticulture graduate, assist me to get the hands-on training she needed for things only experience teaches. I had her read the prints as I explained how we were going to mark.

We measured segments of twine, tied them to the rebar, and determined the placement of the scallops. I showed Amy where to set the center points. Both Barb and Amy watched as I held the twine and the spray can in one hand and drew the arcs on the worn-out sod. We finished one side and the back of the property when Amy asked if she could try the final side. Believing you never really learn something until you do it, I let her give it a shot. I walked with her as she measured and pounded the rebar into the ground. I could feel Barb's blue eyes burning a laser hole through my back. We finished, and then Barb inspected with a meticulous eye.

"Ladies, you have done an excellent job. You may begin the sod removal," she said flatly. Never sure how to take her, I decided to just let it go.

I had the crew grab the sod cutter and begin, making sure they did not hit any of the white spray-painted lines. I personally did them by hand while Barb left to check on the soil delivery. The truck was now late, and she was less than happy. We decided it was a good time to break for lunch. The truck pulled up just as we finished, with Barb following behind as though she was the rear guard making sure the alleged couldn't escape. The driver was still apologizing when I reached them.

"I'm sorry, Mrs. Preston. I'm just a hired hand. I got nothin' to say in the timin' and there ain't nothin' I kin do about that."

"Yes, yes, Ken. I am well aware. I took the matter up with Mr. Roberts. Now be a dear and deposit the soil here." Barb was pointing to a spot on the side of the street.

The crew began tilling and raking out debris. We managed to get one side of the bed completed before calling it a day.

"Tomorrow," I said to Barb, "we will need the rest of the soil and the plants." Realizing the second the sentence left my lips that Barb didn't need to be told what to do, I held my breath, waiting for her response.

"Mr. Roberts has assured me the soil will be waiting for us tomorrow. Have a good evening Abby."

"You as well, Barb," I said as I let out a silent sigh of relief.

I watched as she limped toward her two-tone 1989 Cadillac Coupe DeVille convertible. It was gleaming silver on the base of the car with glistening ebony covering the rest.

"What do ya think?" Amy asked me as we watched Barb drive away.

"I think she has a Bose stereo system in that Caddy that never gets used. That's what I think."

We laughed as we made our way to the truck.

***

The remainder of the week was a blur of soil deliveries, plant material trucks, and mulch drops. A dazzling array of perennials and small shrubs were brought in. Most of the shrubs came from local suppliers, but her choice of perennials were not always found locally. Those were shipped in from Wildflowers & Perennials Unlimited, an upscale nursery in Connecticut that carried limited quantities of newly hybridized plants at a hefty price.

Perennial gardens take about three years to really begin to fill in and become the vision that was intended for them. Barb did her best to hasten the process by purchasing the largest sizes available. She aimed for three-gallon pots, but the specialty items usually showed up in four-inch containers. Still, it was worth the three-year wait to see the final display.

We finished the gardens, reset the patio, and installed the fountain all in seven days. Barb never complimented us on the job, but she didn't complain either, so we figured we must be meeting her expectations.

Upon completion, we loaded up and arrived back at Sapphire late in the day. Steve appeared from his office to inform us he had just gotten off the phone with Barb, and she was extremely pleased with our performance. We were neat, clean, detail-oriented, and professional.

The rest of the season went well for the most part, and the occasional glitches were Barb's to deal with. I got along well with her, yet something about her annoyed me that I never could put my finger on exactly.

Maybe it was her manner of speaking? No contractions, no words run together, no words cut off, no slang, no swearing, no words like "crap."

Maybe it was her over-the-top professionalism? Professionally dressed even in the mud, perfect make-up, perfect smile, perfect hair, exactly the right jewelry.

Maybe it was her impeccable car? No water spots, no mud splashes, no bird crap, no dirt on the thin white walls of her tires.

Maybe it was all of the above rolled into one—like she was condescending without actually being condescending?

Maybe I just felt like she had an air of being better than those of us in the dirt. If she ran into me in a grocery store in an upscale section of town, would she say hello? Or would she pretend she didn't see me and duck down an aisle?

And maybe none of it really mattered since I had nothing to do with Barb beyond Sapphire anyway, right?

Or so I thought.

Chapter 5

I glided my black 1984 Plymouth Turismo into a parking spot at the Sheffield Building, pulled up my emergency brake, grabbed my samples, and headed in. It was mid-March of the following year, and we were gearing up for the upcoming season. Winter was snowy, and any hopes of an early spring seemed less likely with each passing day. I was delivering brick samples to Barb to finalize details for one of her customers and get the order in as soon as possible.

I entered the building and took a left toward Preston's. I hadn't been there since our meeting last year. I stopped at the dark wooden door that had "Preston's Garden Designs" written on the door's smoky glass. "Suite 110" with its matching calligraphy was centered just slightly above the bottom of the window.

Being unable to see through the glass, I was unsure if I should knock or just walk in. I decided both worked, so I knocked lightly and cracked the door open just enough to stick my head in.

"Good morning," I said to Diane.

"Good morning, Abby. Come in. Barb is just finishing up with a call. Can I get you anything? Coffee? Hot tea?"

"No, thank you. I'm good," I said as I took off my spring coat and hung it in the closet.

"Well then, have a seat. She shouldn't be long."

I sat down in the waiting area. It was a small office set up; reception, kitchenette, small conference room, and Barb's office. The waiting area had four high-backed wooden chairs for my butt's sitting pleasure. Two chairs were set on one side of the coffee table and backed up to the wall. The other two were placed on the opposite side of the coffee table and out of the way of foot traffic. The caramel-stained square wooden slats that composed the backrest plunged to the greenish-gray leather seat cushion. The armrests had matching slats that fell all the way to the bottom frame that connected the front legs to the back.

Stickley Mission oak, no doubt, I thought to myself, resisting the urge to kick the table over and look for the name burned into the bottom of it.

Two floor lamps stood at attention next to the chairs against the wall. The lamps were also Mission oak with stained glass shades. They had neutral tones with a black border that encompassed geometric turquoise shapes in the center. *If Stickley and Tiffany had a baby, they would produce these lamps*, I thought to myself.

The generic, short, gray carpet made its way throughout the office, but Barb had a large, wool oriental rug placed over the top in the waiting area. Beautiful canary, gold, ruby, and coffee-dyed threads wove their way through the design's inky black background. The antique-white fringe was combed without a single strand out of place.

I gave Diane's space the once over. Standard reception desk with the workspace down low and the customer sign-in area up high. Behind her was a matching filing cadenza with a fax machine. The wood tone was a close match to the waiting area. Not Stickley, but not a Kmart Bluelight Special either. Above the cadenza was a large brass octagonal clock. The pendulum was housed in a slim box that came to a point at its base and released its ticking sounds as it oscillated. The clock had already chimed nine a.m.

Behind Diane's space, just to my left, was a door that entered into a small kitchenette where the coffee and tea were brewed. Barb's office was to the left of the kitchenette and the Tulip Table, a small conference room, was to Diane's right.

Barb hobbled out of her office and into the waiting area, greeted me, and apologized for the delay. She invited me into her office. It was a large space that also doubled as a conference room. The door was set to the left with a six-seat Mission style table that greeted me as I entered. It appeared that she had a wall taken out to create one large, open area while getting rid of a second small conference room.

Barb's desk was centered between two windows to my right. Her desk was in the same style as the waiting room furniture, except for her beautiful burgundy leather seat. The two chairs opposing her were short-backed and covered with the same burgundy leather. The stained glass shade of her desk lamp matched the waiting room, as did the oriental rugs under her desk and conference table.

Behind her desk sat what appeared to be a china cabinet that she was using for storage. The cabinets and drawers had round, gunmetal gray knobs and were stained the same caramel color that permeated all of Preston's Designs. The lower portion had four drawers that took a vertical path down the middle with two columnar cabinets on either side that were seven feet tall. Above the drawers was a framework of open shelves that connected the two columns and held personal pictures. The personal touch seemed odd to me. I viewed Barb's professionalism as over the top, and personal effects seemed out of place with the Barb I knew.

Two elongated windows, one on each side, paralleled the cabinet. Wooden blinds were tucked neatly under the multi-colored jacquard valances. The muted paisleys meandered their way across the window heads.

She invited me to have a seat, but I had four bricks in my hand of varying colors, and I was unsure where to put them.

"Where would you like me to set these? The floor?"

"We will be conversing at the conference table. I will find something suitable to place under the samples," she said as she rummaged around her desk.

She settled on a cardboard top from a paper box.

Just as we sat down, Diane stuck her head in and in a hushed tone, said, "I'm sorry to bother you ladies, but Mrs. Monihan is here unannounced. She is insistent that she sees you. Says she only needs a few minutes of your time and, of course, has no other time available for an appointment."

Barb furrowed her brow as she lowered her head and peeked over her glasses at Diane. She was aggravated and began, "That woman thinks she can just waltz in here anyti—" she stopped suddenly, catching herself. After a short pause, she smiled and said, "Of course. Please offer her something to warm her up. I will meet with her at the Tulip Table in a moment."

Diane nodded and did what Barb asked.

"My apologies again, Abby. Are you able to extend your time? Or do you have other appointments this morning? I would like to discuss several of our plans for this season."

"No problem at all."

"Thank you. I should not be more than fifteen minutes," Barb said as she grabbed a file and limped out the door. "Judy! How unexpectedly wonderful to see you!" Judy answered with something inaudible to me, followed by Barb's, "Of course, it's no bother."

Yeah, right, I call foul, Judy Monihan. Make an appointment like everyone else. And yet Barb stopped herself in midsentence. I wondered what was like to swallow your aggravation all of the time. Of course, that was something I knew very little about.

I stood up and took a self-guided tour of the pictures hanging on her walls. The wall to my right had several images of Barb over the years. They were of her standing in gardens with different clients. Some I recognized as local politicians and ambulance chasers who advertised on TV. Others I didn't, but knew they must be prominent within whatever field they worked.

I continued following the walls as though I were in a museum. The back wall had four square paintings that took the entirety of the space. The garden paintings looked vaguely familiar to me. By the time I got to the last one, I realized that I was looking at Lynn Cleary's house. Sure enough, her signature was at the bottom corner. *Nice. She's Syracuse's answer to Monet's Garden at Giverny*, I thought to myself.

In the middle of the wall next to the conference table was a black-framed college degree: Barbara J. Clayter, Cornell

University, Bachelors of Science in Horticultural Science, Class of 1959, Magna Cum Laude.

Two family pictures hung on either side of her degree. It appeared she had three sons. The first picture had Barb at one end and her husband on the other with three boys between them. College graduation pictures. The middle son was dressed in a cap and gown, proudly holding his newly acquired sheepskin. The other picture was exactly the same, only with a different son holding the degree. Ivy League, from the looks of it. One was Cornell's coat of arms; the other was Yale's Urim and Thummim. "Ah yes, truth and light," I mused.

Each one of them had a great smile. Judging by the gleaming white, perfectly straight teeth the boys had, I guessed that there was a picture on the opposite wall of Barb with the orthodontist who just paid for his new gardens, courtesy of the Preston boys.

I had to admit that she had a handsome husband and three good-looking sons. My sightseeing tour was suddenly interrupted.

"Hey, Mom. Do you…oh, oops! Sorry!" said a guy who appeared to be son number three.

"No problem. She's in the conference room for a few minutes."

"Got it. Oh well, her loss. I was gonna take her to lunch later today since I'm on spring break."

"It's only nine-fifteen; I'm sure you'll catch her before lunch. Where's school?"

"RPI."

"What's the degree?"

"I got my BS in civil engineering. I'm finishing my master's in the same. How about you? What is someone so young doing in this office?"

"Abby Field. I'm a supervisor at Sapphire. We work with your mom...or for your mom...or something like that," I said, smiling.

"I'm Jim," he said, smiling back. "*For Mom* sounds more accurate. So what's your role in the gala affairs she produces?"

"I was a hardscape supervisor, but they bumped me over to be your mom's go-to. I'm here today with samples to figure out what's in order for the season. Then I'll run the installs under your mom's direction," I said, giving Jim the once over.

He was even better looking in person. Not over the top, but more like his father appeared in the pictures. Handsome.

He was dressed in Levi jeans with a jean jacket over a colonial blue, three-button thermal henley. A pair of worn black Nikes, each with a dirty yellow swoosh covered his feet. Dark brown hair cut short and parted to the right outlined his face. A mustache that looked more like an ailing caterpillar rested on his lip.

"Mustaches still in? I thought we moved from *Magnum PI* to *Miami Vice*?" I said, teasing him.

He ran his fingers proudly over his mustache and answered, "Hey, don't mock! This bad boy helped me purchase alcohol underage more than once. Besides, I'm way more of the Tom Selleck type than a Don Johnson. Too much effort to keep a consistent five o'clock shadow going!" He was smiling and rubbing his fingers on his cheeks where the stubble should be.

"What do you do, besides cater to my mother?" he asked with a smirk on his face.

"Well," I said, tilting my head downward and to the right. "When I'm not landscaping, I enjoy fishing, hiking, cross-country skiing, and watching movies, among other things. Yourself?"

"I like to fish, canoe, down-hill ski, and watch movies. You know, among other things."

I rolled my eyes at him and watched the caterpillar move its front and back ends upwards into a smile.

"I have another idea," Jim continued, "instead of taking my mom to lunch, how about I take y—"

"Jimmy!" came Barb's forceful interruption. She had been eavesdropping outside the door. "You can't get an engagement ring over the knuckle of a woman with fingers like a man!"

I don't know what stunned me more. Her reaction to the thought of Jim and me eating lunch together, or her flagrant use of a contraction! It was a toss-up, but now I knew. If I saw her in a grocery store, she would no doubt avoid me. I was the hired help.

"Really, Mom? An engagement ring? I'm talking about lunch. Calm down!" Jim answered. "Man hands, Mom? It's called work. You know, you used to do that type of work at one time," he said as he gave me a wink, obviously used to her behavior.

Barb's face began to flush with embarrassment.

"Now I'm leaving you two alone. Play nice," Jim continued chiding his mother. "I'll be back at eleven-thirty to pick you up for lunch, Mom," he said as he closed the door.

An awkward meeting followed as we discussed the season's plans. I was so glad to get out of there that I had to refrain from grabbing my coat and *running* out the door.

I crossed the lot to my car and was unlocking it when I heard a vehicle pull up and stop.

"Lemme guess. That's the first time you saw my mom act like that."

"Yup. It's the first time I've heard her use less than perfect English. Does she always talk like that?"

"No, she doesn't. Will the real Barbara J. Preston please stand up! You're getting her work weirdness," Jim announced from his red 1981 Chevy Silverado.

"Hey, how about I take you to the movies tonight? *The Hunt for Red October* looks good. And what woman can resist Sean Connery regardless of his age?"

"I'd love to see it. A friend of mine said it was great. Are you sure the woman in the window behind you will approve?"

"Really?" Jim said as he put his hand over his mouth in feigned disbelief. "Is she staring at us? She doesn't approve of much some days, but don't worry about her. Address and phone number?"

I grabbed a piece of paper from my car and wrote my information down. Jim took it and said he'd call later when he checked the paper for times and theater locations.

He pulled away, leaving Barb glaring at me through the window—which I ignored.

Chapter 6

The *Hunt for Red October* was worth the price of admission. We grabbed a bite to eat at the usual spot for drunken college students. Denny's. Open all night. We talked so long we didn't realize it was four-thirty in the morning. Jim dropped me at my parents' house at five a.m. Yikes. How would I get past two light sleepers? I quietly opened the door and found Jeff in the kitchen getting ready for work.

"Must have been some date."

"Not bad."

Just then, Dad stepped into the kitchen wearing his matching pajama set.

"You just get home?" he asked sternly.

Jeff cocked his head at him and said, "Why are you asking? You were just out here five minutes ago, and she wasn't here. Now she is. You know she just walked in!"

I got a semi-disgusted look from Dad as he retreated to his bedroom, speechless.

"Thanks, Jeff, I owe you. And yes, he's a great guy. You'll like him," I said as I made my way to my room for a short nap.

***

Deborah R. Procopio

I dragged myself into work to meet with Steve and Vicki to discuss the summer plans I made with Barb.

Steve started, "You look tired this morning…so how was yesterday's meeting with Barb?"

"Wellllll, that all depends on what we're talking about. We're almost finalized for all eight projects, minus Mrs. Monihan, who is finishing some details."

"What is the 'depends' part?" asked Vicki. "Good or bad?"

"Welllll, that depends as well," I hesitated, half due to exhaustion and half for comedic, dramatic effect. "First off, Barb does have a nasty streak she tries to hide under her façade of perfect English, perfect dress, and perfect manners—"

"Not all that surprising," Steve interjected as he grabbed Barb's file. "What's the rest of the story?"

"I aggravated her enough to make her use a contraction," I raised my eyebrows as Steve and Vicki laughed. "I met her youngest son, Jim," apparently I smiled when I said it. Vicki gave me a knowing smile back, while Steve looked perplexed.

"And?" a confused Steve asked.

"He asked me out."

"So what's the big deal about that?"

"I'm pretty sure I'm beneath the plans Barb has for him."

"And that's where the contraction came in?"

"Yup."

"When's the hot date?"

"Last night…Did I mention I didn't get home 'til five this morning?"

"WOW! Abby, you brazen hussy!" said Steve using his duck voice and laugh.

"I know, I know," I said as I put my elbows on the table, chin in my hand and rubbed my eyes with my fingers. "You guys do realize it may be a real issue."

"Have you ever known me to take crap from anyone? I'll handle Barb if she has a problem. Honestly, we have plenty of work besides her."

Vicki left to answer the phone as Jay entered.

"Hey, Jay!" said Steve excitedly. "Abby pulled an all-nighter with Barb's son Jim!"

"Wha?" Jay looked a bit bewildered at first and then responded, "Abby, Abby, Abby, what are we going to do with you?" shaking his head with insincere disgust.

I was still sitting with my chin in my hands and fingers over my eyes and nose. I spread my index finger from the other three fingers and tried glaring at the two of them. I knew it was no use as they were having too much fun.

Vicki interrupted, "Barb's on line one looking for you, Steve."

"Of course she is," I said.

We all gathered around Steve's desk, listening and trying to contain our laughter. Steve had a huge grin on his face as he listened to Barb's "concern" about me and Jim and how it could have a detrimental effect on the "partnership."

We listened as Steve asked her how it could possibly affect the Sapphire—Preston working relationship since Jim didn't work for Preston. He asked Barb if she had ever had any problems with my professionalism or work ethic. Of course, she had to say no. Steve ended by telling her that he did not meddle in his employees' personal affairs unless it spilled into Sapphire, at which point Barb alluded to dissolving the agreement. Steve wasn't about to cave to her threat; he politely told her that she was free to do that, as were we.

He ended the conversation by needling Barb with reminders of the work we had done.

"Barb, it's really been a pleasure working with you. Thank you for allowing us the opportunity to provide you with full service. The arbor and pergola constructions we did for you gave us the chance to hone our skills…Wha? Wait a sec, sorry, Barb, Jay is talking to me." Jay was doing no such thing, but Steve was making Barb sweat and loving every minute of it. "What's that, Jay?" he continued, "yeah, I'll tell Barb that. Jay wanted me to tell you he appreciates the time you took with him on the pond installs, particularly at the Trayer's. The small boulders with the waterfall was his personal favorite."

Jay decided to play along. "Judge Cleary's fountain was another one of my favorites," he said loudly as he stepped away from Steve's desk, making it sound as though he was busy in another part of the office.

Steve continued, "I hate to see you left in a lurch. Would you like me to ask around and see if I can get another company to help you in the interim? Spring will be here anyd—" Steve was cut off in midsentence.

He sat in his chair, rolling his eyes and occasionally answering with "uh-huhs."

"That's fine, Barb." The call was coming to an end. "Are you sure you wouldn't like to think about it? I can give you until the end of the week?" Steve was as polite as could be. "No? Well, as long as you're sure. Uh-huh…of course. As soon as the weather breaks, give Abby a call, just like last year…sure thing, nice talking to you, Barb. Bye." And he hung up.

As soon as the phone hit the receiver, we all burst out laughing.

He leaned back in his black leather office chair, clasping his hands behind his head. "Nobody messes with the Master," he said, reaching to tug on his sapphire earring with a huge smile across his face.

"And that's what I love about you!" I said as I stepped behind his chair and leaned my cheek on the top of his wavy hair while tugging on his earring.

"Something tells me we're about to witness what happened to the fifth-grade boys' kickball team," Jay said.

"Yup," I replied, "and it won't be pretty."

***

Jim and I had a busy spring, me with work and him finishing his degree. We met in Utica on Sundays, figuring it was about halfway between Syracuse and Troy. Our days always concluded with a stop at Rosie's Cannolis and More before getting on the thruway. As we chatted over cannolis, I finally asked Jim what was up with his mom. For the most part, Barb kept her snarkyness at bay on the job site, but she was less than thrilled to have me dating her son, and I was curious as to why.

Jim explained that when it came to her sons, she wanted them in the "right college, getting the right degree, and marrying the right girl." Which basically meant the college, degree, and girl of Barb's choosing.

"Couldn't get into an Ivy League? I see your brothers graduated from them along with your mom."

"I got accepted at Cornell and Princeton, but I didn't think they had a strong enough engineering program, so I decided on RPI, much to Mom's dismay. I love RPI. It's a great engineer school. Very challenging."

"Everyone knows that's a great engineering school. Sounds like your mom is just being stupid about that, but I'm guessing you got the 'right' degree."

"Yup, I did, and so did Drew and Sean."

Drew is the oldest and lives in Rochester with his wife Kate, who is expecting in August. Sean is in the middle and lives here in Utica with his wife, Lori. They married last year.

"Like my brothers, I always loved physics, so it was a no-brainer."

"Your mom ended up with three engineers? Not sure what the odds on that are, but then she has the audacity to complain about RPI? So then, what does your mom intend for you?"

"For starters, I get dragged around to the stupid garden parties for her clients while she makes a bit of a jackass out of herself, trying to make sure I meet the daughters of doctors, professors, lawyers, and politicians. Afterward, she quizzes me as to who I'm interested in. So far, it's been no one. The whole thought of living in that world nauseates me. Don't get me wrong, not everyone is like that, but I get tired of it. Twenty-year-old girls with expensive jewelry, Gucci this, Calvin Klein that, too much makeup, too much perfume, brand new cars they didn't earn...I'd rather date someone more down-to-earth with a job their daddy didn't get them."

We were quiet for a moment. I was pondering what Jim said when he continued, "I was offered a job with Insight Engineering on the east side. It's a small firm, and I really like the owner. He seems to be interested in training up new bucks. Mom and Dad don't know yet. Mom is busy pulling some strings to get me a job with the city…as though I'm not capable of getting my own job. She'll hate my choice because the city will pay more and of course, I'll meet 'more important people,' but I'd like to do what I want. I want to know that my success is mine and not my mother's intervention…so don't worry, Miss Abby, she'll forget about you and be mad at me *very* soon!" he said with a laugh.

"What about Drew and Sean? Did they get the 'right jobs and marry the right girls'?"

"Yes and no. Drew works for the city of Rochester, so Mom loves that he meets politicians and government officials. Kate is a secretary for the planning board. Although she doesn't meet my mother's 'professional standards,' she 'knows people.'"

He took a breath and continued, "Sean works for a government contractor, and Mom would rather he work for the government. Lori works in lower management for the event center here. She loves her job, but Mom thinks it's a lowly position. It kind of is, but she's all of twenty-four, and her career has just started. She's a hard worker, and I have no doubt she will move up."

"Do you like your sisters-in-law?"

"I do. They are nice girls and good matches for my brothers. They're also dying to meet you, in spite of what my mother says!" He gave me a cheesy smile as he finished his espresso.

I flicked a piece of cannoli crumb at him. "You're a funny guy, James Preston."

We threw out our trash, turned in our dishes, and we each headed home.

Chapter 7

J im graduated in May, but I was unable to attend due to a
wedding. He made arrangements for dinner at his house
with Mom and Dad. I had not yet met his father and wasn't
quite sure what to expect, but Jim assured me that opposites
attract, and I would get along just fine with him.

I pulled into the Preston's Golden Eagle neighborhood,
where giant houses with perfect landscaping lined the streets.
Seemed a bit sterile, in my opinion; the houses were all similar.
Each one had wood siding, no vinyl. No one had a pool or a
clothesline, and everyone seemed to have the same shed. There
were no boats or RVs in the driveway, and weirder than that, I
didn't see any kids playing in the streets. *Must be all studying
for their SATs*, I thought to myself. *And apparently, no one has
any fun here in the deed-restricted neighborhood.*

I looked at the directions Jim wrote for me; left onto Eaglet
Way, second house on the right. I pulled into the driveway
and parked behind Barb's Caddy. Jim's old red truck was situated behind a Volvo that I assumed belonged to his dad. I was
surprised the neighbors didn't complain about Jim's truck…
then again, maybe they did.

Humongous was the only word I could think of to describe the house. My parents' little three-bedroom ranch would probably have fit inside this puppy three times if I included their basement. The front door sat in the dead center of the house. Two long windows encased the sides of the glass storm door. The wooden front door had an oval opaque leadlight window in the middle with narrow lead cames dividing the glass into sections. On the second floor, centered above the front door, was a rectangular window with a half-moon window directly over that. An upside-down, V-shaped roof was suspended high above the stoop.

The house was completely symmetrical—and completely boring. The white windows were all the same: six feet high, four feet wide, gridded glass with matching shutters. Monochromatic colors finished the look with a beige house, brownish shutters, and off-beige trim…I figured the real color's names were angry mushroom, baby-diaper brown, with a splash of boring gold. Then again, maybe I was just gearing myself up to expect the worst out of our dinner date, and finding fault with their beautiful home was just my way of dealing with it.

***

I walked up the driveway to the awaiting paver-brick stoop. The door had a brass knocker with "The Prestons" engraved on it. I reached for the doorbell, which made a loud, resonating, "BING BONG" sound in the house. I began wondering if a creepy butler would answer, saying, "Yes, Madam?"

The door opened, and Jim said, "Hi. You look perplexed."

"I was half expecting a creepy butler."

"Nope. No butler. Just a cleaning lady on Wednesdays," he said as he let me in.

I entered the house to find a staircase directly behind Jim and an entryway light dangling overhead from the second-floor ceiling. Jim's dad descended the stairs dressed in tan pants and a dark blue, three-button golf shirt complete with the IZOD alligator on it. The pictures didn't lie. Jim looked like his father, only a couple inches taller. Joe's brown hair had gray at the temples with a sprinkling around the rest of his head. Just like Jim, it was tapered at the side and parted to the right. Although the deep Vs had invaded his hairline and he was a bit paunchy, he was still a handsome guy.

"Abby! It's a pleasure to finally meet you! We've heard so much about you. I'm Joe Preston. Like you couldn't guess!" he said with a warm greeting and handshake to match.

I reached out to take his hand, "Nice to meet you as well, Mr. Preston."

"No formalities here, young lady! Call me Joe. I'm going to let Jim give you the nickel tour of the place while I give Barb a hand in the kitchen."

I removed my shoes and set off with Jim on the first-floor tour. I realized the house had nine-foot ceilings, which created the illusion of size. Not that the house wasn't big, but the ceiling height gave it a street appearance of considerable dimensions.

We went to the right of the stairs and entered a living room that seemed so formal to me that I wasn't sure I wanted to step in it, let alone sit down. The pure white short pile carpet was endowed with Queen Anne style furniture set against white walls. The chairs, couch, end tables, coffee table, and a chest of drawers were stained dark walnut. The furniture was uphol-stered in a bronze tapestry with swirls of gold and maroon elegantly entwined throughout.

The curtains were muted garnet with gold-fringed tiebacks that preserved the perfectly spaced pleats and held the panels in their place. Hung on brass rods, the headings met at dead center. A golden scarf draped neatly across a chest of drawers between the windows. A lovely creamy white, antique water pitcher adorned with gilded, gold edges rested on the scarf. Filled with a gorgeous arrangement of silk flowers, it fit the space perfectly.

From the windows, my eyes moved left to where the sofa sat with its two end tables and matching brass lamps.

Walnut frames held three pieces of artwork above the couch, creating a mural of poppies. The long, slender frames each had a fiery flower that surged forth from the canvas in various poses. In the painting to the left, the poppy was positioned in the lower-left corner with its emerald and lime green leaves swirling together and spiraling upward. Parts of the petals were incomplete as the artist intentionally let them "fall off" the canvas. The second showed the poppy exploding from the center with the foliage rushing outward in all directions like an Independence Day firework. The flower on the third canvas was painted in the upper right corner and reminded me of childhood crayon drawings where the yellow sun sat in the corner with its rays pointing in all directions.

In the middle of the back wall was the entryway into the next room. To the left of the entrance, an old grandfather clock sat diagonal to the corner. Next to the clock was a wooden tea cart flanked by two chairs that matched the couch. A stunning three-piece porcelain tea set rested on a second matching gold scarf. The teapot, sugar bowl, and cream pot were all jet black. An intricate gold lily sat in the center of each piece. It was so detailed that the stamen and pistils were clearly embossed in the design. Whirls of golden grasses embraced the flowers in a delicate hug. The evening sun sparkled as it leaped off the gold rims, handles, and spouts.

We left the living room through the back archway and entered a giant family room. The walls were covered in sharp looking blueish-gray wood paneling. Chocolate-colored modular furniture set in a standard horseshoe configuration engulfed the area. A square coffee table was placed in the rectangular space created by the couch with remote controls and coasters neatly sitting in a row. The carpet was a short pile of mottled beige, brown, and black woven together to hide dirt.

The furniture faced a large thirty-six-inch projection TV. Racks of VHS tapes sat on shelves next to the television, with a shelf underneath holding the video player and tape rewinder. An old Atari 2600 and a barrage of games were also scattered in the mix. It was a warm, homey room—the dead opposite of the living room for sure.

To the left was a sliding glass door that led out to a deck.

A second doorway led into the kitchen. We stepped from the family room onto the earthy ceramic tiles of the eat-in space. A standard blond, wooden, oval table with six round-back spindled chairs overlooked the deck. The working part of the kitchen was U-shaped with a counter that divided the workspace from the eating space. Countertops were granite, of course, with cherry wood cabinets lining the walls. The rest was the basic menagerie of kitchen appliances.

Barb and Joe were busy finishing up dinner, and quite honestly, it smelled fantastic.

"It smells wonderful!" I said.

"I hope you like salmon," Barb responded.

"As a matter of fact, I do!" Actually, I had no idea. I had never had salmon, and I was hoping, at the very least, it was something I could eat without wanting to spit it into a napkin.

"Jimmy, finish showing Abby the downstairs and meet us in the dining room."

"Okay, Mom."

We crossed the kitchen where a full bathroom, a giant guest room, and Joe's office was located. Joe was the regional sales manager for Protection Plus Insurance, with a territory covering most of the northeast. He worked from home as well as an office downtown when he wasn't traveling.

We finished the tour with a back door breezeway that led to the garage. We turned around and went into the dining room. Another gorgeous room that was just as intimidating as the white room.

The furniture was an "if you have to ask, you can't afford it" matching set. The enormous dining room table was easily eight feet long and fifty inches across. The two massive columnar legs at each end were surrounded with golden leaves. The tabletop was made of multi-toned woods, which I guessed to be mahogany and rosewood. A beautiful sunburst pattern radiated from the center of the table outward and was surrounded by carvings of five palm tree leaves encircled with a thin line that wove itself from palm to palm around the table. I'm pretty sure I could see my reflection on the tabletop.

La Belle Communauté

Ten chairs, simple in design, were lined up around the table. The top rail had a slight arch with palm fronds sculpted into it. The seats were cushioned in a pale champagne hue with small fleur d'lis in gold brocade. All of this sat on a huge, navy oriental rug with splashes of reds, golds, and whites that covered glowing hardwoods.

Against the wall to my left was a matching cadenza that held crystal, silverware, and table linens. The sunburst top sat upon whittled palm trees. The front doors were plain but beautiful, with light shades surrounding the darker tones. The cabinets had handles that looked like the skeleton keys of old. Dazzling.

A large mirror with its golden border hung on the wall to my right. To the left of that was a wooden, five-sided corner curio cabinet. Its glass shelves were lit and filled with a strange array of decorated eggs, the likes of which I had never seen before—and no, they weren't Fabergé. These appeared to be dyed. Flowers, all sorts of geometric shapes, and various squiggly designs adorned the shells. A few had the word "Mom" with a heart drawn around it in shaky handwriting. Every shelf was full of them. Some were displayed in brandy snifters, others sat on small pedestals designed to hold eggs, while others were cushioned in silky, blue fabric. It was evident that children had made them.

Jim was busy setting the table when I interrupted him, "What are these eggs?"

"Oh, they're Ukrainian eggs, also known as pysanky. Mom's grandparents were from Ukraine, and the tradition was passed down. As kids, we did them at Easter."

I was surprised that Barb would dedicate an entire display case to them. I just didn't view her as the sentimental type, I guess.

I was completely enthralled.

"How are those designs made?"

"We use a kistka. It's a type of stylus with a tiny cup. The cup is filled with beeswax that gets heated over a candle. Any part of the egg you want to stay white is covered with wax. Then it gets dipped in the next lightest color you want. Typically, it's yellow. Anything you want to stay yellow is covered with wax, and so on as the colors get darker. Then the wax is melted by holding the egg over a candle and wiping it on paper towels. Then we blow out the egg and spray shellac on it."

"I love it!" I exclaimed just as Barb and Joe were bringing dinner to the table.

"Abby," said Barb, "you'll have to try it! We'll buy new dyes and beeswax at the Ukrainian shop if you're interested. Maybe a couple electric kistkas as well."

"I would really like that!"

I was taken aback by Barb's willingness to teach me her family tradition. Maybe she was warming up to the idea of Jim and me.

I also noticed Barb acted more like a regular person. Her vocabulary wasn't quite as elegant at home, and she really did use contractions!

***

Salmon amandine, rice pilaf, and fresh seasoned green vegetables were set on the table. Joe filled the water glasses and offered me a glass of wine. Not being a wine fan, I stuck with water.

Joe said grace. "Bless us, O Lord, and these, Thy gifts, which we are about to receive from Thy bounty. Through Christ our Lord. Amen." The three of them then made the sign of the cross.

Barb turned to me with a puzzled look, "Abby, didn't you once tell me your mother is from Italy?"

"Yes."

"Why don't you make the sign of the cross?"

"I'm not Catholic."

"What do you mean you aren't Catholic? How is it your mother isn't Catholic?" Her concern was growing.

"She was raised Catholic, but my father was raised Protestant. They married in a Methodist church, and when my brother was born, Mom and Dad took him to St. Mary's to be baptized. The priest told my father that since he wasn't Catholic and they weren't married in the Catholic Church, he and my mother weren't really married. Then the priest wanted them to sign papers and make various promises to raise my brother Catholic. Dad was pretty angry that the priest told him they weren't really married and wasn't about to sign anything. My mom wasn't thrilled either, so that was the end of Catholicism for my family."

"Then you were raised Protestant?"

"Not really. My parents love God but not religion, so they taught us themselves."

"Really, Abby. I don't see how any person has spiritual guidance outside of the Church and priests. I'm not—"

"Barb," Joe interrupted her, "pass the salmon, please. It smells great!"

I saw him give Barb "the eye" and was glad he had diverted the conversation.

We continued with dinner, and Joe asked about my background: where I lived, went to high school, and what my parents did for work.

"Where did you go to college?" Joe asked.

"Joe, dear. Abby didn't attend college," Barb said in a mildly condescending manner.

I turned to Joe. "Cornell, Class of '88. Majored in horticultural science and graduated Summa Cum Laude."

It was beautiful! Barb stopped dead with a forkful of salmon poised right in front of her gaping mouth and her blue eyes staring blankly at me. She was stunned. Jim wiped his mouth with his napkin to hide his amusement.

I decided to move in for the kill. "My concentration was in public garden management," I said as I sipped water from my glass.

"Good for you! Degrees like that are never wasted," said Joe.

Barb decided to put her fork full of fish back down on her plate. "Abby, dear. You never told me you went to Cornell."

I knew she was feeling a bit foolish with that foot stuck in her mouth.

"You never asked me and, after all, what difference does it make?"

"Why are you a bricklaying laborer?" She was right back to being snotty, spurred on by her own embarrassment.

"I'm not a 'bricklaying laborer' Barb, although I did start as one. I wanted to learn from the ground up. How can I give direction or train someone if I don't know how to do it myself? I started as a laborer after my freshman year of college. The following summer, I was a crew leader. By the time we met, I had graduated and been promoted to supervisor, which meant I handled all sales, design, bidding, and installation of hard-scapes. Now I am the liaison for you. I've learned every aspect of my job, and I continue to learn. I will be building, training, and supervising the pergola at Judy Monihan's house, that's why I have 'knuckles of a man on woman's hand' as you say." I was trying to keep the annoyance out of my voice—while still addressing her "holier than thou" attitude.

"But why do you do this kind of work with a degree like that?"

Joe sensed my weariness.

"Barbara Jean, why don't we clear the table," he said as he turned to me with a smile and asked, "would you like coffee with dessert? Barb made her specialty. Chocolate raspberry mousse."

"No thank you on the coffee. Dinner was excellent!" And it really was.

When Barb and Joe were out of earshot, I looked across the table at Jim, raised my eyebrows at him, and said, "Imagine that. Who knew I liked salmon?"

He was giving me an approving eye over my little zinger at Barb when he said, "Gee, did I intentionally withhold your college degree from my Mom? Now, what kind of son would do that? Oh, yeah," Jim continued answering his own question, "the kind of son who listens to his girlfriend when she tells him not to let his mom in on the 'top secret' Ivy League information. And that's why I love you, Abby Marie."

As he put the water glass to his mouth, I looked through the rim of the glass to see his mustache smiling.

Chapter 8

Barb had finally realized I wasn't going anywhere, so Jim invited me to my first garden party. In all honesty, I had believed they were a thing of the past. Jim explained how he'd been dragged to them since he was sixteen. Apparently, Barb's customers always went through the whole process of renovation and installation, followed by a late afternoon cocktail reception that was usually held the following year. That time delay gave the plant materials a season to root and fill in a bit. Barb and Joe were always the guests of honor, as were the boys when they got older.

"So what you're telling me is you're inviting me to the Grand Unveiling of work I did last summer?" I was lying on my bed trying to untangle the phone cord and pay attention to Jim on the other end at the same time.

"Sure am," he replied.

"Sounds like a yard full of 'Barbs' all jockeying for position."

"It kind of is."

I paused for a moment, really having no interest in any part of it.

"C'mon Abby…please?"

"Welllll…hmmm…I don't know…sounds both boring and annoying all at the same time. Plus, it's out of my social class… so, what's in it for me?" I asked, teasing Jim.

"You get to dress up, watch my mom work the yard, eat weird hors d'oeuvres, and meet some annoying people. All of which I *know* you'll love!"

"Yeah. Again I'll ask. What's in it for me?"

"Me, of course. I'll be looking like a *GQ* model in dress pants, a sports coat, and a dress shirt with no tie."

"Hmmm…will you leave the top shirt button undone so everyone can see your chest hair?"

"Yup. And I'll even give you a quarter."

"I guess I can't resist the quarter."

"The garden party is pretty much just an outdoor cocktail reception. It starts at four on Friday. Do you think you can get out early enough?"

"Yeah, I'll figure it out."

"I'll pick you up at three forty-five."

I hung up the phone, wondering how I got myself into these situations, but because it would be a one-time thing, I decided I'd probably live.

***

Jim picked me up at three forty-five as promised, or maybe threatened, and we headed to Judge Cleary's house. I guess my imagining of the Roaring Twenties was going to catch up to me

89

seventy years after the era. The secrets of this cocktail reception would be kept by the red brick patio.

We parked and made our way to the backyard, where it seemed most of the guests were already gathering. We spotted Barb and Joe chatting with the judge and Lynn. Joe greeted us and re-introduced Jim and myself to them. They both went on about how much they loved the gardens and complimented Barb on her design and me on the installs. I hadn't met the judge before, but he seemed nice.

Barb quietly pulled Jim aside and, in a whisper-yell, said, "Jimmy! Button your top shirt button! You look like a cavone!"

It was all I could do to contain my laughter. Jim was being smart when he arrived at my house and had completely forgotten to button up, making him look like a crude, uneducated person. No clue where Barb picked up the Italian slang, but it was funny.

"Jimmy!" We turned to find the outstretched hand of a city councilor. I was introduced and listened as the two chatted. The councilor congratulated him on his graduation and new job. I didn't pay much attention to the discussion; I was more focused on the progress of the gardens and on people-watching.

It was June, which can be an awkward time for a perennial garden. The tulips' dead foliage was waiting to be cut back completely, while it was still too early for some of the showiest perennials to peak.

White, spikey astilbe feathers swayed in the gentle breeze against a black lace elderberry backdrop. Tangerine-orange and ruby-red blanket flowers were snuggled into the front of the beds while a handful of pale-blue creeping phlox clung to the last of their blossoms. Variegated hosta leaves were in full display, along with coral bells and pink dianthus. Barb was great at making sure the garden had interest from spring through fall, and while many plants were still making their way toward the flowering phase, she managed to fill it in quite nicely.

The waitstaff, dressed in white tuxedo shirts with pants, shoes, and bow ties all in black, circled the back yard offering drinks and hors d'oeuvres. I was hungry from working all day and happily grabbed a soda and a mini quiche as they went by. I watched the guests, all well dressed, chatting with each other while sipping drinks and eating high-end snacks.

Jim and I made our way to the edge of the green space, with both of us hoping to fade into the plants and go unnoticed for the last hour, but that was not to be. Barb came over with a petite, bubbly blonde who appeared to be in her early twenties.

"Jimmy, this is Suzie Cleary, the judge's youngest child. I thought you might like to get to know her better," Barb said in a sickly-sweet voice, all while giving Jim "the eye."

"Um, hi," Jim said awkwardly. "And this is my girl-friend, Abby."

I greeted her, "Nice to meet you, Suzie."

Suzie looked a bit perplexed, said hello, and walked off.

"Your mom did not just try to set you up with Suzie while I was standing here, did she?"

"I think she did. I've never seen her do that before, but then again, I've never had a girlfriend here with me before," Jim said, a bit bewildered himself.

His bewilderment turned to anger as he grabbed my hand and said, "C'mon," and we headed toward his mother.

"Mom!" he demanded, "what was that? What do you think you're doing? How dare you insult Abby like that!"

"Jimmy, I was just—"

"Just what, Mom? Just trying to fix me up with someone YOU want me to be with?"

Jim turned on his heels, and with me in tow, we got in his truck and left. He was fuming, and I was glad that was the first and last of the Grand Unveilings I would have to attend.

***

Just a month later, Jim was headed to the cocktail reception in the garden of the mayor's house. I was stunned he would even consider it, but what was more stunning was when he invited me. Barb had promised to be on her best behavior, or so I was told.

Working with Barb was enough. She was a bit sheepish around me after the Suzie introduction, and I let her sit in it. I spoke politely, but I was short with her. I'd had just about all of her high society crap I could take, and I could not have cared less about anyone she knew. What was most puzzling to me was why Jim would even consider going in the first place and why Barb wanted him there. Nevertheless, I found myself once again suffering through the stupidity of the next reception.

I didn't have anything to do with the mayor's house. Barb renovated the gardens the summer before Sapphire was involved. It was now an election year, so there was no time like the present for the Grand Unveiling. I reluctantly agreed, with the understanding it was the last one I would be at this summer. It was hard to get out of work early, I was tired by the time the end of the work week came, and I'd much rather spend my Friday evening at The

Greatest, shooting darts and eating dinner. Cocktails and snacks weren't filling, and after my first experience, I was done.

***

We pulled up to the mayor's house, which happened to be one of my most favorite houses in the neighborhood. The exterior was red mixed brick with black shutters and a coffee-colored entry door. The driveway sat to the left with a sidewalk that led to the front stoop. At each corner of the house were two weeping cherry trees embedded in pachysandra ground cover. Normally I wasn't a fan of ground cover, but it worked well here. The only odd thing about the front landscape was a giant horse chestnut planted in the middle of the lawn. The tree was as old as the house and must have been popular at the time, as several houses had one. At maturity, they grow to seventy-five feet tall and almost as wide. This one, although beautiful, took up the entire yard. I thought I would be nervous in a gusty wind.

We made our way out back, where I was surprised to see that the yard was much bigger than average for being in the middle of the city. Barb did an amazing job. We entered through an arched trellis loaded with deep violet and pink clematis. One of each color had been planted on either side, and now the two had married to become one. A beautiful, intermingled spray of pastels resulted, making it impossible to know where one plant ended and the other began.

The yard had the obligatory fence surrounding it, creating the backdrop for a perennial border. But due to the yard's size and the space it afforded, there was a second bed that paralleled the outermost border, still leaving room for a large, lush, green lawn. A flagstone corridor wove its way between the two beds. I turned left and entered the space. The flagstone path created a walkway about four feet wide, with the plantings from both sides intentionally encroaching the walk.

Chartreuse from the Japanese forest grasses, mauve speed-well, blue Siberian bellflowers, and the foliage of faded candy tufts spilled out onto the walk. Coreopsis was interspersed with its various varieties with colors of cayenne, lemon, and peach breaking through. Blue leaf hostas rested in the shade of the small hydrangea trees, which anchored the design at regular intervals along the fencing. The young conical flowers emerged in their green tone. Snow white and maroon would follow as the season progressed. Coneflowers and perennial sunflowers burst onto the scene, proudly displaying their white, plum, yellow, and orange petals.

I watched a dozen Canadian tiger swallowtail butterflies as they floated from panicle to panicle on a black knight butterfly bush. The soft, lemony wings were wide open and quite pretty against the dark purple flowers.

A small stand of dark pink Joe-Pye weed with the white torches of liatris stood in the middle of the bed. Bugbane, with its six-foot spikes of blushing pink, shot up from the garden floor like a roman candle. A slew of insects were hustling around the flowers paying no attention to us.

Grasshoppers, startled by our footfall, leaped onto buttery yellow foxgloves to escape us. Monochromatic blues of larkspur dotted the garden and covered the fading lupines. Lupines had always been one of my favorites, and I was sorry I missed the show.

Crimson bee balm, along with peach, and rouge colored rose bushes guided us to the corner of the garden. A beautyberry bush arched over a grouping of lemon-lime hosta. The bush can take up a great deal of real estate, but Barb had the lower branches cut back while letting the upper limbs create a shelter for her shade-lovers. At the moment, the berries were in their infant stage, but in a few short weeks the bush would show off its clusters of magenta berries.

I continued meandering along with Jim in tow. All I could do was whisper "wow" as I walked along. I noticed a familiar smell that I couldn't quite put my finger on. I looked down and noticed that Barb had planted thyme between the irregular shapes of the flagstones. As our feet crushed the herb, a delightful smell filled the air.

We reached the back of the path, where a small hill ascended. Stepping stones took us upward to a rock garden. Yellow alyssum, various stonecrops, hens and chickens, spurge, lavenders, and creeping thyme all made the stones their home. We looped around and stepped down to the last side of the garden.

The path was no longer a tunnel between two beds, just a simple perennial border. Weathered wooden benches were neatly tucked into various locations along the fence with flagstones that led the way to them and invited the guest to sit. Cicada flies buzzing in the treetops bid us farewell as we left the tranquility of the gardens and returned to reality.

We stepped off the path near the house and saw Barb and Joe talking to the mayor and his wife. *Fun's over*, I thought to myself.

***

We walked over to the Prestons, where they greeted us and introduced us to Jerry and Joann McDougal. Jerry was currently the reigning incumbent hoping for reelection in November. The McDougals seemed very pleasant, but I never felt like I knew who they really were. It seemed they were all on their best behavior and sucking up to each other. Maybe they weren't, but it was so hard to tell.

Barb had gone from trying to get Jim a new girlfriend to introducing me with my Cornell degree and major. Occasionally she threw in Summa Cum Laude in an annoyingly fake voice. I'm not sure which I hated more, but I was becoming increasingly perturbed with each introduction. Barb introduced me to a lawyer and his wife.

"Abby Field, I'd like you to meet Peter and Laura Chambers. They're both trial lawyers."

We shook hands while Barb continued, "Abby is a Cornell graduate. She majored in—"

And that's when I snapped. I cut her off and began to speak in a southern accent and act like a southern belle.

"I mayjored in animal husbandry. Ma' last naime is Field because I cut it short," I said, now waving my right hand around while keeping a drink in my left. "It's really Stowfield. As in Stowfield Foods. Y'all are familiar with our pork products like baykin and hams and such? I'm the heiress to it, so ma daddy thought I should get an education from a good school that could teach me about breedin' hogs. Didn't mind it, but sometimes those hogs don't wanna cooperate, and the sows need some help. That's where artificial insemination comes in. Ya git right in up to yer elbows sometimes—if y'all know what I mean." I said with a giggle and right-handed flail at them. I sipped my soda through the red stir stick while batting my eyes at everyone.

There was dead silence for a second or two that felt like forever. I loved it. Barb was stunned. Her bafflement went to rage in about ten seconds flat. Forced to contain it, I watched her face turn beet red with anger. Jim, also stunned at first, tried to conceal his laughter by looking the other way. Then there was Joe. The man would probably be unfazed by an incoming tornado. He casually took the lime off the side of his glass and squeezed it into his vodka tonic. The whole episode left the Chambers uncomfortable and unsure how to extricate themselves from the situation, so I took care of it.

"Well, it was lovely to meet y'all," I continued as my southern belle character. "I think I'm gonna find me some more of those delicious hors d'oeuvres. Will y'all excuse me, please?"

I finished with half a curtsy toward them and a tilt of my head. I then turned and casually headed toward the back corner of the yard, passing a member of the waitstaff with a full tray of hors d'oeuvres. I just couldn't resist one more shot.

"Oh, my my. Looky what we have here. Baykin wrapped scallops! A thing of Stowfield beauty," I said as I took one off the tray. I turned to give everyone a nod and a wink before I sauntered on my way.

***

I picked my spot in the yard and turned to find Joe calmly walking in my direction. He wore gray dress pants with a navy sport coat covering a short-sleeved white dress shirt with no tie. Joe was such a nice guy, but I had no idea what this conversation would hold.

He stepped next to me and turned around, squeezed some more lime, and stirred the drink he'd been nursing. The silence was awkward, but I refused to flinch. He sipped his drink while staring at the activity in the rest of the yard.

"Abby," he began, still looking across the yard, "I really like you. You're smart, hardworking, and you don't pull any punches." He took another sip and continued, "Jim adores you." Silence. "You know you and Barb are more alike than you realize."

It was all I could do to keep my mouth shut at that comment.

"Do you know why Barb started her own business?"

I didn't think Joe wanted me to respond, so I didn't.

"No one would hire Barb. Cornell education. Top of her class among all men, and no one would hire her because she was female." Another pause. "That rejection sparked a drive in her to prove to anyone and everyone that she could make it. She made a vow to herself that she would shatter the glass ceiling and leave the rest covered in her shards. When she started out, she was only twenty-two. She knocked on doors and offered her designs for free if they agreed to let her do the install. She did a lot of the grunt work herself, with her brother and me helping evenings and weekends until she could afford to hire. People began to regard her as talented and hard-working. She was running wheelbarrows around while six months pregnant with Drew. By the time Sean and Jim came along, she was established and had a crew. Her reputation continued to grow, and her customers really liked her, both professionally and personally." He finished his drink and set it on the tray of a passing server. "Sound like a familiar story, Abby?"

I didn't give an answer, but Joe didn't need one; he already knew. I thought about the fifth-grade kickball game. Boys vs. girls, and of course, the girls were just bound to lose. The bases were loaded when I stepped up. I heard one of the boys yell, "Easy out. Everybody move in." I remember thinking that I hoped they'd get good and close. I kicked the ball over all of their heads and left them chasing the bouncing pink orb across the school-yard. I drove in three runs and made it to third before they got the ball to the infield. The next time I was up, every boy on the field moved back.

I intentionally picked Sapphire because I felt the young owner of an upstart would at least give me a fair shot—more so than other more established companies owned by middle-aged men who considered it "man's work." I made sure I knew my stuff well, learned what I didn't know from anyone willing to teach me, worked hard, and when all else failed, I disarmed them with my humor. Barb had definitely had it harder than I did. I supposed the reason I could get a job was because of women like Barb who had paved the way, in some respects.

"Joe, can I ask you something?"

"Go ahead."

"When did Barb change? Why does she judge people based on things like education and social status? It doesn't sound like she was always that way. And what is her problem with me? She tried to fix Jim up with Cleary's daughter last month while I was standing right there!"

Joe thought for a minute and said, "I think Barb's insecurities came to the top once her customers began asking her to come to these receptions. She wasn't any more comfortable here than you are. But after all she fought for, she found it an honor and a way to meet potential customers. Some of these people are from old money, old political families, and old law firms. They're used to this pomp and circumstance with a pinch of one-upmanship. Barb and I grew up together on the south side. No private education and no silver spoons in our mouths. We earned what we have. Sometimes Barb still feels insecure…like she doesn't fit in here. Somehow that seems to have spilled over into what she wants for our boys—Ivy League educations and marrying children from elite families. Some days she forgets where she came from." He paused and then said, "Believe it or not, she really does like you. She already stopped at the Ukrainian shop to pick up supplies for the eggs. She's excited at your interest in her family tradition. She just gets stuck on "stupid" every now and then. It's annoying and frustrating, but sometimes we just have to give her a little room to be a little stupid."

We both chuckled.

"Are you going to ask me to apologize?"

"Nope," Joe said with a big grin. "Stuck on Stupid had that one coming, Miss Stowfield."

Jim was headed in our direction, and Joe decided it was his cue to exit, smiling as he walked away.

"Well. Did you get a 'Dad Talk'?"

"I did."

"He's good at them. He knows how to calm the rest of us down when Mom gets crazy."

I questioned Jim as to why he came to these things. He explained that while he didn't love them, it was only an hour or so out of his life, and it made his mom happy. And as weird as she got sometimes, she was a good mom. She loved Joe and her boys and wanted the boys to reach their potential. No different than any decent parent. I guess I could understand that.

"So now what? I'm sure I made your mom crazy."

"Oh, she's beyond crazy. She is WILD! Dad will have a little chat with her later, and she'll get over it." Jim hesitated for a moment and, in a southern drawl, asked, "Miss Abby Marie Stowfield Ham, might I have the pleasure of yer company at The Greatest? I'll buy you a burger with some Stowfield baykin on it—you fine-lookin' little pork heiress."

And we skipped out without a word to anyone.

Chapter 9

The mayor's house was the last garden party I attended that season. Jim proposed to me in the fall, and we married the following May. The wedding brought the next set of struggles with Barb, as she jumped right in to become our personal wedding planner.

For a while, I simply nodded and ignored her directives while Jim and I quietly made some of our own plans. Eventually, we couldn't avoid her anymore. After my little Stowfield act, any intimidation I had toward Barb was gone. I tried to be respectful, but refused to keep my mouth shut when I didn't agree with her. I kept it out of the workplace and public forums, so long as she didn't start up in public. After the mayor's house, she seemed to have learned her lesson.

I was at the Preston's one Sunday afternoon in early November when Barb informed us she had booked The Cathedral downtown with Father John officiating at six p.m. It would be followed by a black-tie evening reception requiring tuxedos for the men and formal gowns for the women.

"I think a butler serving champagne outside The Cathedral while you have your pictures taken would be a class act...

Becky, who owns Classic Cakes, makes the best cheesecake and carrot cake. I think you should serve that instead of boring white cake. I'm working on the guest list. I have about a hundred and fifty so far…"

I gave Jim the "you better do something, or I will" look.

"Mom, Abby and I reserved the Methodist church on the east side where Abby's parents were married. Pastor Greg, a friend of the Field's, is doing the ceremony at eleven."

"What?" Barb said tersely, "you aren't getting married in a Catholic Church! Jimmy, that's not how you were raised!"

"I know, Mom, but God is God to me. Catholic, Methodist, whatever denomination—he's still God."

Barb was not happy and took the manipulation route.

"If I were a good Catholic, I wouldn't be able to come to your wedding!"

Jim didn't miss a beat, knowing the Catholic Church had gotten rid of those rules years ago.

"That's too bad, Mom. Will you be coming for the reception? We need a count," he said, staring her dead in the eye.

She hesitated a moment, and realizing she wasn't going to win this one, she replied, "I said if I were a *good* Catholic!" To which we all laughed. "Would you at least consider having Father John officiate alongside the pastor?"

"We'll think about it," I answered while moving on to the next set of issues. "A butler serving champagne outside?" I said, trying not to furrow my brows. "Aren't there liquor laws for an open container? Haven't you ever hear of MADD?" I said jokingly to Barb.

She decided I was right and dropped that.

"Mom, we'd like to keep the wedding a little smaller...like a hundred and fifty total."

I could see Barb biting her tongue. Well, at least she was making progress at not running roughshod over us.

"And the cake?" I said, "Cheesecake? Carrot Cake? Really?" I asked.

"Yes, really!" was her response.

And that's where it ended.

***

I got home and flopped on the living room couch, interrupting the Saturday afternoon movie Mom was watching. I turned myself until I was upside down with my feet where my head belonged and my head where my feet belonged, with my hair falling to the floor. Once I settled into my childhood position, I began lamenting to my mother about planning details with Barb. Mom was always a great listener with good answers.

"Honey, consider Barb. She loves this type of thing and has three boys. She will never get to go shopping for a wedding dress, pick flowers or cakes, look at venues, or choose invitations. Was she included in Drew or Sean's planning?"

"No," I said, "my soon-to-be sisters-in-law had a hard time dealing with Barb as well."

"Why don't you consider letting Barb in on this? Ask her opinion on the invitations, let's see Becky at Classic Cakes. Is it terrible to have Father John serve communion with Pastor Greg?

Why don't you ask her to go dress shopping with us next Saturday? We'll grab lunch and make a day of it!"

Mom. Always the voice of reason. I was quite surprised to find that she and Barb got along well and genuinely liked each other. Joe invited Dad to be his partner in a tournament over the summer, and they golfed together frequently. As much as I didn't want to give in, Mom was right, as usual.

"What about you, Mom? I don't want you to miss out on anything because of this."

"I'll be fine! Besides, I think it'll be fun!"

"Fun? Did I hear you say *fun*? Or is it just the blood rushing to my head?" I asked as I flipped myself upright.

"You heard me, Abby," the lecture was rising in her voice. "You are marrying into Jim's family. Better start learning the fine art of compromise now."

I put my hands on my cheeks and pulled my face in a downward motion.

"I'm subject to her five days a week, and now I have to compromise for her on MY wedding. You're killing me, Mom."

"You'll live."

Mom was right, but the thought of it still annoyed me.

***

I decided to run it by Jim first, hoping he would agree with me. Needless to say, he loved the idea and was positive his mom would love it too.

105

So I called Barb and invited her to go dress shopping. She was over the moon, and much to my surprise, it was a fun day. Over the next couple of months Mom, Barb, and I chose invitations, a venue, a menu, and a photographer.

We compromised on the cake. I flipped through the picture book and settled on the simplicity of the four-tiered cakes. Becky suggested we use stargazer lilies for the topper and cascade them down the front. I loved the idea, as did Mom and Barb. I agreed to have the top tier be carrot cake to save for Jim and me on our one-year anniversary. The lower tiers would be classic chocolate and vanilla marble.

We went with a florist friend of Barb's, and Jim called Father John and asked if he would be willing to share the altar with the pastor at a Methodist church. It wasn't a problem because he had known Barb and Joe for years and liked them very much. It seemed we had all finally learned how to get along.

After the planning dust had settled, Joe pulled me aside.

"Thank you for including Barb in the plans. She truly had a great time with you ladies."

"You know I'd be lying if I said it was my idea," I answered, raising my eyebrows at him.

He smiled, "I figured your mother came up with it. Kate and Lori didn't know how to handle Barb's pushiness, so they decided it was easier for them to exclude her from the decision-making process. They would get together and show her their choices, but they didn't ask her opinion beforehand."

"Maybe she just needed somebody who could push back," I said, trying not to laugh.

"You may be right, Miss Abby Stowfield," he said with a wink. "Thanks for making her family."

***

Barb insisted on giving me a bridal shower and picked a lovely venue with a Sunday champagne brunch. The food was excellent, and we all had a great time. Jim, Joe, and Dad showed up at the end to help pack the cars.

As we were finishing up, I thanked Barb for all her efforts. She thanked me with a genuineness that I hadn't seen from her before. She was extremely grateful for the inclusion in the planning. I thought this was a good time to ask her the one thing I never understood.

"Barb, I have to ask you, why were you so upset when I started dating Jim? What didn't you like about me? We seemed to work great together on the projects?"

She thought for a moment before she answered, "Misjudgment is part of it. I really did view you as nothing more than a low-level supervisor—albeit a very good one. I had no complaints about your work. You promoted excellence on the job site and ran a tight ship without demeaning those under you. I didn't want any of my boys marrying women without higher education."

"You realize I knew you were big on that, so I purposely withheld my college information and asked Jim to do the same," I interjected.

"I realize that now, and when I found out you had an education, it only made it worse." She paused and then said, "When I watched you work the first summer, I saw a young version of me: a hard worker who had to earn her spot among the men. I know a lot has changed since I started years back, and men your age are more accepting of women in this field, but I knew you had busted your butt to prove yourself. Unfortunately, it still seems that women work twice as hard and are valued as half as much with a paycheck that reflects that."

I definitely agreed with her on that.

"When I found out you had a degree, I just couldn't understand why you worked *for* someone when you obviously had the drive and talent to build your own business. It seemed to me you were selling yourself short."

"I guess I get it, but Steve has been very good to me. He pays me well, and he took a lot of flack from a couple of guys on his crew when he promoted me. They had seniority, but Steve, being Steve, informed them that they didn't have the drive. He then proceeded to remind them just who owned the place, and if they liked the idea of seniority so much, they should find a union shop. He trusted me enough to team me up with you when he could have done it himself to be sure it was all to his specifications. Speaking of Steve's belief in me, I haven't had a chance to tell everyone my big news!"

I called Mom, Dad, Jim, and Joe over to join us.

"This weekend has been hectic, and I haven't had a moment to tell you all this, but Steve offered me a partnership with Sapphire! The details and legalities will be worked out after our wedding."

While everyone congratulated me, Barb requested six glasses of champagne and offered up a toast. My adult life was off to a great start!

Chapter 10

Hard to believe three decades have passed…enough of Memory Lane," I said as I turned onto my semi-rural road. The road runs the perimeter of old farmland that is still used to grow hay. The houses are a combination of ages and styles—everything from the 1800s through the late 1990s. Unlike tract housing, where an owner chooses from three different style homes, the houses here were built with whatever the owner had in mind creating an eclectic mix.

I pulled onto the Wagon Wheel Path, which is how we refer to our driveway. Two parallel stone trails created by our vehicle tires lead to our house. Grass grows in the middle while the lawn encroaches from both sides. Jim and I closed on this house just before we married. The Cobblestone Oasis is what we call our 1825 cobblestone Greek Revival style home. It sits along the Erie Canal and was love at first sight for us.

The previous owner intended on restoring the dwelling before his passing. Although that didn't happen, he did get the structural repairs done. The coursed cobblestone exterior had been beautifully refurbished. Care was taken to match the existing limestone and mortar colors. Even with my love for stonework, I wouldn't have wanted to take that on.

Our house had a right side gingerbread-colored entry door with two windows to the left. The second floor had three windows, each with black shutters—two over the first-floor windows and one above the entry door.

The stoop and two wide stairs that approached the door were made of large pieces of limestone. The door was encompassed on three sides with dressed stone, as were the windowsills and lintels. As the stone posts of the door made their way to the earth, they met the foundation where it turned to the left and the right, meeting at the corners.

The corners, known as quoins, matched the dressed stone of the rest of the house. One block of stone faced the front, while the next block was stacked on top and faced the side, creating a ninety-degree angle. This pattern continued up the house in an alternating fashion, with cobblestones filling in and weaving their way to the roof.

The gable end faced the front yard with the fascia color matching the door. We ended up having a new roof of architectural shingles put on and did our best to match the house's original character.

Because the previous owner spent so much time and money on the structural issues, he never got to the interior renovations. We loved the house and location and decided it would be fun to restore it. Over the course of a few years, we gutted all the rooms, refinished the floors, and decorated the place. The results were magnificent! The old merged with the new beautifully, and the house became a warm, comfortable place to entertain family and friends.

Then we turned our attention to the exterior two acres, which gave us plenty of room to create our outdoor sanctuary. I built the flat rock wall I dreamed of all those years ago. It stretched across the front of the house and sat twenty feet from the road. I may not have been a pioneer girl collecting rocks from crop fields, but I loved it none the less.

We built a twenty-five by thirty foot flagstone patio out back. I created a sitting area, a small eating area, and an outdoor fire pit. A retractable canopy extended from the house to cover the patio if needed.

Barb helped design the rest of our green space. English cottage-style gardens caressed the house's perimeter, grapevines hung over arbors, and fruit trees dotted the backyard. She also made space on the south side for the vegetable garden we wanted. We love it.

***

I entered the house and found Jim relaxing on the patio, sipping an iced coffee. I grabbed an iced tea from the refrigerator and joined him.

"You know, I think I've really had enough of these things," he said.

Barb had called several times during the week to make sure we were coming.

"I hear ya. Maybe this will be our last of the Grand Unveilings with your mom." We had given up the garden party receptions a couple of years ago when things just got too hectic for us, but this one was an exception.

"I'm tired of the whole thing. You must be exhausted," Jim said.

"I think I passed exhausted a few years ago and I've moved on to complete burnout."

"How's your mom?"

"About the same. Good spirits, deteriorating brain. She said to tell her favorite son-in-law 'hello.'"

Jim smiled. He loves my mom, and she always loves to make him his favorites—lasagna, meatballs, and chocolate chip cookies. It was sad to watch those days fade away into the haze of dementia. She still made an occasional batch of cookies, but they weren't the same. Somewhere along the line, she'd get confused in the recipe she'd made dozens of times. Sometimes there was an extra egg, or she'd make it with some weird margarine blend instead of butter.

We chatted for quite a while, catching up on the week's events. Both of us decided the busyness of that last several years had to stop, but we had no solution as to how to get off the merry-go-round.

Finally, I said, "C'mon Jimmy, let's get ready. You know your mother doesn't like to wait."

***

I went into the bathroom and gazed at myself in the mirror. My brown hair had kept its color, thanks to Paul Mitchell and a great stylist. I straightened my wispy bangs across my forehead and used my fingers to comb the long layer into their correct spot just above my small gold hoop earrings. Next, I made sure the curls that hit my collar were under control. I stared at the dark circles under my somewhat puffy eyes. Reluctantly, I dragged out my makeup in hopes that it could cover my tiredness.

Jim stepped in the mirror behind me. Even in his early fifties, he was still a good looking guy. The mustache was long gone, but the hairstyle remained the same, short on the sides and parted to the right. Gray had intermingled, and much like Joe, the deep Vs had taken their place. He was still muscular and managed to maintain his youthful weight.

Jim combed his hair and left the top buttons of his shirt open with his chest hair sticking out. I turned around to look at him.

He spread his arms to the side and said, "Check it out, baby!"

"Good God, Man! Button up that shirt; you look like a cavone!"

"I hope so; it was the look I was going for!" he said through laughter. "Ready for the all-inclusive, resort living garden party?"

"Ready as I'll ever be," I said with a sigh.

***

We found a spot in the parking lot of Barb's place and headed for the door. The four-story red brick building had a large entry-way overhang that guarded the fake Greek columns. It was a completely symmetrical building with all the gridded windows being the same in size, shape, and number.

"Think Jean-Pierre is at the door today?" I asked.

"With a gig like this? No doubt."

We rang the bell and waited. The door opened, and sure enough, Jean-Pierre was on duty. He was dressed in his usual shiny black shoes, black suit, and white dress shirt. Today's ensemble was completed by a red tie with tiny, white polka dots and a matching pocket square. Judging by his short gray hair, My guess was that he was in his early sixties. Small oval glasses set in silver wire rims rested on his nose. He was a trim man with milky white skin.

"Monsieur et Madame," Jean-Pierre said, holding the door with his heel. He ushered us in with a nod and right arm bent at the elbow, forearm across his stomach, and palm facing the ceiling. "Bon après-midi! Bienvenue à La Belle Communauté!"

"Jean-Pierre! So nice to see you!" Jim said with a big smile as he gave Jean-Pierre a handshake.

"You're looking dapper as always!" I said, grinning at him.

"Merci, Merci," he said to us with a slight bow.

***

We were a bit early, but the hustle and bustle of staff, family, and friends had already begun. We cut across the lobby and headed for the elevator tucked down a short hallway. We hit the button, and the doors opened. After stepping on, Jim hit the number two.

I looked at Jim and stated, "This elevator always has a funk."

"Well, considering the place, it shouldn't be a surprise."

"True."

As the elevator stopped on the second floor, we could hear the music blaring. Jim and I looked at each other and, with grins on our faces, said, "Josiah!" in unison.

The doors opened, and we were met with old '70s song "The Sound of Philadelphia" by MFSB featuring The Three Degrees. Jim and I escaped the funky elevator, walked down the short hall, and made a right toward Barb's room. There was Josiah in the common area, dancing with his mother with the music blasting. We couldn't resist doing our version of a disco line.

The two of us danced side-by-side all the way to Josiah and his parents, Will and Shirley Morris. Jim has no rhythm, and he knows it, so he makes quirky moves that are a combination of walking with head and shoulders moving and arms flailing. He then adds the old '80s "Cabbage Patch" dance—swaying from side to side with his arms out front going in a circular motion.

I have great rhythm, so I decided the old '70s "Funky Chicken Dance" by Rufus Thomas worked well. We danced our way to Josiah while singing lyrics from "TSOP" (The Sound of Philadelphia).

Josiah and his mom, Shirley, stopped dancing, and the five of us broke into laughter. We greeted one another with hugs and handshakes. Jim and I like the Morrises a lot. They are an African-American family we run into almost every time we visit.

"So Josiah, how goes the dance routine?" I asked.

"Oh, you know," he said with a grin, "I'm trying to teach Mom all the moves. I'm not sure she's getting it. That's why I keep coming to visit them. I know she can do it!" We all chuckled.

Josiah wasn't particularly tall for a man, only my height. He was in his late fifties, with his black hair beginning to gray. His sharp haircut left curls on top with a fade to his ears and a neatly trimmed beard surrounding his jawline. Every time I ran into

115

him, he was in jeans, a baggy T-shirt, and a pair of sneakers, and today was no exception.

Shirley stood, wiping the sweat off her forehead and adjusting her curly gray hair that fell to her ears and across her eyebrows. At five foot three and probably a hundred and fifty pounds, she was a spitfire. Spry and upbeat with very natural-looking makeup that accented her features.

"I'm going to get it, Josiah. Don't you worry, I'll be ready for the wedding!" she assured him.

Josiah's daughter, Trinity, was set to be married in two weeks, which is why they were practicing a dance routine.

Will sat on the sidelines, bobbing his head and tapping his cane while they practiced. He was a victim of arthritis in his hip due to an old injury. His doctor had been encouraging him to have it replaced, but he has yet to do it. A well-built man, Will stood six foot three. He shaved his head when he began to go bald and kept a neatly trimmed gray goatee.

We chatted for a few minutes before Jim and I continued down the hall. We didn't get far before we heard Rose Marie calling out to Jim.

"Hey, big boy!" she said while making a clicking sound out of the side of her mouth. She gave him a wink.

Rose Marie lived in an apartment on an adjacent wing. A small woman at just five feet one, she combed her thinning brown-ish-gray hair straight back over the top of her head. Rose Marie was also missing a tooth or two—maybe three. She cracked us up with her "Mae West" attitude and always called after Jim in the same manner.

She moseyed on by us, and we heard her stop to talk to the Morrises. She gave Will the same, "Hey big boy!" greeting. We heard Will and Shirley laughing.

***

We finally made it through the place just as Barb was shutting her apartment door.

"Hello, Mother Superior!" I called to her.

She turned to me with a laugh and said, "That's right! You better watch yourself!"

Realizing she wasn't quite ready, Jim asked where she was headed.

"I'm looking for your father. Did you see him on the way up?"

Jim answered, "We didn't see him. Why don't you go in and finish getting ready, and we'll go look for him."

Barb was now in her early eighties. The dyed brunette was long gone, and her hair was now a very pretty silver color. She still kept it short to show off her earrings but had longer layers in the back that rested at her collar. The Yves St. Laurent glass frames are the same shape with golden rims.

"I can't believe Joe," Barb continued as she reentered her apartment, pushing her walker in front of her. "He knows this is important and now he decides to go visiting. He needs to get ready."

"I'll go see if I can find him," I responded. "You just get your makeup on, and I'll be right back."

***

117

I closed the apartment door behind me and headed down the hall where I ran into Dave Dalton. Dave's nickname is Sheriff. When I asked him how he came to be called Sheriff, he informed me he was a retired sheriff and the title just stuck, even after retirement.

"Hi, Sheriff!" I said as I met him in the hallway, "How's it going? You look a little perplexed today."

"I had my old badge out, and now I can't find it," he said as he shuffled down the hallway. Sheriff stood about five foot ten inches and was probably fifty pounds overweight. He was bald with white fringe traveling around his head from one ear to the other. He looked to be in his late seventies

"You're kidding! Did you check with the laundry service?"

"Good idea," he said.

"You never know what you leave in your pocket sometimes. If I see it, I'll let you know," I said, continuing down the hall on my quest to find Joe.

I returned to the common area. The Morrises were now gone and likely getting ready. In their place were Bob and Kathleen Martin, a couple that I would guess were also in their seventies. Bob was a wiry guy. He was wearing a pair of belted khakis with a red, white, and blue plaid short-sleeved shirt. His short, thinning gray hair was combed to the left, and his soft green eyes spotted me through his glasses.

"Abby! Nice to see you, sweetheart. How are you?"

"I'm well! How are you two? Where's Shelley?" I asked as Kathleen rocked the baby, who was all snuggled up in a peach crocheted blanket.

"She just ran back to retrieve the baby bottle we left in the apartment," answered Bob.

"Got it," I said. "How's the baby, Kathleen?"

"Just precious!" she said to me as she stopped rocking for a moment and pulled the blanket back so I could see her.

"She's beautiful, Kathleen! You should be very proud!"

"I am." Her gaze returned to the baby, and I was left looking at the top of her gray head.

Just then, their daughter Shelley made her way back with the bottle.

"Abby!" she exclaimed

"Shelley!" I replied.

Shelley and I are roughly the same age. She is also about my height and has a similar hairstyle. People started telling us we look like sisters.

"No doubt you guys will be down shortly," Shelley said to me.

"We will. Barb is finishing her makeup, and I'm off to find Joe," I said to her over my shoulder as I walked away.

"Good luck with that!" Shelley replied with a laugh.

"I know, I know!" I said, shaking my head.

I did a lap and made my way back to Barb's room, where she was just finishing up her lipstick.

"Get your walker, and let's go!" Jim told her.

Although she had her knee replaced almost twenty years ago, Barb's limping put stress on one of her hips, forcing her to reluctantly rely on a walker.

As she pushed her walker toward the door, she asked where I had gone.

"I ran into Dave," I answered.

"Who?" asked Barb.

"Dave, you know, Sheriff?"

"Ohhh," she said, in an unconvincing voice. "Did you see Joe?"

"No. You know Joe is a people person. He probably just got gabbing with somebody. I wouldn't be surprised if he is waiting for you at the courtyard door."

Chapter 11

We left the apartment and headed toward the elevator. Barb made sure to point out the interior renovations to us. The hallways that went from the apartments to the common area had all been refurbished. Old carpeting had been replaced, and the smell of fresh paint still hung in the air.

"Look at how beautiful the floors came out!" Barb gushed, "Dark Brazilian mahogany, you know," she said quietly as though she didn't want to brag on her knowledge of such things.

"They're nice," I said. "I really like the paint color." A new coat of "corn silk" brightened the place.

As we walked across the common area, Barb stopped and turned to Jim. "You know, this is where the orchestra was playing when I came here to visit with your father."

"That must have been nice," Jim replied.

"*Very* elegant," Barb whispered again.

Now the place was a flurry of activity. Residents, staff, and family all headed outdoors for the Grand Unveiling. Along the way, we caught up with Sheriff and squeezed onto the elevator with another resident and their family from an upper floor. We hit the button for the ground floor and headed to the courtyard door.

The door opened, and we observed the busyness of the last-minute preparations that were wrapping up. White event tents extended upward like snowcapped mountains against the bright blue skies of a warm day that says summer is here to stay.

Several staff members were operating the grills while happily greeting guests. Tantalizing smells rose into the air and swirled throughout the courtyard. Pans of fruits and salads were taking their place on the serving table. Staff members were lighting the cans of Sterno and placing them under the chafing dishes readying them for what the grill was about to produce.

The tent was long and took up a good portion of the courtyard. Numerous tables and chairs were arranged under it. Coolers full of ice sat on the ground with their bevy.

We found the table with our name on it and took our chairs along with Sheriff. Will, Shirley, and Josiah were also at our table. I took a drink order from the Morris crew while Barb and Sheriff chatted.

"Barb, what would you like to drink?" I asked.

She didn't hear me and kept talking with Sheriff.

"Barb," I repeated, trying to get her attention.

No response.

Finally, I said, "Barbara Jean," and immediately realized what I had done. Jim gave me a sharp look as I closed my eyes and I tilted my head backward, quietly saying, *Oh no*, to myself.

That did it. She stopped dead in her tracks and turned to me.

"WHERE is Joe?" Barb demanded. But this time, we had no answer. Her blue eyes squinted, narrowing into a fixed stare. After a few long seconds, she turned to Jim.

"He's dead, isn't he," she said softly, more of a statement than a question.

"Yeah, Mom, he is," Jim replied with all the comfort his voice could muster.

She stared for a few more seconds before blurting out, "THAT BASTARD!" Her outburst caught us all by surprise and left stunned looks and gaping mouths in its wake.

"He couldn't help it, Mom."

"Oh, bullshit, Jimmy!" she snapped back.

I was sitting on the aisle with Barb to my left. I had to turn my back to her so she wouldn't see me laughing. Never in thirty-plus years have I ever heard that woman swear, and she had just broken that streak twice in two sentences. Jim started to laugh. Then Barb started laughing, with everyone at the table joining in.

Chapter 12

C an I have everyone's attention, please!" yelled Kelly through a small megaphone, "I just want to take a minute to welcome you to Sunrise Memory Care Facilities' annual picnic! It's always a pleasure to see all of you, and dinner is almost ready! We will be calling you up by tables. In the meantime, enjoy the music provided by Teddy the Music Man!"

Ted finished setting up his acoustic guitar and PA system and played instrumentals that lasted through dinner. Afterward, he played some oldies, took requests, and encouraged sing-a-longs. He was very engaging, and the residents love him.

Karen, the case worker for the second floor, stopped at our table to say hello and let us know it was our turn at the buffet line. Barb put one hand on her walker and the other on the table. She rocked back and forth a little before pushing herself up.

We got in line with Sheriff in tow. Pans of hamburgers, hotdogs, Italian sausage, and rolls began the food procession, with fruit salad, macaroni salad, and baked beans ending it. Jim juggled his plate and Barb's while I handled mine and Sheriff's.

We returned to the table where I again attempted to take the drink order. This time I was successful.

I rummaged through the cooler to retrieve everyone's requests. Upon returning to the table, I set the drinks down and opened a can of orange soda for Sheriff. According to the staff, it was his favorite. Jim and I had assumed Sheriff had no surviving family members. Apparently this was untrue.

Sheriff had been a widower for five years before arriving at Sunrise, where he has now lived for two years. We have never seen the father of two and grandfather of five with a visitor. No one comes to family picnics or Christmas parties.

We found out that his daughter and her family live in the Silicon Valley area, where her husband works in the tech industry. They have two kids in high school and one in college. She calls her father twice a week, but memories fade as time moves on, and Sheriff has a hard time understanding who she is. Out of sight, out of mind is all too true when it comes to the dementia brain.

It turns out that Sheriff was never actually a sheriff. He was employed for forty-five years by a local DPW and was also the part-time village constable. Because of this position, people started calling him Sheriff and the nickname stuck. His daughter told Karen that her dad loved the old westerns as a kid, and it seems older memories and newer ones made mush soup in his brain, and he now believes he really was a sheriff.

His son Ryan lives locally with his wife and two kids. Ryan is the one who took on the responsibility of finding a facility and moving his father. On move-in day, Ryan went to the business office and made Sunrise the representative payee. Representative payees are a third party that manages social security for a mentally incapacitated person, thereby making it Sunrise's responsibility to pay Sheriff's bills—not Ryan's. They say he walked out of the business office, never to be seen or heard from again at Sunrise.

It happens more often than anyone realizes. We've seen more than one resident without any visitors. And as hard as I try, I just don't understand it. How do you leave the one who raised you? I try not to get judgmental about it because I don't know their story. Sheriff seemed like a nice guy, but maybe he wasn't always. Maybe he was a miserable father, and Ryan had had enough. Maybe Ryan figured Dad got what he deserved. Or maybe the disease is so cruel that Ryan just couldn't watch it steal his father from him, wanting to remember him the way he was. Maybe he figured Dad wouldn't remember him for long and decided it just didn't matter, or maybe Ryan had a child with special needs, and he can only handle so much. In any event, I guess it's something I'll never know.

Whatever the reasoning, Sheriff had no visitors, and he and Barb pal around a lot, so we let him tag along. When we found out chocolate chip cookies were his favorite, I made a batch for him. We heard he loved to hunt, so we brought our black lab puppy for a visit. He snuggled and hugged the dog for so long that we weren't sure we would get her back! At Christmas, we wrapped a box for Sherriff with warm socks, new pajamas, and candy.

***

We worked on our burgers and salads while the staff scurried along amongst the tables greeting guests and serving residents that needed help. As we were finishing dinner, the rest of the Morris clan showed up. Their five children made them grandparents to fifteen and great-grandparents to three. They didn't all show up, which is probably good because they would have needed their own tent!

Josiah's daughter Trinity and his soon-to-be son-in-law, Daryl, took their place at the table.

"Trinity!" I said. "How are the final wedding plans coming along?"

"I will be so glad when this is over!"

Daryl nodded in agreement.

"Yeah, me and Jim felt the same way."

Shirley leaned over to us, and making sure Josiah was out of earshot, she said to Trinity, "Baby, we've been here every day practicing the father-daughter dance. I think it's starting to stick in his brain."

"Thanks, Nana. I appreciate it. I think he'll be fine. He's such a great dancer that even if he doesn't remember the routine, he'll wing it, and no one will know the difference." A tinge of sadness crossed Trinity's face.

Shirley put her arm around Trinity's shoulder and kissed her. "Don't let it bring you down on your big day, Sweetie."

I leaned in to the two ladies and said, "The hardest thing in the world is to live in the moment. Have someone record the dance on his phone. Then he can re-watch it and show everyone here how his big day went! Make sure tons of pictures are taken on his phone too, and use one of them for the phone's wallpaper."

"That's a good idea!" Daryl chimed in.

"Always remember," I continued, "just because his memory is fading doesn't mean he won't have a great time and create good memories for you guys. Enjoy your day, and make sure I see the video!"

"We will," Trinity said with a smile.

Just as we finished our conversation, Josiah returned from getting another soda.

"Hey, Baby Girl!" Josiah said as he hugged Trinity.

"Hi, Daddy, how's it going? Have you been dancing?"

"Baby, you know I'm teaching Nana for the wedding. When is the date?"

They continued chatting away, and I moved back to my spot at the end of the table. Will and Shirley were high school sweethearts during one of the most tumultuous times in American history—the sixties. Originally from Birmingham Alabama, they tired of the non-stop violence and Jim Crow laws of the south.

Will had a cousin in Syracuse who worked at the Chrysler plant and got Will in. They bought a house, and Shirley happily settled into motherhood, raising a total of five kids. Three of their children went on to college, producing a teacher, an accountant, and a paralegal. Another became a realtor, and Josiah followed his father into the plant, where he became a skilled machinist.

Family started to notice Josiah's memory problems when he was in his early fifties. Several trips to the doctor confirmed the issue: early-onset dementia. Over the course of two years, he was forced to retire, sell his house, and move in with Will and Shirley. As horrible as it is to watch the disease progress in older people, I can't fathom the heartbreak of a parent watching their child fade before their eyes. In their mid-seventies, Will and Shirley became Josiah's caretakers.

They enrolled Josiah in an adult day program to keep him occupied for most of the week, but eventually, his care became too much for them. Will needed a hip replacement but refused to put any more stress on Shirley, who would have had to take care of them both. Stress, exhaustion, and burnout were overtaking them. Shirley had gained thirty pounds and was constantly worried that Josiah would wander off or find the hidden car keys and drive off somewhere. Last year they made the agonizing decision to find assisted living, and six months ago, Josiah moved to Sunrise.

Josiah was angry at being moved, believing he "wasn't that bad," and became withdrawn, depressed, and lost his sense of humor. His anger was directed at his parents, as well as any family member who came to visit. Will and Shirley already struggled with the guilt of not being able to care for him, and Josiah's tirades reinforced it. The first couple of months were really unbearable. Will and Shirley would ignore his phone calls and turn down the answering machine so they didn't have to hear him. They then deleted his messages, having never listened to them.

Like many residents, Josiah complained to his family how miserable he was at Sunrise, only for them to find out from Karen and the recreation staff that he was having a great time. His anger and depression began subsiding in a matter of weeks, and his fun-loving personality returned. He teased the staff and was known to hide anything they left lying around. That meant they needed to watch where they set their phones, medicine logbooks, and binders. The problem was, he couldn't remember where he hid them! The staff has been on more than one wild goose chase over his antics.

Growing up, Josiah had a passion for music and loved *Soul Train* and its host Don Cornelius. He was also a great dancer. Shirley said he was a natural, and whenever *Soul Train* was on while she was around, he would grab her for a disco dance line. He loved to go out to the clubs and dance, which is where he met his wife, Cyndi. Josiah married at thirty and had his only child, Trinity, before divorcing fifteen years later. Trinity, the bride-to-be, is now twenty-five and working as a nurse practitioner.

For the father-daughter dance, Trinity and Josiah decided to go with one of Josiah's favorites, none other than "The Sound of Philadelphia" by MFSB. This song was also the intro to *Soul Train* in the mid-1970s, and of all the intros *Soul Train* had, it was his favorite. More often than not, it was blaring through the second floor of Sunrise. It was not unusual to see other residents dancing and swaying to the tune. On one visit, we saw a couple trying to do the bump while getting lower to the floor with each successive move. Jim and I were sure there was going to be a hip injury. Destiny, one of the aides, came along telling them they better stop before they got too low and wouldn't be able to get up. Josiah had definitely brought life to the floor.

Will and Shirley had been at Sunrise almost daily, working with him on the dance. They were hoping that eventually the repetition will stick. So far, it seemed to be working.

***

After scanning the crowd to see if Jenny had arrived, I found her at a table near the back and plopped myself in the empty chair beside her.

"Jenny! I haven't seen you in a while. Glad you made it!"

"Abby! How's it going?"

"Oh, you know. 'Bout par for the course. You?"

She smiled, causing her freckles to rearrange themselves across her cheekbones and fade into the sides of her shoulder-length auburn hair.

"Same as you. Par for the course."

Jenny is the only child of Don and Rose Marie Germane. I feel bad for only children. Talk about bearing the brunt with no one to lean on. Of course, having siblings doesn't guarantee help either, as it usually falls onto one person anyway. Jim and I know about that all too well.

Don is a tall, lanky man and a retired accountant. He still looks sharp with neatly combed white hair. He took Rose Marie's diagnosis hard, but then again, who doesn't?

Jenny told me her mother had been raised by a harsh man. Although not physically abusive, he ruled the family with an iron fist, dictating what they could and could not do. When Rose Marie was young, she was allowed to go to the Saturday matinees with her older sisters. Movies became her escape and her love. The sex symbols of those times, Jayne Mansfield, Brigitte Bardot, and of course Marilyn Monroe, became her idols. She saw them as women to be emulated with what she perceived to be their qualities of sophistication, strength, and control over their own destinies. They were a far stretch from what she had witnessed in her own home.

131

Rose Marie's desire was to become a hairstylist and makeup artist, but her father would have none of that. She was quite beautiful in her younger years and caught the attention of more than one man. She secretly dated a young man named Glen, who worked in a warehouse. Her father found out and forced her to break up with him to date Don. Don fell in love with Rose Marie, but it was one-sided. He asked Rose Marie's father for permission to marry her, and dear old dad would not pass up the accountant he had hand-picked.

Their marriage was a tumultuous one. Rose Marie told Don she didn't love him and didn't want to marry him, hoping he would call it off, but Don was a bit like her father—controlling. He figured that with enough time, she'd learn to love him.

Jenny came along two years later as Rose Marie and Don continued to live in disharmony. After ten years, Don finally decided that maybe treating his wife the way she deserved to be treated was the way to go. Jenny said their fighting cooled, and they seemed to become friends, even if it wasn't Rose Marie's plan for her life.

I stared at Don as he finished a hotdog while gazing at Rose Marie. The sadness in his eyes was obvious as his wife swayed and hummed to "The Candy Man." She was paying more attention to the Music Man while unintentionally ignoring Don. Mike, a maintenance worker at Sunrise, stopped at the table, passing out ice cream sandwiches. Rose Marie tugged at one of the side pockets of his cargo shorts and went into her Mae West routine.

"Hey, big boy!" she said, giving Mike a click from the side of her mouth and a wink.

"Hi, Rose Marie!" He said with a warm smile. "Here's your ice cream."

Another family's guest walked by.

"Hey, big boy!" she said, reaching out for him with the same click and wink.

"Hi," the man said with a smile.

Another man walked by.

"Hey, big boy!" A grab, a click, and a smile as she continued to sway to the music.

Don hung his head. Heartbreak, grief, and embarrassment over Rose Marie's behavior was overwhelming him. Jenny put her arm over his shoulder to comfort him.

"Can we go now?" Don asked softly.

"Sure, Dad," Jenny said. "We'll take our ice cream for the road. I'll see you next time, Abby."

"Sorry, Abby," Don said to me.

"No apologies necessary, Don. I'll catch up with you two next time."

I unwrapped my ice cream and made my way back to the table where the Preston, Morris, and Sheriff crew were engrossed in conversation. Music Man was taking requests, and someone in the crowd yelled out, "Patsy Cline."

"How about Walkin' After Midnight?" was his reply.

The power of music will never cease to amaze me. I don't care how far down dementia takes a brain, I'm convinced that remembering lyrics is the last thing to go. The younger people didn't know all the words, but the older crowd didn't miss a beat, singing all the words to the classic song.

Chapter 13

The picnic was wrapping up, so we decided it was a good time to tour the newly renovated courtyard with Barb. Silver chain-link fence surrounded the area with a sole gate that was safely padlocked. The old asphalt paths that led to a paved area in the middle of the lawn had been renovated. The old trail had cracked and heaved, creating uneven ground and tripping hazards. The new area was expanded and produced a space under the tent that was smooth and level. No more rocky tables and no more fears of walkers and canes that support feeble knees catching on the pavement edges.

We stopped at the first of four large wooden gazebos that had been added to the perimeter of the yard. All had seating areas underneath with flower boxes saddled over the side rails.

"Aren't the flowers beautiful?" Barb asked softly as she reached out and carefully ran her fingers over them. I could tell her mind was drifting off to somewhere nice as a slight smile and a trace of sadness crossed her face.

"They are. Let's see what we have. Hmmm…I wonder what these bright purple, yellow, and red ones are?" I asked, eyeing the million bells that intertwined and splashed their colors against the dark wooden sides of the gazebo.

"Calibrachoa …hybrid," Barb correctly replied, identifying the plant by its Latin name.

"I love them, Barb!"

Barb smiled wider and her thoughts returned to the moment.

"Let's go look at all the huts!" Barb said with excitement returning to her voice.

"Okay, Mom," Jim said, "you lead the way!"

She hobbled around the courtyard, pushing her walker ahead of her. Once my height, the aches and pains in her lower extremities caused her to bend at the waist, making her seem much shorter than she is.

We stopped at the next gazebo with flower boxes full of red geraniums that sprung up from the cascade of small white bacopa flowers. We waited as Barb made her way to each box. She steadied herself with one hand on her walker while the other hand removed the dead geraniums.

She carried the dead flowers to the next gazebo, where we were met with containers exploding with ivy geraniums. The shades of pink, lavender, and burgundy were stunning. Again, Barb wanted to deadhead the flowers. Jim and I gave each other the eye, trying to figure out how to redirect her. Deadheading ivy geraniums is far more time-consuming than cleaning up standard zonal geraniums, and we didn't want to hang around all evening.

"Barb! Look over there at the last gazebo!" I said excitedly. "We haven't seen that one yet, and the colors are crazy! Let's go have a look!"

Thankfully, that distracted Barb, and we headed to the last set of flowers. Gerbera daisies. Their bright and cheery colors made them Barb's personal favorites. She had always loved their simplicity and planted them in pots on her deck at home every summer.

"My favorites!" she exclaimed. "Do you think anyone would mind if I cut a few for my apartment?"

"No, Mom, I don't think so. What colors do you want?"

With Barb picking the colors and Jim cutting them for her, I walked to the buffet table and grabbed a bunch of napkins.

"Barb really did a great job picking out the flowers," Kelly said to me as she was helping clean up.

"Yeah, she did!" I answered as I dipped the napkin in the water created by the melting ice in the coolers.

Knowing Barb's background, the staff brought in spring catalogs and let Barb choose the flowers. The maintenance crew filled the boxes with soil while Barb, along with other residents, planted them.

"Does the courtyard get a lot of use now?" I asked.

"Oh yeah," Maggie, the recreation director, answered. "Every nice day there is."

Her staff also loved the new outdoor space. It is a welcome respite from the "gated community" that kept all exterior doors under numeric keypad lockdown. Should a resident attempt to exit the place, they were met immediately with blaring alarms.

I returned to the final gazebo where Jim was just finishing the bouquet of yellow, pink, and crimson flowers. I wrapped the ends of the stems in the damp napkins.

"Perfect!" I said.

"You know what would be nice?" Barb asked whimsically.

"What's that, Barb?"

"I think it would be nice to have a garden that we could come out and pick flowers from. Then we could take them back to our rooms and have flowers! We could put tall zinnias in it and the tall ones that grow on spikes…what are they called? They come in lots of colors…" she said, her voice quietly trailed off while her brain desperately tried to think of the word *gladiolas*.

"I think that's a good idea. We could call it 'Barb's Cut Flower Garden,'" I said.

Barb thought for a moment as she stared at her gerbera daisies.

"No. I think it should be called Joe and Barb's Place," she said, her voice fading. "I miss him."

"We know you do, Mom. We miss him too," Jim said as he put his arm around her and guided her toward the entry door.

Chapter 14

I held Barb's flowers as she pushed her walker back into the building. We stepped off the elevator on the second floor to find Shelley, Bob, and Kathleen back in the common area. Kathleen was still holding the baby and swaying back and forth as she talked to Shelley.

"You're sure you're okay with it?" Kathleen asked.

"Of course, Mom! I trust you. The baby will be fine with you overnight."

"Oh, Shelley!" Kathleen said with tears balancing on the rims of her lower eyelids, "Thank you!"

Bob was staring at the floor and shuffling his feet.

"It's okay, Dad. It really is," Shelley whispered to him with quiet reassurance.

"Do you want to see the baby?" Kathleen called out to Barb as we walked by. "She's beautiful!"

We had no choice; Kathleen was already next to us. Barb looked at the baby and told her how precious she was. Kathleen beamed as she returned to Bob and Shelley.

As we made our way down the hall, Barb said, "You know what I think?"

"No, Mom. What do you think?"

"I think that woman's NUTS!" Barb said as she stopped mid-stride.

She pointed to the side of her head with her index finger and began making circular motions. Just to add to the antics, she stuck her tongue out, rolled her eyes, and began swaying her head.

"MOM!" Jim whisper-yelled as we both tried to stifle our laughter, "Quiet!"

We were grateful that Kathleen was down the hall and out of earshot.

"Quiet what? That's no baby! It's a doll! She's nuts! She brings it to breakfast and tries to feed it!" she said, completely oblivious to her own mental condition.

By now, Jim and I were laughing so hard we had to wipe the tears from our eyes. We weren't sure which was funnier—the doll or Barb, who was so sure she was sane while pointing out another person's decreased mental capacities.

Make no mistake; dementia is a horrible disease, but the things we've seen dementia patients do and say have caught us off guard more than once. We decided we could either be depressed or laugh. We chose laughter, but not in a way that mocks or disrespect a person. Trust me; there is enough heartbreak with this disease, so we laugh when we can.

***

La Belle Communauté

We got Barb's live flowers in water, finally threw out the dead geraniums, and said our good-byes. We closed the door behind us and headed toward the elevator. Shelley was in the common area waiting on her father, who was escorting her mother back to her apartment.

"Well? How's the baby?" I asked Shelley.

She looked down the hall to make sure Bob wasn't nearby.

She put her hand on her forehead and said, "Oh my God! Almost as good as Joe. Did you find him?"

We all laughed.

Bob and Kathleen have been married for fifty-three years and have three children and seven grandchildren. When Kathleen's memory began to slip, Bob covered for her. He didn't want their kids to know, fearing they would put Kathleen in a facility, thereby separating them. He did a pretty good job for the first three years. Even when the kids noticed, he still managed to make it seem like less of an issue than it really was. He took over the driving and sold her car.

Finally, it was Bob's heart attack that blew the house of cards apart. Kathleen was having a "good day," and when Bob wasn't acting like himself, she called Shelley. Shelley called 911. It was determined that at some point in life, he had suffered a silent heart attack. He had no symptoms that he could recall, but it left his heart damaged. This episode exacerbated the previous one, weakening Bob considerably.

His kids held a family meeting and decided it was best that he didn't live alone. He certainly couldn't take care of Kathleen, plus his doctor didn't want him driving anymore. Shelley and her family had a guest room and volunteered to take them both in, with the understanding that Kathleen would need the help of assisted living because they just couldn't meet her needs.

The transition was hard on Bob and Kathleen. But it always is. Bob felt like a failure and lamented to his kids that he had taken a vow of "in sickness and in health." He felt as though they were denying him the right to keep that vow.

Bob and Kathleen were wonderful parents and grandparents. The kids tried to find a facility where they could both live. After much searching, they found out that when it comes to assisted living, dementia is its own animal. Assisted living will take in people in the early stages of the disease, but it won't be long before they have to move to a place that specializes in memory care. Kathleen was already past the early stage, and memory care only allows those with a dementia diagnosis to live there.

Not having Bob around stressed Kathleen out immensely. She paced, fretted, and lost her appetite. Maggie suggested doll therapy to Shelley. They found an amazing doll you'd swear was real if you didn't look twice. The doll gave Kathleen a sense of responsibility and structure. Of course, Kathleen had to come to meals now because she had to feed the baby. Shelley kept the baby in clothes and supplied facial wipes to clean up the mess that "feeding times" created.

Nine months into her time at Sunrise, the kids were worried more about Bob than Kathleen. Losing Kathleen's daily companionship, combined with his guilt and his own health woes, sent him into a depression that he still hasn't defeated. Their three children all live in the area and take turns bringing him to Sunrise, making sure he sees Kathleen at least five days a week. Her deterioration saddens him even more.

***

We said our goodbyes to Shelley and took the funky elevator to the ground floor. As we turned the corner of the short hall from the elevator to the lobby, we ran into Randy and Val. Literally, we almost walked right into them as they came off a first-floor wing. We all headed toward the door.

"What? No Jean-Pierre holding the door and wishing us a 'bonne nuit et merci d'être venu à La Belle Communauté'?" I said, teasing Randy and Val.

"Not tonight," answered his older sister Val as she adjusted her silvery ponytail. "I think he's tired from welcoming everyone!" she said with a laugh.

Randy and Val had recently retired from running their small carpet cleaning business. Randy was well over six feet tall with chestnut brown hair and a bushy beard. He always reminded me of a lumberjack. Val was no slouch either at five foot eleven; she was still slender and youthful.

Jean-Pierre, whose real name is Peter, is an extremely intelligent man. Val said he was smart enough to be anything he wanted, but developed a love for languages and cultures in middle school. He became fluent in Russian as well as the five most common romance languages of Europe. His first degree was a BA in foreign language, while his last degree was a PhD in linguistics.

His favorite language and culture was always that of the French. After finishing his undergraduate studies, he spent a year in the country perfecting his vocabulary, grammar, and accent. Of course, he also had a great time exploring the neighboring European countries and crashing in hostels with friends.

He returned to the US and continued his schooling, eventually becoming a college professor and the department chair. He spent his summers in France and rented an apartment in the Montmartre district of Paris. Situated upon the Right Bank of the Seine, it was once known as the bohemian section of the City of Lights. At last year's Sunrise Christmas party, Val, Randy, and Pete showed us pictures of their time spent together in Paris. Pete loved Christmas and really wanted his sister and brother-in-law to join him and experience Paris at that time of year.

The trio took in two classical Christmas concerts; one at Sainte-Chapelle and one inside the Eiffel Tower on Christmas Eve.

"Which concert was better?" I asked.

"Sainte-Chapelle," replied Pete. "Giant stained glass windows."

"Are there a lot of windows?" I queried.

"Sixteen. Huge. Six hundred square meters…I think there are six hundred square meters? Val, how many square meters are at the Chappelle?"

"You're right, Pete, six hundred."

"Yeah…yeah…six hundred…"

"The glass makes the place glow," Randy interjected.

"But the Eiffel Tower on Christmas Eve? C'mon, that *had* to be great," I stated.

"Tourist!" Pete said to me, causing the five of us to laugh.

We flipped through pictures of their Christmas trip along with his other French adventures as Pete recalled the places and Val translated.

"Côte d'Azur."

"French Riviera."

"Le Palais des Princes."

"Residence of the Sovereign Prince of Monaco, not part of France and the second smallest country in the world."

"Monte Carlo Casino," Pete continued.

"Part of Monaco."

"Palais de Papes Avignon."

"Palace of the Popes. After the great schism they moved to Avignon."

Cities and regions passed by through the pictures until one in particular stopped the procession.

Pete turned a page in the photo album where I caught a glimpse of him with a woman. He stared for a minute and gently touched the picture. He then slammed the album shut and threw it on the ground.

"Enough!" was all he said as he rested his elbow on the neatly pressed crease of his dress pants. With his chin in the palm of his hand, he began sulking.

Jim and I looked at Val and Randy, knowing there was more to the story that we weren't going to hear in Pete's presence. Val put her arm around her brother in quiet consolation.

Val turned to me and said, "Abby, let's head to the dessert table and see what goodies they have. Pete, I'll bring you a plate of your favorite sugar cookies!"

Pete looked up, and a smile returned, "Love sugar cookies!"

One thing about dementia is that bad memories only linger for a minute, and then, just like the rest of the memories, they are snatched away in an instant.

Val and I perused the table and picked out a plate of cookies for all of us. She told me that Pete had never married and never had a serious girlfriend until he was in his early fifties.

Pete and Margaux met through mutual friends in Paris. Margaux, who also never married, was in her late forties. Val and Randy met her several times and said she was lovely and that they were a perfect match.

Margaux grew up south of Paris along the Bay of Biscay in Bordeaux. La Sorbonne, a prestigious university, brought her to Paris thirty years prior, and she never left. Pete used the name Pierre in France, but it was Margaux who began calling him Jean-Pierre. Jean-Pierre Claris de Florian was one of her favorite French poets and romance writers, and she thought the name fit Pete well.

They were together for two years when he purchased a padlock. On one side, he had two intersecting hearts engraved, and on the other, he had the words from Claris de Florian's poem Plaisir d'mour:

> "Tant que cette eau coulera doucement
> vers ce ruisseau qui borde la prairie,
> je t'aimerai"

> *"As long as this water will run gently*
> *Toward this brook which borders the meadow,*
> *I will love you"*

Val explained that the poem is actually about losing love, but Pete etched the best part of it onto the lock. It was spring of 2013 in Paris. He took Margaux on an evening stroll over the Pont des Arts, also known as the Love Lock Bridge. With daylight fading and the city coming to light, he got down on bended knee. He held out a beautiful diamond ring and asked Margaux to marry him. She said yes. Joining thousands of other locks, they put the hasp through the fence links and locked it. Then they threw the key into the river, symbolizing their "locked love." The picture that caused

Pete to slam the album shut was taken on the bridge that evening, complete with the lighted Eiffel Tower in the background.

They began to plan their life. Pete was going to finish another year and a half of teaching. That would make him fifty-five and eligible for early retirement. Margaux had visited the US a few times but just couldn't get used to it. Pete wanted to retire and live in France anyway, so it was a match made in heaven.

While in the States, Val noticed her brilliant older brother seemed to be slipping. He would misplace items and forget appointments, which was definitely out of character for him. Her initial concern was the possibility that he'd had a small stroke. She talked to Pete about getting checked over, but he brushed her off. He returned to Paris that summer and the following Christmas. At Christmas, Val became increasingly concerned. Before returning to Paris, she called Margaux and had a challenging conversation with her, asking if she noticed Pete's forgetfulness. Margaux had, but also told Val that he had always been a bit forgetful in the time she had known him. Now Val wondered how long his memory issues had been going on.

Val forced Pete to go to a doctor the following spring. One year after his engagement, he received the devastating news: dementia. He retired as planned, but that was the only plan that was fulfilled. He traveled to Paris that summer with Val and Randy, and the four of them sat together in a puddle of tears in Pete's apartment. There would be no wedding. The dementia seemed to be moving relatively slow, but it wouldn't be fair to Margaux. They exchanged letters for a while but eventually, they both let go.

Chapter 15

Barb and Joe decided to retire at sixty, and Barb sold Preston's to Sapphire, which naturally became my responsibility.

The first thing Barb did when she retired was get her knee replaced. After that, she and Joe had a great time traveling. They made good use of the Eurorail Pass and traveled extensively throughout Europe. Italy was one of their favorite countries, and they loved seeing Pope John Paul II at Vatican Square.

They ventured through the British Isles, Australia, the Caribbean, Hawaii, Tahiti, and Bora Bora. They traveled between Rochester and Utica, spending time with their grandkids. As the grandkids got old enough, we did the family vacations at Disney World and cruised the Caribbean.

Barb and Joe were still invited to occasional Grand Unveilings, as was I. The four of us decided that we weren't willing to spend half the summer at those things. Although I'm more comfortable now, I still don't care for them and managed to get myself down to just one or two appearances a year.

Then, without warning, the unbelievable happened. Our parents got old. And then they got sick. It started with my father ten years ago when he was diagnosed with esophageal cancer. They said he wouldn't beat it. He was a very healthy eighty-year-old, but eighty is still eighty, and the body wears out. Even in their forties, people don't have much of a chance against this type of cancer, and the best-case scenario is five years.

The doctor prescribed both chemo and radiation for my father. He refused chemo and went solely with radiation. This decision aggravated the oncologist, who explained that it was all or nothing. He still refused chemo, and at the end of six weeks the oncologist stared at his results in disbelief. The tumor was undetectable. The doctor warned that just because they couldn't see it didn't mean it wouldn't return.

He finished all his treatments in time for golf season. When the following winter came, Mom and Dad decided to head for slightly warmer weather. Jeff, an auto mechanic, took a job with a Mercedes dealership in North Carolina. He and his family had lived there for fifteen years, and I think Dad knew it was the last trip they would make.

Spring returned, and so did golf. For Father's Day, I made his favorite dessert, coconut cream pie. I heard him make an off-handed comment stating, "At least I can eat that." I don't know why it didn't click at the time, but it didn't until four weeks later. He was having problems swallowing, and the doctor confirmed that the tumor had returned.

He spent the rest of the summer doing what he always did. Monday through Friday, he met a bunch of his retired friends at the golf course, where they picked teams and played eighteen. His last day of playing was a beautiful November day. Mom informed me the lack of food was making him pretty weak, and she was surprised he could golf at all.

He had a couple of medical procedures in early December. I pulled the doctor aside and asked her how long. She gave him three months, and she was right on the money.

***

It was late February when the switch flipped. I left on a Monday evening, and when I returned Tuesday morning, he was a different person. For the first time during this whole ordeal, he didn't get out of his pajamas and robe. His mental abilities suddenly declined; he was extremely fidgety and refused to sleep. I sat on the couch holding his hand, trying to distract him from the perpetual motion he was experiencing. He kept playing with the buttons on his pajamas and pulling on the feeding tube in his stomach. I noticed how thin he was. His one-hundred-and-ninety-pound frame had slowly wasted away until he weighed maybe one-hundred twenty. I hugged him and could feel his protruding shoulder blades. Mom had a nurse who was helping on occasion. She stayed overnight Tuesday and left Wednesday morning.

At noon Wednesday, Mom called, asking me to come over. Dad was entirely mentally incompetent and kept trying to wander the house. By now, he was so weak that he could barely stand. I arrived to find him sitting on the edge of his hospital bed in the living room, picking at the carpet and muttering something.

"What is he doing?" I asked Mom.

"Go ahead and ask him," she said with a half-smirk.

"Dad. What are you doing?"

He looked at me, and I knew he didn't know who I was, and answered, "Playing marbles. What does it look like?!" He was gruff, as though I was the one with the problem.

149

I began to chuckle.

I turned to Mom, "Are you kidding me?" I said in complete disbelief. "Do you know who he's playing with?"

"His brothers along with a childhood friend."

Wow. The mind does weird things. He was back to being a boy.

"Give him a minute. He'll be fishing next."

Mom was correct. He sat on the edge of the bed with an imaginary pole. Occasionally he would cast his line and hold a conversation with God only knows who. Then he switched again and began looking back and forth as though he couldn't find something.

"What are you looking for, Dad?"

"My putter."

"I think the caddy took it," I said to him. Dad never had a caddy, but I couldn't resist.

"Why that rotten, lousy, no good caddy!" came his angry response.

I was sitting on the stool next to his bed laughing, and he was oblivious.

"Abby Marie! Stop that!" Mom said, trying not to laugh herself.

As I continued to watch him "golf," I thought back to when Dad retired. Not one to sit around, he worked part-time on the weekends at the course. Before I was married, I would often join him late in the afternoon. We'd play the front nine and be done in time for dinner.

"Here, Dad. I found your putter," I said, handing him an invisible putter.

He took it from me. I watched him go through his usual putting ritual of lining up the shot as he sat on the edge of his bed. Then he seemed to watch intently for a few seconds.

"Good one, Abby!" He put his arm around an imaginary me and finished, "Five o'clock. I'm hungry. Let's go see what your mother's making for dinner. I hope it's something good!"

This is exactly what he said every time we finished nine holes, and it would be the last words I would ever hear from him.

He laid down in bed but wouldn't relax. His talking stopped, but his motion didn't. We finally had to admit him to the hospital. Three days later, he was gone.

***

While I was dealing with my father, Barb and Joe continued bouncing between Drew in Rochester and Sean in Utica. Just before my father's initial diagnosis, Barb became concerned with Joe's forgetfulness and had him tested for dementia. As it turned out, he just needed hearing aids.

But then Drew began noticing Joe's odd behavior. On one visit, Drew caught Joe relieving himself on the side of the house. Drew also noticed Joe's struggle to find words. Sean became concerned too, so Barb had him reevaluated. This time, their concerns were valid. At seventy-five years old, Joe was diagnosed with dementia.

Dealing with my father was enough for me. It seemed Barb was doing okay with Joe at the time, but then we found out the rest of the miserable story.

Joe was two years into his diagnosis, and my father was three months from death when we all attended a November wedding reception. Jim, myself, Barb, and Joe were standing in a circle working on small plates of appetizers when Sister Martha walked up to say hello. She had been a family friend for longer than Jim could remember.

Sister Martha greeted us with "Prestons! It's great to see you!"

"Sister Martha!" Barb said, leaning to give her a cheek hug. "Have you met my son, Jimmy?"

Jim and I looked at each other, completely mortified.

Jim recovered and said, "Yeah, Mom, we've met."

We made small talk for a few minutes before grabbing Drew and Kate and Sean and Lori and huddling in a corner.

"Uh, what's up with Mom?" Jim started.

"What? Why?" asked Sean.

"She just introduced me to Sister Martha as though we've never met!"

Drew answered, "Oh…we haven't seen them as much as we used to. We figured it was too much with her dealing with Dad. Kate said she thought maybe forgetfulness was creeping in…"

"I didn't think much of it at first," Kate explained, "it was just little things that didn't seem like Barb. I passed it off, figuring it was just the stress of dealing with Joe. But then she didn't remember going to dinner with us. The kids were all home…it had only been a week, and she didn't remember it."

The last few years had already been crazy enough. Besides Dad, Jim had ventured out on his own eight years ago and founded Preston's Engineering Group. Five years later, after becoming established in Syracuse, he partnered with Drew and Sean to expand Preston's Engineering into Rochester and Utica. The three of them were close and decided a partnership in other markets was something they were all up for, but upstarts are always a lot of work.

***

The reception ended, and we headed home.

"You're quiet, Abby. What's wrong?"

I exploded, "What's wrong? What's wrong? Are you kidding me? We have a dementia patient taking care of a dementia patient, and apparently no one bothered to tell us that? And SHE'S DRIVING! That's just great. No safety issues there. How long before she confuses red lights and green lights? Someone's going to get hurt!"

"Abby... it'll be okay."

"No, Jim," I continued in my anger, "it won't be okay. Who do you think is going to end up taking care of this crap? Your brother in Utica? Oh, no wait, maybe it's your brother in Rochester? Yeah, that's it. They're going to take time from the Preston upstart and come right down here, and alternate days so I can go back to work full time come spring. You know, after I finish taking care of my dying father. Yup. That's probably what's going to happen."

I was already on part-time leave dealing with my father because my own brother lives seven hundred miles away. I snidely continued, "Maybe everyone will at least let me watch my father starve to death first. You think everyone will do that for me before I have to deal with *your* parents? That would be nice," I said, my voice becoming soft. Jim knew better than to answer.

La Belle Communauté

I probably should have been more concerned with Barb and Joe—they were the sick ones—but at that moment, all I could think of was myself. I'd already spent the last two years running on and off with my father. Now it was on with no off. X-rays, PET scans, CT scans, oncologists, radiologists, radiation, and surgeons, along with trips to the ER and trying to keep Mom calm. I'd already had enough, and now I was headed into the last Thanksgiving and Christmas with a man who is unable to eat. The worst is yet to come, and when I'm done with that, Barb and Joe will be dumped on me for an encore. Just great.

Little did we know, it would be another eighteen months before we could get the two of them into an assisted living facility.

Chapter 16

Barb seemed to be holding her own despite the Sister Martha incident, and my hands were full enough. The boys began conversations with Barb regarding assisted living. They were met with anger and adamant refusals. She was fine, her memory was fine, everyone was against her and didn't understand it was just stress, etcetera, etcetera. I have found that many dementia patients rarely believe that they have the disease. I've heard more than one say how glad they are to still have their faculties, while family stands by rolling their eyes. Never mind the stoves that are left on, bills that go unpaid, or doctor appointments that are forgotten.

It took fifteen months after the Sister Martha introduction for Barb to become just disoriented enough to begin the process in earnest. We had to wait until her brain couldn't quite comprehend what was going on.

She had refused to transfer power of attorney over to Jim, but now a lawyer friend, Tom Dowery, sat at the table drinking tea and talking about old garden parties. Once the conversation started, the lawyer pulled out papers and began sliding them across the table to her. Tom never missed a beat while talking and pointing to the "sign here" lines. Jim signed his part, and Joe did his best while the notary stood by stamping and dating the papers.

We asked about forcing them to move, and Tom informed us that it is technically illegal. I protested that they were both unable to make decisions and should not be driving. Tom explained that while that was true, in the eyes of the law, we would have to go through the court system to have them declared incompetent.

"You don't even want to know how long that process takes," Tom said to me as he got in his SUV. "You will just have to force them. Joe won't be the problem. Barb? Well, good luck with that!"

I researched several places, but Jim and I only visited two that we felt would be a good fit. We went to a beautiful private pay facility but didn't care for the staff. They seemed to be more interested in name dropping those who were once influential members of the community and acting like they knew them.

Then we visited Sunrise. It was in need of a remodel and took both private pay and Medicaid. Although it couldn't compare to the upscale private pay facility, the staff was warm and welcoming. We watched as they interacted with residents. They loved on them and treated them with a genuineness that seemed to be lacking at the other facility. We checked out a couple of the apartments and decided it was a good fit.

***

Joe already had a dementia diagnosis and saw a specialist, not that the specialist could do much for him. However, Barb didn't have an official diagnosis, and we needed one to move her into Sunrise.

Jim called ahead to her primary care doctor and explained the situation. We had to wait four weeks for an appointment. The doctor already saw the signs but said she needed to have a brain scan to rule out any other problems. Another five-week wait. Great. It was finally determined that no other brain issues were going on, so dementia was the official diagnosis.

We called Sunrise to find out there was a waitlist, and that Joe and Barb were third in line. We waited another ten weeks. In the meantime, she was getting worse, and Joe was becoming increasingly difficult. Barb still did a decent job hiding the struggles she was having.

Jim and I showed up at the house for a visit to find Joe eating cereal that Barb had just set down for him. I picked up the milk container and checked the date. It was two weeks out of code, and the sniff test confirmed it. Joe sat there eating cereal with a brain that couldn't process what his taste buds were saying. Jim tried to remove everything without Barb noticing, but he was unsuccessful. She started yelling at Jim, telling him the milk was fine, and that she cooked Joe a steak dinner last night. The problem was, there was almost no food in the refrigerator.

We started dropping by with meals, but they weren't home half the time, which was also upsetting because the woman had no business driving. We figured out that Joe had begun to wander, and Barb couldn't keep up with him. Although she had her knee replaced, her hips had begun giving her trouble, causing her to use a cane.

We also found out from a police-officer friend that they had been called to find Joe. Apparently, Barb visited the dentist and told Joe to sit in the waiting room while she had her teeth cleaned. She came out, and Joe was gone. Thankfully he didn't get far. He wandered to a neighboring store where the clerk realized he had a problem and called the police. When Barb saw the police, she went to see if they had Joe.

We gave up on telling her about moving. She had dug in her heels and informed us she wasn't stupid or crazy. You cannot reason with dementia. Reasoning skills are stolen pretty early in the game. We didn't know this in the beginning but figured it out quickly. From that time forward, we simply lied and didn't tell Barb that she and Joe would be moving.

***

The night before they moved, Drew came in and stayed overnight with Barb and Joe. Sean stayed with us, and he and Jim headed to their parents' place in a rented U-Haul, while I followed behind. On the way there, Drew texted me saying he told Barb that today was moving day, and informed me that it was our job to peel her off the ceiling. She was angry and confused about what was going on around her.

We decided to divide and conquer. I was in charge of gathering clothes, toiletries, and any medicine I could find. Every time one of us passed by Barb sitting at the kitchen table, she asked why they had to move. The four of us decided to keep the focus on Joe. We told her the doctor wanted Joe to be in a facility that could help him, and she needed to go to support Joe.

She didn't believe it and argued in an infinite loop as we gathered their belongings. The boys broke down the bed, hauled the dresser down the stairs, and decided the couch, chair, and TV were next.

"Why is this happening?" she said to me as I passed her again.

"Barb, if something happens to Joe and he ends up in the hospital, they can decide to send him to a nursing home. None of us will have any say in it. They could move him seventy miles from here. You wouldn't want that. You want him to be with you, and we want you to be with him."

"Joe could come home. He wouldn't have to go anywhere. They can't do that."

"Yes, they can." And the loop continued.

That wasn't a lie. In New York, if someone goes to the hospital and the attending physician realizes they aren't safe at home, they will send them to a nursing home. They have a seventy-mile radius and will take the first available bed. If Barb was well, Joe would be able to return home. But she isn't, and the lawyer and her doctor warned us that if Joe ended up in the hospital, they would do precisely that.

"Barb, why don't you join Joe on the deck?" I suggested, trying to refocus her. "It won't be sunny for too much longer. Thunderstorms are headed this way."

***

I opened the hall closet to see what they had for soaps, shampoos, etc. I was met with a cascade of shampoo bottles and cans of shaving cream that bounced off me before crashing to the floor. Drew stuck his head out of the bedroom, took one look, and started laughing at the pile of bottles and cans on the floor. I counted fifteen bottles of shampoo and twenty cans of shaving cream.

"Know what the best part is?"

"No, enlighten me, Drew," I said with a smile.

"Dad uses an electric razor."

"Yeah, and?"

He responded through his laughter, "You don't use shaving cream with an electric razor."

I opened closets and dresser drawers only to find a mess. Everywhere upstairs was a mess. Downstairs seemed fairly neat, but none of us ever had a reason to go upstairs. Barb had stuff all over the place. I did my best to find matching sheets, matching socks, underwear—and the list went on. Now it was an all-out scavenger hunt. The four of us turned it into a game.

Has anyone seen toothbrushes or toothpaste? Check in the kitchen.

Medicine? Try the kitchen cupboards, the medicine cabinet, and between the couch cushions.

Joe's socks? We might need to go to Target and buy some because we can't find two of a kind. And let's get some sheets while we're there.

Two hours later, we had collected all we thought we'd needed to get them through the first few days. Jim and Drew hopped in the U-Haul while Sean took Barb and Joe in their own vehicle.

Jim stuck his head in the front door and yelled to me, "Hey, Abby! We're leaving now. See you at the place. The storm is almost here."

"Okay," I yelled down the stairs, "I'm going to make a quick run through the house to make sure windows are shut and doors are locked."

I made a quick final sweep through the upstairs rooms checking the windows. I headed down the stairs and took a left through the White Room and into the family room. I pulled the French swing-out patio doors closed and heard the low rumbles of thunder moving into the area. The wind had picked up, and the skies were darkening quickly. I cut through the kitchen, grabbing Joe's favorite baseball cap off the table. I ran out to check the garage as giant raindrops began to fall. From there, I checked the guest room and stuck my head in Joe's old office to find random papers blowing off his desk and onto the floor.

"How many rainy days have you been through, Old Filing Cabinet?" I asked as I reached across it to shut the window. Water damage on his old wooden bench filing cabinet told me the window had no doubt been open for months.

I left the office and stopped in the hall to turn off the air conditioning. The gathering storm clouds were creating darkness in the house, and I noticed an odd glow that seemed to be coming from the kitchen. I got to the kitchen and realized the dim light was coming from the dining room. I stood at the dining room threshold, staring at the curio cabinet in the front corner. Barb had left the light on, and it was shining brightly amid the gloom.

I set Joe's cap on the dining room table and slowly approached the cabinet full of Ukrainian eggs. Sadness was overtaking me. I stood before the glass shelves that now displayed "the good old days." The pysanky that captivated me thirty-something years ago had become a yearly tradition at the Preston's. The case containing brandy snifters cradling eggs made by young versions of Jim, Sean, and Drew was now bursting at the seams with eggs added by them, their wives, and their children.

Barb had increased the number of snifters, along with wine glasses of varying heights and sizes to show off the eggs. She had also bought several egg trees that displayed seven eggs each, along with various pedestals that lined the front of the case. All six shelves were jammed full, forming a cacophony of color and design.

La Belle Communauté

The rain was now pounding on the front windows and running down them in sheets as I stared at each shelf. Geometric shapes, pin-drop flowers, and wheat stalks were dyed sunshine yellow, burnt orange, brick red, turquoise, magenta, green, and ocean blue. Some eggs were stunning; others were made by little hands having fun. Each year brought sharper designs as our nieces and nephews grew up. I smiled as I recalled the days we made them.

The entire Preston crew would gather on a Saturday. Barb would have the dyes, kistkas, beeswax, candles, and paper towels set on a thick layer of newspaper across the kitchen table. As the family grew, she added a second fold-out table. We'd spend a few hours designing and dying eggs while chatting and laughing with each other. It always ended with Joe bringing in a stack of pizza boxes and bottles of soda for dinner.

"God, I miss this," I said with tears rolling down my cheeks.

I reached behind the cabinet and turned out the light.

Chapter 17

The storm had moved through by the time I pulled up to the "all-inclusive gated community" that is Sunrise. Sean was just getting out of the car with Barb and Joe. The front door is always locked and alarmed with a numeric keypad to allow people in and out of the building. That code was given to family members with a warning to never say the number out loud near a resident. They've had residents who could retain the numbers long enough to get out the door. Additionally, that same code was used to lock the stairwell doors to ensure residents use the elevator and don't sit on the stairs or get hurt climbing them.

Not having the code yet, we rang the bell. Barb was quiet for the moment, completely befuddled by what was happening. The first of the double doors swung open, and we were greeted by Nyasia, a young African American woman who was the receptionist.

"Good morning, everybody! You must be the Prestons!" she said, giving us a warm welcome while punching the code into the second set of doors. "It's so nice to meet you all! You'll love it here. We have a great staff!"

Barb had snapped partway out of her funk by then and replied in a nasty tone, "Love it? Oh, Sweetie, I don't think so. We are NOT STAYING!" She turned to Sean, "Do you understand me, mister? We are NOT STAYING!"

Before Sean could answer, Karen showed up.

"You must be Barb and Joe! We're so glad to have you here!" Karen and Sean shook hands and exchanged names.

Now Barb began yelling, "I SAID, WE'RE NOT STAY-ING HERE!"

Nobody in the place noticed except for the staff, who gave us a look and a knowing smile. No doubt they go through this routine with almost every resident.

"Okay, Barb," Karen continued, "we're just going to give you a quick tour." She turned and gave Sean and me a wink as she led the two of them away.

Just then, Mike, the head of maintenance, stopped and intro-duced himself while Jim and Drew finally arrived. During the rain, they had decided to stop for coffee.

"I'm going to help move their belongings," Mike explained. "Have them pull around to the back door, and we'll use the eleva-tor from there."

Mike was a nice guy. He was in his forties and struck me as the teddy-bear type—a little pudgy with cheeks just begging to be squeezed. He loved the residents and knew them all by name, stopping to say hello to each one he passed by.

***

Barb and Joe were given a tour and taken to lunch while the four of us set up their apartment. They had a decent sized living area. We fit a couch, two chairs, a coffee table, an end table, and a TV with its stand. On the wall to the right was a small refrigerator positioned under a set of two-door hanging cupboards. New short, gray commercial carpet ran through the entire apartment except for the bathroom. Beige vinyl was the color of the day there, and a fresh coat of off-white blanketed the walls.

The gridded windows had dark beige valances with small, multi-colored flowers splashed on them. Metal venetian blinds were lowered until they met the top of the window sills. Their slats were open to let the sunlight in.

A left out of the living room took them to a large built-in closet, a bathroom, and a bedroom. I hung their clothes and put extra blankets on the top shelf, making sure not to breach the red-tape line, which is a violation of fire codes.

I unloaded the toiletries onto the top of the decorative radiator shield in the bathroom. The bathroom was fairly big to allow for walkers. Handrails were on both sides of the toilet, as well as the walk-in shower.

The boys were assembling the bed when Karen came to the door with the two of them. Joe, who was almost completely incontinent, and by now needed a new diaper. Barb was headed into one of her tirades, so I pulled Jim aside and told him I was off to get drinks, snacks, and pizza for all of us. I had had enough. It was now mid-afternoon, and none of us had eaten since six a.m.

***

I returned with the goods to find that Sean had hooked up the TV and made sure the landline phone was working. Joe saw the pizza box and smiled. It was his favorite, so Drew handed him the first slice. I grabbed a slice and watched Joe. He was as happy as could be. He loved people, and even in his deteriorated state, it was obvious that he missed the social aspect of life. Although he could barely speak anymore, Karen told us that while on their tour he would smile and tip his non-existent hat as he walked by residents and staff.

I missed Joe. He was like a second father to me. I missed his encouragement. I missed him squeezing lime into the vodka tonics he nursed. I missed him at his backyard grill. I missed his voice. And right now, I missed his "Dad Talks" when Barb got to be too much. And Barb was definitely getting to be too much. Not that she could help it.

Barb was sulking in the corner, still working on the same conversation we'd all been having with her all day. Lather, rinse, repeat. I couldn't take it anymore.

At Jim's encouragement, she wandered the apartment with her cane in hand, complaining about everything. She didn't like the shower curtain. She didn't like the window valances; she didn't like the carpet, didn't like the closet, I hung the clothes wrong—and then she repeated her complaints over and over and over.

Mike stopped to visit and welcome Joe and Barb. Joe stood up, his baggy pants concealing a diaper, and managed a smile, a handshake, and a "hat tip." Barb just glared at him. Mike saw the pictures we brought for the walls and offered to hang them for us. We gladly took him up on that. He promised they would be done by the end of the week.

It was dinnertime before Sean and Drew headed for their respective cities. Jim and I were still working on the last details and left around eight—completely exhausted.

***

We didn't get to bed until almost eleven and then we were startled awake at four-thirty by the phone. I rolled over and squinted at the caller ID. It was Barb. I poked Jim and made him take the call. I could hear her yelling from my side of the bed: How dare the boys move her, there was nothing wrong; she could handle Joe and herself, she wasn't stupid, and then demanded that Jim pick them up immediately. Jim tried in vain to explain things to her. Of course, she was having none of it.

He managed to get her calmed down, and we both rolled over only to have the phone ring three minutes later. Same conversation. Same outcome. The phone rang back again. This time when Jim finished his conversation, he took the phone off the hook. Later in the day, we found out that Drew was next on her call list with Sean shortly after. We began to wonder if the phone was such a good idea.

I called Karen that morning asking for advice. She said it was normal, especially since we basically "shanghaied" them out of their home. Change is very hard for folks with dementia, and Barb had gone from being completely independent to having her house and car taken from her, as well as being "locked in," all in a matter of hours.

She told me not to have family visit every day. We had no intention of doing so to begin with, but she warned us to keep it to two to three days a week to start. Too much visiting, and they won't get into a routine. We were also told to brace ourselves for more backlash from Barb for at least a good month.

***

Barb didn't disappoint. For the first two weeks, we would get home to find our answering machine full and the phone ringing. It started with her yelling at us: she wanted to go home, Joe was fine, she was fine, she wasn't stupid, we were not to sell their house, we had to come to get them, she couldn't find her car so they were going to walk home. Messages changed from yelling to crying and begging. We didn't bother listening to them anymore, and the delete button became our best friend.

Between three and four weeks, things calmed a little. We got fewer messages, and by week five, we had a day when she never called. Finally!

I talked to Karen to see how they were adjusting. Joe was having a great time. He loved the music programs and dancing. Barb was doing pretty well. Sunrise's recreation staff worked to introduce residents to each other with similar interests. Barb had two women, Betty and Lucy, whom she started to pal around with. She was enjoying the activities, and the two of them were busy for a good part of the day.

"Why are we still getting these phone calls?" I asked Karen.

"Usually, it's two reasons. First, she is just being a bratty teen and wants you all on a guilt trip. Second, pay attention to the time-stamps on the phone. I bet she's calling during our downtimes around meals or near bedtime."

Karen was correct. That's precisely when she was calling, and yes, she was manipulative. It was a relief to the boys. At least they knew their parents were doing well, and Barb was just being a punk. It made life so much easier knowing that.

***

Jim and I struggled through the summer trying to figure out Joe and Barb's financial situation. We couldn't find mail, bank statements, or investments that we were sure they had. I went to the house a week after the move to clean out the refrigerator. I snooped through all the rooms and the garage. I happened to walk past Barb's car when I noticed the backseat. It looked like a mail truck. From there, I unlocked the garage to find small stacks of mail sitting on shelves and garbage cans.

"You've GOT to be kidding me," I said out loud.

I gathered all the mail and dropped it on the gorgeous dining room table. I took a picture and texted it to Jim with the caption, "Breaking News: Mailman's Stolen Mail Bag Found in Swanky Section of Town!"

"OMG! R u kidding me???" was the text back with the bi-line: "Woman in Question: 'I didn't do it! The mailman and I are personal friends. He GAVE me his mailbag!' ROFL! Did u text my bros?"

"Just sent it."

I got the same stunned responses from them as I was sorting the mail into three piles: junk, unknown, and keep.

I tossed the junk in the recycle bin and went through the unknown stuff. Most of it was junk as well. Then I started going through the real stuff: bank statements, investments, uncashed dividend checks, an uncashed IRS tax refund, unpaid utility bills, unpaid car insurance, unpaid homeowners, and unpaid health insurance. Thankfully, most items had not made it as far as cancellation.

I checked bank statements, looking for social security deposits. I found Joe's, but couldn't find Barb's. I spotted a pile of mail I had set on a chair as I sorted. At the bottom of the stack, I found a statement from a completely different bank. Its sole purpose was for depositing Barb's social security checks.

I put the important stuff in my SUV and headed back into the house for a second tour. I began opening cupboards and drawers throughout the house. Downstairs wasn't terrible. Things were not in their usual spots, but still not terrible. A lot of outdated food and the stuff in the refrigerator was nasty, but that was to be expected. Joe's old office was somewhat of a dumping ground for the first floor. There was old junk mail, dead plants, and a half a case of adult diapers.

I went into the basement. Nothing seemed out of sorts, and most things had been cleaned out years back. It was difficult for Barb's hip to trek up and down the stairs, so a first-floor laundry was installed.

I went upstairs, turned right, and went down the hall to the master suite. I opened Barb's jewelry armoire. Usually full, it was now half-empty. I frantically began pulling open the side doors of the chest. Nothing. I went through the drawers of the remaining furniture in their room. Nothing. The closet was a disaster, with shoes thrown on the bottom and purses piled on the top shelves. Clothes that fell off hangers were left where they landed.

I went down the hall to the other three bedrooms once occupied by the boys. Jim's old room had boxes full of shoes stacked on the bed, gift wrap and bows on the floor while the closet was full of their clothes and just as messy as the master suite. I went through the dresser drawers hoping to find the jewelry, but instead, I was met with junk drawers full of random crap: candles, scissors, eyeglasses they had supposedly lost, greeting cards, Christmas ornaments, plastic grass for Easter baskets. You name it, I found it.

I went into the other two rooms, which were about the same—a giant mess with barely any room to walk through. I opened the hall closet. I already knew it was a mess but hoped I'd find missing bracelets, rings, necklaces, and earrings. Nothing.

I texted the boys. Everyone was in agreement not to get too stressed out. No one thought they were given away, probably just lost somewhere in the mess. I took what I found home for safekeeping.

***

We made it through the rest of the summer, and in mid-fall, we began discussions about the house. It needed to be emptied, cleaned, and sold. Of course, this became mostly my job. As the season ended, I talked to Steve and went part-time. Steve had done a fantastic job growing Sapphire over the years. Years ago, we added residential and commercial snow removal to our long list of services. Jay ran that. Not being in love with midnight snow calls in one of the snowiest metropolitan cities in America, I mostly skipped that part of the business. I would fill in for drivers as needed and did some daytime removal, but the dead of the night is for owls and raccoons.

I was four years into caretaking, and Steve, Vicki, and Jay knew I'd had enough. They unanimously decided I would go part-time, whether I wanted to or not, and take a leave if needed. I was tired of those options. I had already done this with my own father.

I went part-time in October and began cleaning out their personal effects. I tackled Joe and Barb's master suite closet, starting with the top shelf and Barb's collection of purses. I worked my way through the hanging clothes and felt it was like an archaeological dig—one layer at a time.

I decided to organize clothes in each closet as "his" or "hers"—Barb's stuff on one side and Joe's on the other. I then started picking up belts, ties, scarves, and sweaters off the closet floor. Under all this was a pile of mismatched sneakers, shoes, and slippers. Many were well worn and should have been thrown out long ago. I started tossing them to the floor outside the closet when I noticed weird rattling sounds coming from some of the shoes. I grabbed a pair of Joe's old dress shoes that hadn't been used since his insurance days. I held the worn black wingtips vertically, and down slid one of Barb's necklaces.

"Oh, good Lord," I said to no one.

I crawled around the bottom of the closet, grabbing shoes and tipping them upward. It was like getting three sevens on a Vegas slot machine. The one-armed bandits dropped coins, and Joe and Barb's shoes dropped jewelry. Missing rings, earrings, necklaces, brooches, and bracelets all dropped into the heel slot. Sometimes one item, sometimes two, sometimes three, sometimes none. By the time I finished the closet, I had found all the missing jewelry.

I spent three weeks throwing stuff out, organizing closets, and cleaning out the cars and the garage. Once that was done, we all gathered to decide who wanted what. Then we hired a company that did estate sales. We got the house emptied and on the market the following spring. Thankfully, it was a decent market, and the house sold within a month.

***

The house was the easy part; finances were another story. Joe and Barb, who were once organized, had managed to make a mess. At one time, they had one joint checking and savings account. Somewhere along the line, they opened a second one, but Joe's monthly retirement money was being deposited into Barb's account. Then there were two different transfers listed that returned the money to Joe's account. Meanwhile, Barb had opened a new account at a separate bank to deposit her social security checks.

I found a total of twelve small CDs strewn across eight different investment houses. We figured the two of them opened the CDs with friends that worked in various banks and investment firms. We found two IRAs held by two separate entities plus stocks that paid dividends. Of course, Joe had life insurance on both of them, as well as investment accounts for the grandkids that weren't transferable until twenty-five. We wondered how long Barb had dementia before we noticed. In hindsight, we think she had it before Joe, but hers progressed at a much slower rate, making it more difficult to spot.

I easily spent eighty hours on the phone figuring out how to navigate and condense the disaster. I faxed POA paperwork to numerous places while Jim ran to the banks, closing accounts and cashing and consolidating their investments.

Then came the two most difficult places to deal with—the Securities Exchange Commission and the Social Security office.

The stocks were a nightmare. Something called a medallion signature guarantee was needed. The medallion signature is a special stamp required to transfer securities. It confirms that the signature is authentic and the signer is authorized to transfer items. But most banks don't hold the stamp, and others have one but don't want to guarantee anything, especially if you don't have an account with them. We found one bank in our city that held the stamp. No one had an account there, but it turned out that I had designed a huge project for the manager. No clue what people do if they don't have an account and don't know the branch manager.

Social Security was a joy. The feds are a fun-loving bunch full of misinformation. I called the toll-free number, and a nice southerly woman informed me that the federal government does not recognize power of attorney papers. She gave me all the information Jim would need for a trip he would have to personally make to our local office. It's first-come, first-served, so he got up early and still had a two-hour wait. The best thing was that the nice southern lady gave him all the wrong information. Now he had to collect all the right stuff and return in order to become a representative payee for his parents. Another trip and another two hours downtown, and he was informed that they could deny his request to be the payee. Of course, they didn't do that, but apparently, they like to tell people these things.

It was almost three years from the day of Jim's introduction to Sister Martha that all was said and done with the house sale and straightening the finances.

But just when you think things have settled down, they get crazy again!

Chapter 18

With the finances straightened out and the house cleaned up, cleaned out, and sold, we thought we'd get a breather, but it didn't last long. Only three months later, Joe had become increasingly worse, and Barb got in the way of his care.

He was completely incontinent and couldn't wash or dress himself. The staff at Sunrise was there to help with all those things, but Barb, who still didn't think anything was wrong with her, insisted she could care for him. She wouldn't let anyone help with Joe, and the staff had to get pushy concerning the diapers. They had had enough of cleaning up needless messes that spread themselves throughout the apartment and sometimes down the hall.

Barb wouldn't allow them to wash Joe and was insistent that she already had. It was obvious that she hadn't, and his clothes weren't cleaned or changed. The staff was reporting bruising on Joe's hands and forearms from an unknown source. Aides began waiting outside their apartment for any sign that Barb needed help. Joe's ability to follow instructions was diminishing while Barb's frustration was increasing.

The aides reported that Barb was yelling at Joe when he couldn't follow her directions. She had gotten to the point where she believed there was nothing wrong with Joe and that he was just stubborn. They concluded that Barb was pulling on Joe trying to get him out of a chair, resulting in the bruises. Older people bruise easily, but assisted living is under state scrutiny, so something needed to be done.

Karen finally requested that Jim and I come in for a meeting. She explained the situation to us and came up with an option. There were no apartments open at the time, but they were in the middle of some minor construction. The giant supply closet at the end of the hall was going to be moved. It had a bathroom and would fit a twin bed, dresser, and chair.

We all agreed it was best, and Sean came in from Utica to help me move Joe. It wasn't a big physical move, all I needed to do was take his clothes down the hall, but it was a big emotional move for Barb. For the first time in over fifty years, they would no longer be in the same bed, and there was no way I was taking the brunt of that.

They still dined together and went to activities together, but they no longer shared an apartment. This allowed the staff to "toilet" Joe, which means they took him to the bathroom every two hours. Barb took it reasonably well, and we all suspected she was secretly relieved not to have those daily responsibilities.

***

Joe's stay in his own apartment was also short-lived. In early September, Karen called to inform me that we needed to find a nursing home for him. He could no longer feed himself (a task

Barb had now taken on) or follow instructions of any kind. We knew it was more than Sunrise could handle, and we held no grudges. All in all, they do a great job every day. Assisted living facilities usually aren't the place people live out their final years; nursing homes are. Assisted living is simply the midway point between life at home and death in a nursing home.

Karen explained to me that we first needed to choose up to five nursing homes. From there, she would call and send Joe's information to them. The first one with an open bed would be the winner. Oh, joy. Sunrise was part of a group that owned several living facilities, including a nursing home called Sunset. What a stupid name for a nursing home. Why didn't they just name it "Waiting for Death" or maybe, "Death Bed?" I liked the name Sunset about as much as I liked Jean-Pierre calling Sunrise "La Belle Communauté."

The Beautiful Community? Hardly. At least not in my book. Don't get me wrong, they have a great staff who love the residents where they're at each day, but I hate the place. I hate the smell of the halls; I hate the smell on the elevator, I hate the smell of the stairwells, I hate the "easy-to-clean" vinyl chairs, I hate the vacant eyes wandering aimlessly, I hate the pain in the eyes of the families, I hate watching residents crying at the doors begging to go home, I hate that anyone has to come here, I hate that they can't stay, and I hate that Joe and Barb are numbered among them. The nickname "La Belle" has stuck, but there's nothing beautiful about it, and I refuse to refer to Sunrise in that manner.

***

The boys only picked three homes due to their proximity to Sunrise, but they really were hoping for Sunset. Sunrise and

Sunset are close together and would make visiting easier for everyone. A week-and-a-half later, Karen called to inform me that Sunset had a bed on the dementia floor. This time Drew came to help me as Jim had a meeting he couldn't get out of.

Drew's job was to distract Barb while my job was to take Joe to Sunset. We showed up around nine-thirty and made plans with Karen. Barb and Joe were finishing breakfast, so we decided Drew would take Barb to the ten o'clock activities while Karen and I got Joe in the car. I headed for Joe's room to collect his clothes.

All five of us took the elevator to the third floor for activities. We all got off the elevator and headed toward the activity room. Drew and Karen distracted Barb and walked her in, while I stayed back with Joe. Drew got Barb settled for the entertainment while Karen and I led Joe back to the elevator and out the front door. The two of us managed to get Joe in my car, with Karen fighting back tears while handing me his paperwork and saying goodbye. I never stopped to think how much the staff must get attached to the residents.

***

I headed up a block and took a left at the stop sign. In front of me stood the fifteen-story rectangular building known as Sunset. I pulled up to the front door to get Joe out. Staff from the fourteenth floor were supposed to be there waiting with a wheelchair. Joe was mobile, but it was almost impossible to get him to follow any directions, so we decided it would be the easiest way to get him to the floor.

I didn't see anyone, so I went through the double doors to the reception desk and explained the situation. Of course, they knew nothing but told me I could take a wheelchair from the lobby. I grabbed one and went to retrieve Joe. I opened the passenger side door. He was sitting with his arms crossed and eyes closed, sunning himself on a perfect fall day.

"Joe. You need to get out of the car."

Nothing.

"Joe." This time I patted him on the arm to get his attention.

Still nothing.

"Joe." I tried gently shaking him, thinking he may have fallen asleep.

He looked at me and smiled.

"Hi, Joe." I smiled back at him. "You need to get out of the car."

He went back to his original position in the sunshine, so I gently shook him again and again. All I got was a smile out of him.

"Joe, come on now. You need to get out of the car. Let's go," I said softly.

He continued staring at me with a smile. I reached in and tried to physically swing his legs out—that worked, sort of.

"Joe, you need to stand up."

Nothing. I tried asking him more times than I could keep track of, with no luck. I tried gently pulling on his arms, hoping the motion would trigger something in his brain that would cause him to stand up. It finally worked. Now my concern was that he would sit back down in the vehicle. Thankfully that didn't happen, and I got him into the wheelchair after a mere fifteen minutes of coaxing him.

We took the elevator to the fourteenth floor. The doors opened to a desk where a nurse looked up at me.

"Hi. This is Joe Preston. You should be expecting him."

The nurse stood in her blue scrubs dotted with butterflies and flipped through the paperwork until she found his.

"Got it," she said as she made her way around the desk to greet Joe. "You can park him right here. We have a meeting scheduled with Dustin, who will be his case manager. Can you make one o'clock this afternoon?"

"No, but their son Drew will be here along with Joe's wife, Barb, who is also a resident at Sunrise."

"Oh, wow. I'm sorry to hear that. It must be tough having both of them with dementia."

"Understatement of the year," I replied with a smile.

"Let me give you a quick rundown of how things go here," she said, brushing her blonde hair out of her eyes. "We call for everything. If Joe rolls out of bed, we call. If he falls, we call. Even if he isn't hurt, we are required to let you know. We do bed checks every half-hour during the night. We prick his finger. It's just enough to make him move, but not enough to wake him up. That's it!" she said with a smile.

"Got it, thanks."

I left Joe and made my way back to Sunrise. I found Drew and told him they had a one o'clock next door. He decided he'd take Barb to lunch and then over for a visit. Meanwhile, I made my way to work.

***

The transition to Sunset was a nightmare, and we got more than one phone call that Joe had rolled out of bed. The beds were lowered to the ground at night, and another mattress was set on the floor. He never got hurt, but our phone rang at all hours to let us know.

To add to that, Barb called the house constantly, wanting to go see Joe. I took her late on a Tuesday morning, and we stayed through lunch with him. Although he smiled at us, I have no idea if he knew us or not.

I sat at a cafeteria-style table while an aide named Zaire fed Joe. I watched as he ate mashed potatoes and other soft foods. He was no longer given anything that was difficult to chew or swallow, and he was getting very thin. His hand rested on the table with his bones and veins protruding through his skin, now speckled with dark spots. He ate with his eyes closed and Barb gently stroking his hair.

I looked around the room. Every resident was in a wheelchair. Some could feed themselves, and others couldn't. Some were on a diet of baby food—completely pureed, no chewing required, and like Joe, being spoon-fed.

I couldn't help but wonder—who were these people really? Were they married? Did they have children? Grandchildren? Were they kind? What were their hobbies? Fishing? Cooking? Sewing? Were they funny? What did they do for a living? Were they smart? Educated? Good looking? Did anyone miss them? Did they get visitors?

"All set! Good job, Joe!" Zaire said, which broke my thoughts.

"Thanks," I said with a sad smile.

"Joe seems like a nice guy. What did he do for a living?"

I had no idea how Zaire figured out he was a nice guy in his current condition, but in some ways, he maintained his "Joe" demeanor, still smiling.

"Insurance," I replied, "he was a regional manager. Has three boys and seven grandkids…loved to golf and one of the nicest men I've ever know…"

Zaire gave me a small smile back.

"Alright, Barb, time to go," I said, pushing out my chair.

She kept staring at Joe, still stroking his hair. "I have to leave," she said to him. "I'm sorry I can't stay…" I handed her a tissue to wipe her eyes. "I love you, Joe." She kissed him on the cheek, and he smiled back at her.

"Bye, Joe," I said quietly as I kissed him on top of his head.

We left the cafeteria and walked across the hall to the elevator. I hit the down button and was happy to see the elevator was only one floor away. The doors separated, and Barb and I got on and turned around.

Just then, I heard Zaire yell, "Louis! LOUIS!" I saw a man just across from me next to the cafeteria door. He was in pajamas and slumped over in his chair. Drool stretching from his mouth to his lap. "NURSE! NURSE!" he yelled frantically, "LOUIS!" he was shaking his shoulder, "NURSE, LOUIS IS CHOKING!" A nurse came running as the elevator doors closed.

***

From there, I took Barb out to eat, knowing she had missed her lunch, and then took her back to Sunrise. I decided to head home and get some things done around my own house.

Jim had gone to Rochester to meet with Drew and a potential client. I knew he'd be home late. At five-thirty, the phone rang. It was Barb.

"Hi, Abby. Can I talk to Jimmy?"

"He's not home yet."

"When is he coming home?" she demanded.

"Late. Probably close to nine."

"Oh, that's just great!" she said in an angry tone. "I want to go see Joe! No one has taken me over in three days!"

"You and I were there earlier today," I gently said, hoping to jar her memory a little.

"What? The HELL I WAS! No one cares about me or Dad! Tell Jimmy to call me."

"Okay, I'll have him call you, but it will be late."

"Fine!" she said as she hung up.

I began counting out loud, "One Mississippi, two Mississippi, three Mississippi, four Mississippi," and with five Mississippi, I pointed to the phone and waited half a second before it rang back.

"Hello."

"Hi, Abby. Can I talk to Jimmy?"

"He's still working."

"When is he coming home?"

"Probably not till nine."

"Oh, that's just great! I want to go see Joe! No one has taken me over in three days!"

"I'll let him know, Barb, bye." And before she could get a rebuttal in, I hung up.

It always amazed me how she got to the end of a sentence and repeated herself with the exact same words, exact same tone, and exact same body language.

The phone rang back. I let the answering machine get it.

"JIMMY! IT'S MOM! I WANT TO GO SEE DAD! NO ONE HAS TAKEN ME OVER IN THREE DAYS! Call me back!"

This time I took the phone off the hook and left it off the hook until Jim got home at eight-thirty.

"Still afraid to hang it up?" Jim chided me.

I had talked to him earlier on my cell phone, giving him an update on today's nonsense.

"Actually, I forgot I left it off the hook," I said as I hung it up.

It rang within seconds.

"Don't even bother," I said.

"Wasn't planning on it. It's been a long day."

When the machine picked up, I grabbed the phone, being careful not to hit the wrong button and accidentally pick it up. I looked at Jim and lip-synched with Barb making sure I had all my facial expressions correct, "JIMMY! IT'S MOM! I WANT TO GO SEE DAD! NO ONE HAS TAKEN ME OVER IN THREE DAYS! Call me back!"

Jim shook his head and chuckled. "She's tiring."

"Some days…Did you eat?"

"No. I just wanted to get home."

184

"I took your mom to Little Italy's Pasta House for lunch today. I might have gotten you chicken riggies and Utica greens."

Jim had just kicked off his shoes, pulled the knot of his tie down, and unbuttoned the first two buttons of his shirt. He was now on the couch, putting his feet up on the table.

"Yes! My favorite!"

"You didn't hear me. I said *might*, as in maybe," I taunted him, leaning over the counter and looking into the family room at him.

"Why are you so mean to me?"

"I am a *mean* woman James Preston," I said as I held out the Styrofoam container in my right hand, shaking it at him.

"I don't suppose you'd heat them for me, would you?"

"Hmmm…What's in it for me?"

"I'll give you a quarter."

"Jim, we've been together for like thirty-some-odd years, and you always offer a quarter. Inflation Jim, inflation. Time to up the ante."

He put his chin to his chest and looked down at his shirt. "Okay, a quarter *and* I'll show you my chest hair," he said, giving me a look out of the side of his eye as he rubbed the little tuft of chest hair sticking out. "Huh, huh, how 'bout that?"

I had just put his dinner in the microwave. I leaned over the counter to look.

"Nah," I shook my head and scrunched my face, "that chest hair is turning gray." Mimicking Barb, I continued, "Makes you look like a cavone Jimmy."

185

"You are a mean woman, Abby. Just plain mean. Think I'm gonna tell your mom on you."

***

For the next six weeks, Jim and I traded off taking Barb over to see Joe. It was exhausting, and she just didn't stop. We'd take her; she'd forget and then start calling the house relentlessly. Between that, work, and trying to run our own house, we'd just about had it.

Jim took her over on a Sunday and returned home sadder than usual.

"What's the matter?" I asked as he was making a cup of coffee.

"Every time you think it can't suck more, you find out you're wrong. It does get worse."

"What happened?"

"They had a woman for entertainment. She was playing an acoustic guitar and asking residents what they wanted to hear. Dad is sitting in his wheelchair, wearing his diaper. You know, the usual. Eyes closed and completely oblivious to us or anything else going on. The woman asks us if he has a favorite song. So I say, 'Yeah, do you know "Let There Be Peace on Earth?"' She says, 'yeah' and starts playing it." Jim had put cream in his coffee and was now sipping it. "Abby, I looked at Dad, and he had tears rolling out of the corner of his eyes and down his cheeks…when we got there, an aide was trying to get him to swallow the water he was chewing." Jim stopped for a minute and then turned to me and said, "When does this end?"

One thing we've both learned. There are fates worse than death.

Chapter 19

Just before we went to bed that night, Jay called. He asked me if I'd do snow shoveling at an office park in the morning. It was mid-November, but the weather was cold, and three inches of snow was expected by morning. Jay hadn't finished hiring the snow shovelers yet, so I agreed to be there by six.

Jim had to be in the office very early and left at five-thirty. I laced my boot and was in the middle of searching for matching gloves when the phone rang. It was Sunset.

"Hello."

"Hi. Can I speak to Abby?"

"Speaking," I said, putting the phone against my shoulder so I could continue rummaging for gloves.

"This is Renee at Sunset. I'm just calling to let you know Joe is unresponsive."

I stopped rummaging for a second, "Um, okay. What does that mean?"

"Well. He's unresponsive."

"What does that mean?"

"I checked on him just after five, and when I came through around five thirty-five, he didn't respond to the finger prick."

"So, are you telling me he died?" I said, trying not to sound stupid, but if he had a stroke, wouldn't that be unresponsive as well?

"Yes, he died…" Renee continued rattling on about death in the most pleasant manner she could, but I wasn't paying much attention. Honestly, I just couldn't understand how someone who deals with death on a daily basis couldn't explicitly tell me that Joe died.

Renee continued, "I have his file here. It says he is going to be cremated. Would you like us to hold off on calling the funeral home so the family can come to see him before the undertaker comes?"

"Good question. Can I call you back? Two of his sons are out of town, and Barb is at Sunrise. If they want to come, it will be a while…" I gave up on my gloves and was now sitting on the stairs.

"Sure. The waiting is no problem. Just give me a call back."

"Ok. Give me fifteen."

I hung up and dialed Jim, who was just pulling into his office. "Hi, Hon…hey, I just got a call from Sunset."

"Did he roll out of bed again?"

"No." I paused for a few seconds, "He passed away. She said his heart just stopped beating."

Jim let out a big sigh. It sucked, but I think it was a sigh of relief. No more suffering.

"Ok. I'll call Drew and Sean."

"There's more. Since he's going to be cremated, she said you can all come to visit before the funeral home comes for him. I need to let her know if you guys want to do that, and do you want to bring your mom? I told her I'd call back in fifteen or so."

"Let me see what my brothers say. I'll call you right back."

I called Jay to let him know I was running late but would be at the office park. He insisted I stay home, but there was no reason. We weren't going to see Joe for at least three hours, so I might as well stand in the cold, wet snow in the meantime.

Jim called me back. They all decided they were coming and it would be best to bring their mom over. They were concerned she would have a harder time processing his death if she didn't get to see him.

***

I called Karen and told her about Joe and asked if there was any chance they could get Barb her breakfast a little earlier. They did, and I met Jim in the parking lot of Sunrise at nine. He got out of his truck.

"How are you doing?" I asked him.

"Sad," he said, wiping his eyes, "but glad it's over. How do you think she'll take it?"

"I don't know. It's so hard to tell."

We got off the elevator and headed down the hall where most of the residents were seated for breakfast. Sheriff was headed to his table.

"Mornin', Sheriff," Jim said.

"Have you seen my badge? I can't find my badge."

"Sorry Sheriff, but I—" Jim started to reply.

"As a matter of fact, I did pick one up by the elevator," I said, sticking my hand in the pocket of my winter coat. I pulled out a gold, six-pointed metal toy badge with the word "Sheriff" written in the center. "Is this it?"

Sheriff's brown eyes got as big as a kid with a new bike at Christmas. "Oh! Oh! That's it!" He was almost in tears.

"Here, let me pin it on you." I pinned it through his flannel pocket, "There you go! All set!"

"Thank you! Thank you so much!" he said, turning toward the breakfast table. "Look! Look! I got my badge! I got my badge!" he announced to Destiny, the aide on duty that morning.

"Wow! Look at that! Now you can join the rest of us," Destiny replied while she looked at us with a smile, shaking her head back and forth.

I shrugged my shoulders, grinned, and with outstretched arms said, "Hey, it's the little things."

Destiny looked in both directions before saying, "We heard the news. I'm really sorry. He was such a sweetheart."

"Thanks," Jim answered, "it's a 'sorry-not-sorry' situation."

"I know you guys are glad it's over," Destiny replied.

"Trust me. We are."

He then turned to me, "Is that what came from Amazon? Toy sheriff badges?"

"Yup. Twenty-four pack."

"Wow. I guess you're only mean to me."

"Yup!" I said, putting my arm around him and my head against his chest. "And I'm all yours."

***

Jim knocked on the door to announce us as we walked in.

"Oh, hi Jimmy. Can I go see Dad?"

"Yeah, Mom. We're going to go see Dad," he hesitated a minute. "Mom, the place he lives at called us a little while ago. Dad died this morning." We held our collective breath.

Barb was sitting on the couch and looked a little confused at first, "He died?"

"Yeah, Mom."

She looked at the picture of the two of them that sat on the window sill. "He's gone? What happened, Jimmy?"

"He died in his sleep. His heart just stopped."

She hung her head and began to cry, "That poor soul."

Jim put his arm around her and asked if she wanted to go see him, which she did.

***

We dropped Barb at the lobby door where Drew and Sean were waiting. After parking the truck, we made our way to the fourteenth floor and down the hall to Joe's room. Drew stuck his head in first to make sure there was nothing disturbing to see. There wasn't, so the rest of us went in.

Joe was lying on his back with his eyes closed and covers up to his chin. Finally peaceful. I saw Zaire pass by, so I stuck my head out and asked if we could get a couple more chairs.

"Of course. Sorry about Joe."

"Thanks, but it's okay."

"I know what you mean."

We stayed about an hour.

"Jimmy," Barb said, "pray for him. He doesn't look good."

The rest of us began looking back and forth at each other, unsure what to say.

Jim finally answered, "He died, Mom."

"He did?" she said, and then the tears started. "That poor soul."

That conversation would be had three more times before we left.

***

The boys decided the calling hours and funeral Mass would be all together at St. Margaret's. The church was in the city, and Joe and Barb had both gone there their entire lives. They were baptized there, married there, and the three boys were baptized there as well. Father John, who was now in his early seventies, officiated. He'd known the two of them for decades.

Not surprisingly, the place was packed, and Father John did a great job. He made the funeral a true celebration of Joe's life. He had Barb stand up, as well as the kids and the grandkids. He asked the grandkids to share their favorite memory of Joe.

Stories of blanket forts and pizza, Ukrainian eggs and pizza, trips to the playground and pizza, vacations, and attendance at their milestones all echoed off the stained glass windows of the church.

We all greeted visitors offering condolences for well over an hour as they made their way out of the church. Karen and Mike from Sunrise managed to sneak out of work long enough to attend

Mass and circumvented the line, giving us a wave and motioning that they had to get back.

We followed the limo to the cemetery where Joe was placed in an old family plot. I read the names of people I'd never heard of. The boys knew some of them, and others were far beyond their years. We headed to lunch afterward, where we socialized with many of Joe and Barb's friends and family. It was nice to see everyone. Weddings and funerals, that's how it goes.

***

It was a long day, and we all escorted Barb back to her apartment. The boys decided to donate the funeral flowers to the fourteenth floor of Sunset, with the exception of one. Barb loved the simple arrangement of white roses, blue belladonna delphinium, with a single blue hydrangea, all set in a sapphire blue vase with a silver bow. Of course, it was sent by Steve and Vicki.

Sean set it in the middle of the coffee table, and everyone settled down for a few minutes.

"Those flowers are beautiful," Barb said.

"Aren't they?" answered Drew.

"Where did they come from?"

"Dad's funeral."

"When did he die?"

"We buried him today."

"Oh…" she ended in a slightly confused state.

Drew and his clan said their goodbyes and headed for home. Barb sat back down.

"Those flowers are beautiful."

This time Sean answered, "Yes, they are."

"Where did they come from?"

"Dad's funeral."

"When did he die?"

"We buried him today."

"Oh…"

Sean and his family left, with Jim and me just a few minutes behind. We didn't escape quickly enough.

"Those flowers are beautiful."

"Your turn," Jim said to me.

"Aren't they? I love the blue colors."

"Where did they come from?"

"Joe's funeral."

"When did he die?"

"A couple of days ago. Today was the funeral."

"Oh…"

We hugged Barb and headed home.

Chapter 20

L ife after Joe didn't go as badly as we expected. Much to our surprise, Barb adjusted quite well. Somehow her brain seemed to retain Joe's death to a point, but she occasionally asked about his whereabouts. She usually remembered on her own that he had died, but as time went on and her memory got worse, sometimes "the news" came as a surprise.

Jim took Barb out for Saturday drives. Every Saturday became too much, so he went to every other Saturday. He took her to the cemetery to see Joe's grave hoping the repetition would keep his death in her brain. Jim returned home on one particular Saturday, shaking his head on his way through the door.

"That good, huh?" I asked.

"Yeah...I took her to 'see Dad.' I grabbed a cheap bouquet of flowers for Mom to put on his grave. We get in the car to leave, and she says to me, 'Now, Jimmy, when I die, I want to be buried on top of your father.' So, I said, 'okay, Mom,' and she says, 'Wanna know why? So I can keep him right under my thumb!' at which point she takes her thumb and puts it on the top of the dashboard and makes a grinding motion."

"Oh my God!" I said through laughter, "You've got to be kidding me."

"Oh no, I'm not. Then she starts laughing and says, 'You got that, Jimmy?' Oh yeah, Mom, I got it!"

***

A week after the annual picnic/garden party was held, Jim and I showed up on a Saturday to take Barb out to breakfast. We stopped to talk to Moriah, the RN on duty. She was a petite woman who was born in Puerto Rico but had been in the US since elementary school. She loved her job at Sunrise and had been here for over twenty years.

We asked how Barb was doing. Moriah informed us that the aides were having a difficult time with her hygiene—or lack thereof.

She would wear the same clothes day after day, and since she was becoming incontinent, the clothes could be pretty disgusting. To combat this, they removed the hamper from her bathroom and kept her clothes in the laundry room. Each morning they would bring her a clean outfit. She would not allow them to dress her, but she seemed to do okay dressing on her own.

They asked us to make sure she had deodorant, which we did, but they couldn't make her wear it. They also couldn't get her to shower and wash her hair. Although Sunrise provides all those services, it is assisted living, and in assisted living facilities, staff cannot force someone to bathe or do anything against their will. The aides do their best to coax them into what needs to be done, and one aide sometimes does better than another. It can come down to personality and the way they handle the resident.

The three of us assessed the current strategies, trying to come up with one to get Barb in the shower. Jim told Moriah he'd think about a new plan of attack.

"One last thing," Moriah said, "she's back to her cane."

"Ugh," Jim replied, "I'll see what I can do."

Barb came to Sunrise using a cane, but her physical therapist decided she would be better with a walker. Of course, Barb insisted she didn't need a walker, and the battle began. She got to the point where she was alternating between them, so Jim removed the cane from her room altogether. What he didn't realize was there was a second one in the back of her closet.

**

We continued on to the apartment, where Jim knocked on her door. Unsurprisingly, she didn't answer, so we let ourselves in. Jim called for his mom as he walked to her bedroom. I stayed in the living room and was checking the refrigerator to see if she needed any drinks when I heard Jim freak out.

"Hey, Mom…WHAT THE?"

I turned toward the bedroom just as he emerged from the hall with his hand on his forehead.

"Jim, what's wrong?" I asked, fearing the answer.

"I can't even…I just…no, I did not just see that," he said, shaking his head.

Not getting an answer from him, I walked down the short hall and cautiously stuck my head through the door to look. I burst out laughing. Jim was right on my heels.

"Mom, geez. Really?"

"Barb, Barb, Barb," I said, shaking my head, "what will Father John say?"

"It's not funny, Abby," Jim said, upset by the situation.

"Oh, you are *so* right…it's not funny…it's HYSTER-ICAL, Jim!"

Barb was lying in bed looking at the two of us when she said, "Shush! You'll wake him."

Sharing Barb's queen-sized bed with her was Sheriff. He was still spooning her when we walked in. The commotion began to wake him.

"Mornin', Sheriff. Did you have a good night?" I asked.

"Shut up, Abby!" Jim said to me.

There was no way this little rendezvous was slipping by me.

"I think so," Sheriff answered, completely confused at the question.

"So, Barb…are you and Sheriff an item? New boyfriend, maybe?"

Jim was leaning against the wall glaring at me when Barb said, "Well, you know, Jimmy always wanted a little brother!" and then she started laughing.

I burst out laughing, and Jim finally relented and laughed himself.

"Calm down, Jim. Nothing is going on; they're just sharing the bed and snuggling up."

"I know, I know. It's just so…so…"

"Weird?" I said.

"I was thinking disgusting. I just can't unsee that!" he said with a laugh.

"You get your mom up and moving. I'll escort Sheriff to his room and see Moriah about clothes for Barb and let her know Sheriff was here."

"Deal."

Jim turned to his mom and told her it was time to get up and get moving. She sat up slowly, nursing her aches and pains.

"C'mon, Sheriff. Grab your six-shooter and let's head back to town," I said.

"Really, Abby? His six-shooter? Can you just stop for a second?"

"By six-shooter, I was referring to his cane Jim…what were you referring to?"

"Just get out of here with him, will you please?" he said, laughing.

***

I got Sheriff out of Barb's apartment and shuffled him in his brown plaid pajamas toward Moriah.

"We were wondering where he went. We just came out of his room," Moriah said with her hands on her hips and a smile on her face.

Residents have a room check every two hours, twenty-four hours a day. Sheriff couldn't have been in Barb's room all that long and had somehow managed to sneak by Moriah, who was probably in someone else's room at the time.

"Can I get Barb's clothes du jour? We're headed to breakfast. Is it okay to take Sheriff?"

Moriah called to an aide and asked her to get Sheriff ready to go out to breakfast and grab an outfit for Barb.

"So, what's up with Sheriff spooning my mother-in-law?" I asked Moriah.

"It's a first for them."

"For them? Is it common?"

"VERY common. More common than people realize to the point where Sunrise is now in the process of writing up what's called a 'Sexual Expression Policy.'"

"Are you kidding me?"

"Nope. Just because dementia kicks in doesn't mean the sex drive kicks out."

By now, I was wearing my emotions on my face in a contorted sort of way.

Moriah laughed. "Most of the residents have children who make the decisions concerning their parents' care. Most children can't comprehend their parents' sex lives. Especially at an advanced age and with this type of disease."

Now I had my hands on both cheeks and was pulling my face toward my ears. I was pretty sure I was mimicking Edvard Munch's famous painting, "The Scream." I wasn't really sure I wanted to hear anymore as I am a visual thinker, but curiosity got the best of me.

"How do you guys handle that? Are they able to consent? What if they have a spouse? Do you let the kids know?"

"That's why the powers that be are working on a policy. There has been a lot of discussion by those who make up policy over the issue of consent. When we find residents in each other's beds, we return them to their room and notify the family caregiver. Some say that it should be private and up to the resident to make the decision without family notification."

"Sorry, but that doesn't make sense to me being the family. If Barb was able to make her own decisions, she wouldn't be here."

"Exactly. Dementia throws the monkey wrench in. If it was assisted living due to non-dementia-related issues, it's pretty easy. Consenting adults can do what they want, but whether a dementia patient can consent is another story. And you're right; someone is making all their financial and medical decisions, so they do have a right to know what's going on."

"I gotta know two things. First, Barb and Sheriff were just snuggling up. Have you had residents who actually have sex? And if so, how do the kids react? What about a case where one spouse has dementia, and the other is fine?"

"Yes. We have caught residents having sex."

I cringed a little more when Moriah said that.

"And most kids freak. We are still looking at an older generation that has taught their children that pre-marital sex is wrong. So, yeah, the kids do flip sometimes, but we have to remind them that they are also dealing with a degenerating brain. Morals that they once taught are no longer remembered. As far as a spouse with and a spouse without dementia goes, I'm sure it goes on. They visit in the private apartment, and who's to say otherwise? They have usually been married for decades. Did you see the news about a man named Henry Rayhons? His wife was in a dementia unit in Iowa. He was charged with third-degree felony sexual abuse and went on trial at seventy-eight years old for having sex with his wife. The doctor said she didn't have the capacity for consent, and a stepdaughter had him charged. He was found not guilty, but the result has been a push for policymakers. The next problem is dementia has its good days and its bad. She may have been able to consent, and it was her own husband, but her kids didn't like it."

"Sounds a little complicated," I said.

"And then some. We've also dealt with residents who decide to take up with members of the same sex. That's when the kids *really* freak. Did they hide their homosexuality all those years, or is it just due to the disease? No one knows for sure. And then there's something we call the Sandra Day O'Connor Syndrome. When the former Supreme Court Justice Sandra Day O'Connor put her husband in a memory facility, he found a girlfriend. He just didn't remember he was married. The need for relationships never leaves, even when the mind does."

"Huh. Thanks for the info."

"Sure! Aren't you glad you asked?"

***

I returned to Barb's apartment, and then we all headed to breakfast on the overcast spring day. We drove through areas Barb was once familiar with but now struggled to understand.

"The Berlin Theater," Barb said as though her voice was trying to get her brain to understand the place.

She failed to notice the triple X's that followed the word *theater*—as in an adult theater.

Barb continued, "You know what, Jimmy? Dad and I used to come here all the time."

It's a good thing I was in the backseat with Sheriff. Jim redirected the rearview mirror to see me sitting behind Barb. He gave me a wide-eyed, deer in the headlight look. Of course, I was laughing and wondering what Jim was going to say to that!

"Well, Mom…you'll always have Berlin!"

"I suppose you're right, Jimmy…I'll always have those memories."

Jim was stifling his laughter while I pulled my sweater up over my mouth, trying to be quiet.

Just then, we passed by a sign that Sheriff began reading. "Ka-ra-te…" We listened as he sounded out the word like a six-year-old who is just learning to read. While dementia patients can read, often they cannot comprehend, but that was not the case this time. "Ka-ra-te," he said faster and finally, "karate!" which was followed by a yell of "HI-YA!" complete with karate chops.

"Oh, good Lord!" Jim said as we all laughed.

***

We got to the diner and requested a table, figuring the chairs would be easier for Barb and Sheriff than a booth. Jim and I sat across from each other. Barb was to my right and Sheriff to my left. Barb and Sheriff looked at the menu, but both were completely unable to order for themselves. As soon as they finished reading an item, it was forgotten. We asked both of them if there was anything they would like, and we got a reply in unison of "whatever they bring."

They were used to sitting down and having whatever Sunrise had on the menu that day, so we decided to get them both a mixed plate: scrambled eggs, a pancake, toast, bacon, and coffee.

It was busy in the diner, and Barb and Sheriff seemed to be content with people-watching. Barb was sipping her coffee and bobbing her head to music from the ceiling speaker. A teenage busboy went by, and Barb remarked that he was cute. Barb decided she wanted more coffee, although her cup was nowhere near empty. On the young man's return trip she reached out in his direction while whistling at him. She managed to get his apron and refer to him as "Honey."

"Sorry," Jim said to the kid, while grabbing his mom's arm, "Mom, you can't do that."

"Can't do what? He's a cutie, and I need coffee," she replied through laughter.

"No, you don't grab at people. Or whistle at them. And don't call him honey."

"Relax, Jimmy," she said as she tried to whistle at the kid again.

"Funny how things change," I said to Jim. "She's grabbing at a kid. Remember how mad she got when Rose Marie called Joe 'big boy' and grabbed at him?"

"Oh, yeah, I do!"

***

When Joe was still alive, I took Barb to a dentist appointment. She had wanted Joe to come with us, but Joe wandered and was incontinent and it would have been way too much for me to handle. On our way home, Barb started getting snotty with me about not driving fast enough. I was doing the speed limit and asked her what the hurry was.

"That nutsy witch! That's the hurry!" she answered, quite aggravated.

"Huh? What are you talking about?"

"You know, the one always calling Joe 'big boy.' She just wants to get down his pants!"

I had to lean against the car window with my hand over my mouth, trying to act casual so she wouldn't see me laughing.

We made it back to Sunrise and got in the elevator. Barb was extremely antsy and began banging her cane on the floor and telling the elevator to hurry up. We got off the elevator with her asking, "Where is he?" in a loud voice.

"Barb! It's okay. It's lunch. I'm sure he's at the table waiting for you."

Which he was.

"If I find that nasty nutsy woman near him, she's getting a sock! And it's not the one on my foot!"

We were close enough to the dining area that the aides heard her and started to laugh.

"She's all yours!" I said to them, "I'll drop her paperwork off to Karen and see you all another day!"

They wished me well and sat Barb down.

La Belle Communauté

Things calmed down in the diner for about two seconds. Sheriff and Barb stared at each other for a moment when Sheriff started up.

A smile crossed his face as he leaned in toward Barb and said, "Quick draw!"

Barb got a huge grin while Jim and I gave each other a puzzled look.

"Inside joke?" I said to Jim, who shrugged back at me.

We didn't see that both had reached for their canes and began lifting them straight overhead. We did notice as they began to bring them down across the table at each other. They were about to have a "sword fight." Jim and I both jumped up to grab the canes and stop them.

"Holy sh—NO! MOM!" Jim yelled as he grabbed her cane.

"Sheriff, NO!" I yelled simultaneously, grabbing his cane as well.

The tables around us erupted in laughter, as did Barb and Sheriff. I took their canes and hung them near the door, and sat back down, shaking my head in disbelief.

Jim looked to his left at Barb and to his right at Sheriff, and then back at me and started singing "Stuck in the Middle With You" by Stealers Wheel.

***

We returned to Sunrise and got off the elevator just in time to hear Frank Sinatra finishing "My Way."

Barb joined in for the finale before telling us, "You know I once danced with Ol' Blue Eyes…but don't tell my mother. She wouldn't approve."

"Your secret's safe with me, Mom," Jim was trying not to chuckle.

Sinatra gave way to Gene Kelly, and Barb was "Singin' in the Rain."

We slowly walked along with her when I asked Jim, "What kind of music do you think they'll be playing when our generation hits this age?"

Without hesitation, he replied through laughter, "Madonna. 'Like a Virgin.'"

"You know," Barb said, "this is where they had the orchestra when Joe and I visited."

"Wow," I said, "they let them set up on this Brazilian mahogany floor?"

"Oh yes," she gushed, "Joe and I danced the night away."

Neither Jim nor I have yet to figure out where she got the idea of an orchestra, but it's been stuck in her head since she got here.

"Abby," Jim assured me, "pretty sure the brown vinyl plank flooring can handle the orchestra." He gave me an eye roll.

"That's good to know. Not sure it'll hold up for River Dance, though."

We met Moriah as we neared Barb's wing. She informed us that cane fighting at the O.K. Corral has become a favorite pastime for them both.

Jim and Barb were ahead of me while walking down the hall to her apartment. I watched as she used a cane with her left hand

and the wall rails with her right. It was becoming harder for her to walk, and we needed to remove that cane as well.

We also desperately needed to get that woman in the shower. Her hair, once styled, was now greasy, and honestly, she just smelled. Her clothes, once professional and classy, were now wrinkled elastic waistband jeans and baggy sweatshirts.

We got her into her apartment, and somehow Jim finagled her into taking a shower. He asked me to get one of the aides to help wash her and shampoo her hair. I went down the hall into the common area but found no one. I checked the activity board and realized they were likely escorting the last of the residents to the activity room one floor up. I looked up and down the halls and couldn't find anyone, so I took the stairs up. Sure enough, they were just settling the residents into their seats. I found Moriah and explained the situation. She said to give her five minutes, and either she or an aide would be down.

I hit the code for the stairs and ran back down them two at a time, jogging back to Barb's room.

"Hey Jim, sorry it took me so long," I said as I rushed through the door. "Moriah…" I stopped, seeing Jim sitting slumped down on the couch, hands laced across his chest with eyes in a fixed gaze at the ceiling.

I slowly continued, "Moriah is upstairs…what is going on?"

"What's going on? What's going on? Do you want to know what's going on?" Jim said. He was incensed as he turned his eyes from the ceiling to me.

I gave him a full-body shrug and said, "Did she change her mind on the shower?"

"Oh no. No. Nope, THAT didn't happen." Now Jim's right leg was nervously swinging back and forth.

"Then what's the prob—*Ohh*," I said as the revelation hit me.

"Yeah, *ohh* is right."

"So, then," I began, but Jim put his hand up to stop me.

"Don't speak a word to me...not a single word, Abby."

I stood there pursing my lips and biting my tongue, but it just wasn't gonna work. I sat next to Jim on the couch where I tried hard to be quiet, but then a song went through my head about rubber ducks and taking baths, and my brain couldn't stop me from leaning into Jim and singing into a pretend microphone. "So, was shower time a lot of fun?"

"Not FUNNY, ABBY! I told you I didn't want to hear anything from you!"

"No. You said you didn't want me to speak a word. You didn't say I couldn't sing. Not my fault I watched too much TV when I was little. So, did you close your eyes *real* tight?"

"So tight I think I dislodged my retina."

"Where is she?"

"Getting dressed."

Moriah knocked and entered. She took one look at Jim and apologized, and went to help Barb finish up.

"Can we go now?" Jim asked.

"Yup. Gonna say goodbye?"

Just then, Moriah came back through and left. Barb was right behind her.

"Okay, Mom. We have to get going now."

"Okay, give me a hug."

As we turned to leave, she asked us to straighten up Mr. Frog, a stuffed animal she won at bingo. She must have been crushing it at bingo because there were several stuffed animals scattered throughout the place. Her favorite was a green-and-yellow stuffed frog who used the backrest of her sofa as a lily pad. It had slumped over, probably when Jim flopped down.

"Jimmy. Do me a favor and fix the frog, will ya?" Barb asked.

Jim reached over and straightened it out.

"Not like that, Jimmy! Geez, now everyone can see his—"

"MOM!" Jim interrupted her, knowing what she was about to say. "It is NOT an anatomically correct stuffed animal!"

"Oh, good Lord," I said, shaking my head and laughing as I stepped into the hallway.

Barb was still laughing when Jim shut the door.

Chapter 21

We got in the car and headed home, discussing Barb's overall physical and mental health and wondering how much longer Sunrise was going to be able to keep her. We guessed her biggest issue was going to be what's called "the inability to transfer," which is when a resident can no longer get up from a chair or bed by themselves. Although she still can, it's becoming increasingly difficult.

Mentally, her slow decline has continued. She is in her seventh year at Sunrise and now asks Jim if he's checked on her mother. Her mother has been gone for close to fifty years, dying when Jim was a toddler. She can no longer recall my name, although I am familiar to her. Jim told me that while I had been talking with Moriah that morning, Barb asked who he was. She knew his name was Jim, but she didn't understand that he was her son. She then asked what her last name was. Jim told her it was Preston. He said she flipped out and couldn't believe she was a Preston and had married Joe.

"The dementia brain is like a flickering candle. It brightens for a second and then dims down," I said with a sigh. "So sad."

"Sad is an understatement. Sometimes I think it's the family that suffers more than the patient. I just pray Mom dies before we have to move her to Sunset. Once was enough," Jim remarked.

"True."

"What's on your agenda for the rest of the day?" Jim asked as he turned down our road.

"Dementia Part 2: Mom Goes to the Grocery Store."

***

I called Mom to make sure she was home and ready to head to the store. I pulled into her driveway and entered the kitchen. She had her coat and purse ready to go, which was a good sign. She doesn't always remember, even after a phone call. It's been a year since she had the car accident, and "Running With Mom" became my new pastime. Grocery stores, drug stores, and a never-ending stream of doctor appointments were beginning to wear on me.

The first eight months after the accident weren't terrible. Although the dementia was bad enough to end her driving, she still functioned fairly well. She kept a grocery list and paid her bills on time but struggled with the checkbook. But then winter came. I suspected the short days and lack of outings with her siblings due to bad weather exacerbated her mental condition. Or maybe it was just the speed the disease was moving? Hard to say, but in a little over a year, she was deteriorating quickly, and I was unsure which way to go.

Mom emerged from the bathroom, rubbing lotion on her hands.

"Hi, Honey! I'm ready to go!"

"Hi, Mom," I said while rustling through her cupboards. I learned the hard way how to grocery shop.

At first, I took her to the normal store she shopped at and we ended up wandering around in there for over an hour for forty-dollars worth of stuff. She would go through produce and be unable to decide what she wanted. Then she needed tea. Every. Single. Time. From there, she stared at the meat counter before making her way around the perimeter of the store through dairy and frozen foods. Then we meandered through random aisles, often returning to the same one more than once. She would say, "Okay, I'm ready. Let's go," at least ten times, only to wander off to another aisle. Finally, I got so tired of it I forced her to get in line. On the ride home, I noticed she wasn't talking to me, which was odd. She got snippy and told me that she wasn't going to the store with me anymore because I pushed her too quickly.

Next, I learned to avoid the Walmart Supercenter. Not only do they have a grocery section, but they also have an "everything section!" Mom always did like to shop. I always hated it. Somehow I managed to lose her in Walmart every time. It was way too big for me to circle the store and look up and down all the aisles. She got mad at me there as well.

I learned to look through her cupboards and refrigerator to see what she really needed and then take her to a small store with a limited selection. It worked great, and she seemed to like it as well. I took her on off-hours when it wasn't as busy and let her go up and down all the aisles. It definitely kept my sanity and stopped her from getting mad at me each time we did grocery shopping.

***

We headed to the "little store," as she calls it. It was a bit busier than I like it, but it was the only time I had. She made it around the store, but I was beginning to notice the next set of changes creeping in. She just couldn't make a decision.

"Mom, do you need bagels?" I asked, already knowing the answer.

"Yes…I think so…"

"What flavor? Cinnamon raisin or blueberry?"

She stood there frozen. Her brain just couldn't compute. She took both packages in her hand and looked back and forth at them, not sure what to do.

"How about cinnamon raisin? I'm pretty sure you got blueberry last time."

"Oh yeah, that's right," she answered, sounding like she knew that was the truth, but really having no idea what kind of bagel she had last week.

Barb and Joe would do the same thing. They answered with confidence but truly had no idea. Often they would fall back on one particular line. Joe's answer to everything was, "Okay." Barb's was, "Of course I know! I'm not stupid!" and Mom's is, "Oh yeah, that's right."

"Mom, do you want some chips?"

"Yeah…" she said as she stood completely overwhelmed by the wall of snacks. "Do they have plain potato chips?"

"Right here."

"Put them in the cart."

This went on all the way around the store.

We made it to the checkout. I learned to make sure she was near the cashier and had her wallet out and ready to pay as her groceries were rung up. If I didn't, the cashier would give the total, and then the slow process of opening her purse, finding her wallet, and counting out the bills began. I realized she could still count the bills, but she could no longer count the change. She would dump the coins from her wallet into her hand and then stick her hand out for the cashier to take the change.

I took her home and helped her with the groceries. Then I snooped through her desk while she was in the bathroom. I found a past-due insurance bill and a past-due utility bill. I stuck them in my pocket to take home with me.

"Before you leave, will you look at this mail? They want me to cancel my accounts!"

"Sure, Mom. That seems odd. Let me see them."

Of course she couldn't find them. Eventually, even to her own aggravation, she located them on a table. I thumbed through them, trying to explain it was junk mail. The cable company wanted her to add Internet, the bank had a new credit card offer, and an extended warranty was available for the car she no longer owned. She was sure she owed money, or something was being canceled. She was losing her comprehension and reasoning abilities.

I knew it was time to start looking at places to move her.

Chapter 22

I began my assisted living search for Mom in June. I looked within the Sunshine Group, which owns Sunrise, Sunset, and several other places in the city. They have many options. Some I took off the list due to location, which made the list very short. I toured two places. One was quite nice, but Mom was expected to share a bathroom. I was not about to do that to her, as I wouldn't want that done to me.

The second was a large place. She would have a private room with her own bathroom. I spoke with intake and explained her physical and mental condition. I was informed that a dementia diagnosis didn't always mean they needed to be in a memory-care facility at first. Most of their residents had some type of memory issue.

My biggest concern was Mom walking off the property. She took walks in her neighborhood almost daily, and on a nice day, I have no doubt she would take a walk in her new neighborhood and get lost. I've also witnessed more than one Sunrise resident who thought they were "fine" and tried to leave. I knew Mom would eventually get to that point, and intake told me that if she stepped off the premises, they would consider it wandering and transfer her to Sunrise. I didn't feel she was ready for Sunrise yet and decided to take my chances.

In the meantime, things were getting worse with Barb. She had fallen twice. While she wasn't seriously injured, it did require two trips to the hospital and intensified her hip problems. The second time she fell was last Saturday, and the aides at Sunrise along with the ambulance crew were unable to get her to move. At first, they thought she had broken her hip, but that wasn't the case. She was X-rayed and sent back to Sunrise.

Monday morning, I received a call that they were having a hard time getting Barb off her bed and out of chairs. They were allowing her to use a wheelchair for the moment, but that could not continue. They were hoping the stiffness of the injury would wear off in a couple of days.

***

It was a beautiful Wednesday morning. I was in my car and headed to the business office with Mom's paperwork when my phone rang. It was Karen.

"Hi. Abby?"

"Hi, Karen. Should I ask?"

"No. You and Jim won't like it," I could hear the disappointment in her voice. "Barb is going to have to move as soon as possible."

We just couldn't catch a break; our mothers were running us ragged. I let out a sigh and said, "Ugh."

"Ugh is right. It's going to get worse. We already put in a call to Sunset...no beds. In fact, I called five skilled nursing facilities, and no one has an opening," she hesitated and then said, "except Dusen's..."

I could almost hear Karen cringing on the other end, waiting for me to flip.

"OH NO! We are NOT taking Barb there! The only reason there's beds there is because it's a rat trap, and *everybody* knows it!"

Dusen's had been in the news on and off for the last two years with unending complaints from family and staff. They have had so many issues with state compliance; it's surprising they were allowed to stay open.

"Sorry, Abby, we don't have much choice. The staff has had to lift her more than once, and she's not getting better. We can't keep doing that."

"You know us well enough by now. You know we'll get Barb out as soon as we can, but how can you move her against our will? How is that allowed?"

"We have to do it because it goes beyond the boundaries of what we are allowed to do, and we can get in trouble...You can be put on the transfer list to Sunset and move her when a bed becomes available."

"Yeah, that's nice. This is our fourth move with Joe and Barb; we'd love to do a fifth."

"Sorry, Abby, there's just nothing I can do about it."

"No, I'm sorry, Karen, I know it's not your fault. When do we move her?"

"This afternoon."

"Are you kidding me? I can't just cancel my afternoon business meeting! No one can just stop their plans for the day! What the hell, Karen?"

"I know, Abby. No one needs to be here. We'll arrange for transport and make sure she has her clothes with her. Jim can stop and sign her paperwork on another day."

***

I called Jim and gave him the low down. He exploded over Dusen's and the short notice. He had an important meeting as well, and while I could have probably changed mine, I simply refused. I was tired of constantly rearranging my schedule to run for Barb and Mom, and before that, Joe and my own father. It had now been nine years, and I had had enough. If Barb had to transfer to Dusen's with no family, then so be it. She was not my mom, and I had done far more for her than any of her flesh and blood. I was having this conversation while sitting in the parking lot of the Sunshine Group's business office, waiting to drop off Mom's paperwork.

Jim said he would call Drew and Sean to let them know. Twenty minutes later, Drew called me and let me know that he was on his way to Sunrise. Karen agreed to wait for him so he could go with Barb. He begged Karen to make one more call to Sunset before the move.

An hour later, as I was just about to go into my meeting, Drew called me back. A bed had opened at Sunset, and since Barb was considered an emergency placement, she got it. We all breathed a sigh of relief.

Drew ended up spending three hours at Sunset waiting to talk to her caseworker. He gave me another call back, and the two of us decided he would stay overnight at our house, and in the morning, the three of us would return to Sunrise to clean out Barb's apartment.

I called Karen and told her we would be there at six a.m. if that was okay with Sunrise. She was surprised at how fast we were willing to do the cleanout. We knew the waitlist all too well and knew that the maintenance staff would have to clean, paint, and replace the carpet for the next resident. Karen said six was fine, but Mike didn't come in until seven, so we'd have to wait if we needed help.

**

We arrived at six and quietly made our way to Barb's apartment. I was in charge of cleaning out any food and drinks as well as throwing out the trash. Barb had picked up a habit of sticking dirty napkins, tissues, and washcloths everywhere. They were in drawers, kicked under the furniture, shoved in the refrigerator, and stuck in empty cups that sat on the heat registers. The trash cans, however, remained empty. Jim and Drew broke down the bed and handled the furniture.

Ten minutes into our cleanup, there was a knock at the door, and Mike entered. We loved Mike, and Mike loved the residents and their families. He dropped onto Barb's couch and rested his arm on the back. He was braver than the rest of us who dared not sit on the couch of an incontinent woman!

"Can't believe Gramma Barb had to leave," Mike said, referring to her by the nickname he gave her. "I'm gonna miss her…

220

and you guys…and all the grandkids. You all have been one of our most involved families and you guys almost never complained about anything in all these years…"

Although Mike was head of maintenance, he had such a great rapport with the residents that he was called in more than once to help calm someone down. His voice had the soothing tone of Barry White, and his warm bear hugs calmed the savage beast— or an irate resident who was homesick and insistent on leaving. I witnessed him hugging "Grandpa Ed" and assuring him every- thing was going to be alright while redirecting him to another activity. He took Ed over and sat with him until he got involved and forgot what upset him in the first place. Mike then quietly got up and returned to his job.

"Here," Drew said to Mike while handing him a gift- wrapped box.

"What is this? You know we aren't allowed to take money or gifts from residents *or* their families."

"Since Mom isn't a resident anymore, you're off the hook," Drew replied with a smile.

"Oh, man. You guys didn't need to do this."

Jim answered, "We wanted to do this. You've dealt with the sometimes-ornery Barbara J. Preston better than we could, and we so appreciate it, Mike."

Jim and Drew ran to the mall the night before and bought Mike a navy baseball hat that matched the color of his Sunrise shirts. Tucked in the hat was a gift certificate for a sporting goods store.

"Wow," Mike said, "my son is playing in the little league major division and needs some new cleats." He got up to hug us all, "Thanks, guys, I'm sorry to see you go. Anything you need help with?"

"Can you get us a couple of the giant garbage bags?" I asked, "I'm going to put all the stuffed animals in a bag for Maggie."

"That woman cleaned up at bingo! Sure. I'll also bring a couple carts up to get the furniture out as well."

The three of us went back to our respective duties. Years back, when we moved Barb and Joe, we didn't go through their dresser drawers well. I've cleaned most of Joe's stuff out and took inventory on occasion, but that was about it.

Now I was parked in the living room making two piles of clothes—ones that were too disgusting to keep and ones that were fine. I found a bunch of shirts and sweaters that weren't hers. Laundry frequently gets mixed up, even though their names are written on the tags in permanent marker.

I bagged the trash and set it in the hall but was unsure what to do with the rest. She still had quite a few sweaters that she never wore. I decided to pack four pairs of elastic-waist jeans and seven sweatshirts. The rest were headed to other residents, along with some new socks I found hiding in the closet. They had belonged to Joe and were a hot commodity.

The boys each had trucks. Drew's became the "dump" truck, and Jim's became the "save" truck. All the living room furniture, along with the mattress and boxspring, made the dump truck. We donated the TV and its stand along with a coffee table and end tables. The only thing we took home was Joe and Barb's bedroom set, along with a couple of lamps. Sean's oldest had just graduated college and was moving into an apartment next month and had decided she wanted her grandparents' bedroom set.

Drew double-checked the high boy. Barb had a liner in the bottom of each drawer. I didn't bother to pull them out, but Drew did.

"Score!" He yelled after finding sixty bucks. "How 'bout this? Probably more valuable than the money," he said proudly, displaying an old S&H Green Stamp. We all laughed.

"I can't imaging Barb collecting those things," I said.

"Yup," Drew answered, "not for long, though. My last memory of gluing those things in the book was probably when I was in kindergarten."

"I don't remember them at all," Jim chimed in.

"Yeah? Well, I've got something for you guys," I said. I had been pulling rosary beads out of every single drawer and amassing them in a Target bag. "Here," I said as I threw the bag at the two of them, "the Pope called. He wants his beads back."

They opened the bag and laughed.

We finished up and turned in the keys. Drew decided to visit Barb quickly before he headed to the dump and then home. I handed him a bag of Barb's clothes with Mr. Frog's plastic brown eyes peeking out the top. Drew stared at the bag for few seconds, with the green-and-yellow frog looking back at him.

"You know," Drew started, "they had good careers, lived in a nice neighborhood, and had a giant house full of stuff. Some of it was pretty expensive. And now all Mom's belongings fit in a little garbage bag, and her prized possession is a stuffed frog... and she doesn't even know where the frog came from..."

Chapter 23

The summer dragged on into September as Mom's physical condition got worse. She had pain on her right side that her doctor thought he had figured out, but apparently not. She could hardly breathe some days with the pain radiating into the right side of her chest, back, and shoulder. It was so hard for me to sit by helplessly. Then it came. The call I was waiting for and dreading all at the same time. Assisted living had a bed, and now they needed to evaluate Mom before they could officially admit her.

During the summer, she had begged me to find a facility for her to live in. Through tears, she informed me that she was a burden and should be put into a nursing home. I told her she wasn't a burden, but an apartment with a nurse on duty was coming in the near future. One minute she thought it was a great idea, the next minute, she wasn't leaving her house, and five minutes later, she had no recollection of the conversation.

I tried explaining to her the nature of the nurse's visit and evaluation. She didn't like it and got defensive, refusing to answer some questions while completely lying on others. I always let her answer first to the best of her ability and corrected things after, if need be.

She started saying crazy things: she had cancer twice and lost all her hair; she had been in a facility once before for three months; she broke her hip and had a rod inserted in her abdomen. No idea where any of that was coming from, as none of it was remotely true, other than having a small basal cell carcinoma removed eons ago. Her brain had stuff so mixed up it was staggering. When I corrected the information, she argued with me. Much to my disbelief, they allowed her in.

****

Three days before I was supposed to move her, I went to her room and made the bed. It was hard to imagine her in one room, but it was worse to imagine her at Sunrise. This place had wheelchairs and walkers everywhere. It was so much bigger than Sunrise. A giant cafeteria fed the residents. I was sure Mom wouldn't come out to socialize, and I questioned how much one-on-one interaction she would get from the staff.

Discouraged about the living situation, I left. On the way home, it occurred to me that the immense pain in her side would likely become a problem. When residents complain about chest pain, an ambulance becomes their next ride.

I called the intake manager and explained the situation. What caused the pain was called esophagitis. Too many years of nonsteroidal anti-inflammatories had inflamed the esophagus where the stomach meets the intestine. It had become so bad that it was close to becoming a stricture. Her doctor prescribed an antacid twice a day, which seemed to help at first, but then it stopped working, creating the chest pain. I was informed that they would send her to the ER regardless of the diagnosis and they would do it with each complaint, so I withdrew her application. Unbelievable. There was no way I could put her there—or anywhere for that matter. The only place she would be accepted would be a nursing home.

Jim came home to find me moping on the couch.

"What's the matter? Mom's move?"

"No. Mom's non-move."

"What's that mean? What happened?"

I explained the whole story to him.

"Abby, she's not really ready for Sunrise, let alone a nursing home."

"I know. But what am I supposed to do? Leave her suffering in pain and alone?"

"She could live here," Jim answered.

"No, she can't. Physically, she can't navigate the stairs in the house. We have a wood stove and a gas range, and we're not home all day...even if I was home, I couldn't put up with the repetition and constant care. Sorry, I love my mom, but I know my limits, and after the last nine years of dealing with everyone, I've long since reached them." I said, now leaning back on Jim's chest.

"There has to be an answer, Abby."

"Yeah. Running away from home comes to mind."

"How about dinner? Dinner's a good answer. Let's start there. I'll take you out."

"I guess. Where we off to?"

"Hmmm...how 'bout we get a drive-thru Happy Meal?"

I knew he wasn't serious but gave him one of my head-tilting glares anyways.

"Wha? No Happy Meal? You never know; we may find an anatomically correct stuffed male frog for a toy surprise!"

***

I stopped at Mom's on the way to work the next morning because I forgot to check her medicine for refills. I had no idea why it didn't occur to me before, but I suddenly realized she wasn't taking her meds correctly.

I called Jim on the way to work. He got on it and found a tamperproof medicine machine. It came two days later, and I made sure I understood how it worked before heading to Mom's. She hated it because she was perfectly capable of taking her own medicine. Just ask her, she'll tell you. I filled the machine and set the timer. I waited with her to explain how it works. The timer went off and the medicine dispensed.

"There you go, Mom! Now just take your pills!"

She took the pills and said, "These are for later."

"Huh? No, Mom, these are your pills for tonight."

"No, they're not. I already took them."

I decided to skip the argument but wasn't sure what to do next. I watched as she put the pills in a tiny cup where she kept her meds. Then I realized what was going on.

For years she had a habit of having her morning pills in a cup. When she took them in the morning, she opened her evening meds and put them in the cup. In the evening, she took them out of the cup and then filled the cup back up with the morning meds. She was always pulling one dose ahead. When she wasn't looking, I took the meds out of her cup and decided to get there before the morning alarm.

The next morning I arrived ten minutes before the alarm. Once the beeping started, Mom informed me she didn't need the machine; she just needed her medicine.

"Your medicine is right there, Mom," I said, pointing to the newly dispensed pills.

She reached for her little cup to find it empty.

"I already took them."

"No, you didn't. I emptied the cup last night."

"No. I took them already."

"You couldn't have."

"I did."

The experts will tell you never to argue with a dementia patient. I'd love to see them show me how, as she really needed her medicine. I came up with another plan.

"Oh!" I exclaimed, "These ones are *different!* I called the doctor, and he sent these for your pain."

"Oh, that's right," she said, using her fallback line as she got a glass of water and took her meds.

She needed her inhalers as well, but I already knew how that was going to go, so I didn't bother. Jim agreed to meet her for her evening medicine. He went around with her a few times, but she finally took it for him. He also took the little cup out of there, hoping it would solve part of the problem. The two of us continued this routine, and after three days, we noticed a huge improvement. I stopped to take her to the grocery store and found her outside doing yard work. She hadn't done anything all summer due to the pain.

"How's it going, Mom?"

"Great! The pain on my right side is almost gone! It still hurts a little, but I can breathe!" she said with a happiness that had been missing for weeks.

The doctor was right, the antacid did work, but she hadn't been taking it correctly. Now that she was taking all her medicine on time, we saw a "new Mom." If nothing else, we figured we could get her into assisted living without the threat of non-stop trips to the hospital.

***

We hoped that three weeks of repetition with the pill dispenser would do the trick, but it didn't. For Jim and me, it meant two trips a day to Mom's as she just didn't get the medicine machine. When we were there, she would get up and take it, but if we weren't, she'd shut it off and find a cup for her medicine. We tried leaving notes for her as well, but that didn't work either. Notes just become part of the background that doesn't stick out to the dementia brain.

Four weeks into this, I stopped just before the evening alarm. The beeper went off, and she sat there and let it beep. I waited to see what she was going to do. Almost five minutes went by.

"Mom, do you hear that?"

"Yeah. But I already took my medicine."

"I don't think so; that's why the machine is beeping."

"I took my medicine."

"Okay, let's go have a look."

We checked the beeping machine to find the pills sitting in the dispenser.

"See, Mom, they're right here," I said quietly.

"I ALREADY took my pills!" she replied, now becoming agitated.

"I'm not sure how; they're right here," I was trying to tell her she was wrong without being forceful about it.

"I already TOOK them!" she said as she sat down at her little kitchen table, trying not to cry. "Nobody believes me...I'm not crazy...and you don't believe that either."

I shut the machine off and sat down across from her, "Sometimes your brain doesn't work right, and you forget things."

"Honey, tell me I'm not crazy," she said through sniffles.

"You're not crazy, Mom."

"Thanks."

She got up from the table and took some homemade chocolate chip cookies out of the freezer. She opened up a cupboard and set two glasses on the table.

"Water or milk?" she asked me.

"Water is fine."

"I'll nuke the cookies for a second," she said as she put them in the microwave.

This whole thing was becoming too hard to deal with, and I just didn't know what to do. I watched as she struggled to get the time set. *Just one of the hundreds of things she struggles with*, I thought to myself. She has so many other health issues, and I always thought they would kill her before dementia would. She put the cookies on the table and took her seat. I stared at her for a second.

My mom. Sweet, loving, and always ready with an encouraging word was now disappearing before my eyes, and there was nothing I could do. The harsh realization that she was going to end up like Joe and Barb hit me like a ton of bricks, and now I was the one trying not to cry. Some things I still couldn't hide from her.

She looked up from her plate as I was staring at mine. "Honey? What's wrong?" I could see the pain in her eyes.

I couldn't answer. I knew if I opened my mouth, I would start crying for real. I shook my head to say "nothing."

"Don't cry," she said to me through her own tears, "it'll be okay."

"It's never going to be okay, Mom," I said with tears now running down my face.

She came over and put her arms around my shoulders and her cheek on my head, "Don't cry, don't cry, don't cry, Abby. It's going to be okay. Don't cry."

I gained my composure, "I'm okay, Mom."

"I worry about you...I'm becoming too much. Maybe I need to go live someplace for people like me."

I didn't even know how to answer that, so I changed the conversation to dinner, telling her I needed to get home and make dinner for Jim. I finished my cookie, gave her a hug, and left.

***

That visit put me in a funk for the next three days as the reality of Mom slipping away was approaching faster than I realized. I wasn't happy, I wasn't sad—I was just "there." I didn't show any signs of snapping out of it, which concerned Jim. It was out of character for me. Not that I haven't had bad days, but that's all they ever were—just a day. More than one, and Jim began to worry.

On the third night, I quietly made my way upstairs and went to bed early. I figured sleep would be a nice escape. I have always slept pretty well in the midst of all the craziness and decision-making with our parents. That night, I had a dream.

I dreamt I was in a room with a black, cube-shaped wicker basket. It had a top on it that began to move, and I knew it wasn't good. A creepy guy emerged, and I knew he was a serial killer. He was sneaking up behind people and choking them with a shoelace, but he wasn't killing them; he was killing their joy. I was trying to avoid him when a man stepped between us and said to me, "Abby, this man is here to kill your joy. What scripture did your mom always say in the midst of her hardships?" I answered, "The joy of the Lord is my strength." The man continued, "If you lose your joy, you will lose your strength to move forward through this. You will end up bitter and depressed." Then the dream ended.

I woke up immediately and lay there in the dark pondering the dream. Mom always told me God spoke through dreams and cited several biblical examples. This one seemed too vivid to ignore, so I shook off the funk and moved forward. Moping around wasn't going to change the circumstances.

***

I couldn't get back to sleep, so I got up early and started scouring new options. I looked into day facilities but knew Mom wouldn't go due to her physical pain. Sometimes it's just too much for her. Jim suggested looking into the "Rise and Shine" program that is part of the Sunshine Group.

Rise and Shine's main focus is to keep seniors living independently as long as possible. They offered transportation, wellness checks, a day center, housekeeping, meal prep, bathing, and onsite medicine reminders. It sounded like a match made in heaven to me, so I gave them a call and made an appointment.

Mom turned out to be a great fit for their services. Of course, she refused them all, but I enrolled her anyway. Because they were part of the Sunshine Group, it would make any moves into one of their facilities fairly seamless, and I could use a break.

A nurse showed up in early December for a final analysis. I watched as she was once again given the Mini-Cog, a three-minute recall test I've watched Joe, Barb, and Mom fail countless times. It always begins with three words, then a series of questions, and then ends with the nurse asking what the three words were. It is followed by the patient being asked to draw a clock.

Nurse: "I'm going to give you three words and then I'm going to ask you for them in a few minutes. Ready?"

Mom nodded.

"Ball, bat, honesty. Got it? Ball, bat, honesty."

Mom repeated them back to her.

Nurse: "What day is it?"

Mom: "Mmmm…Tuesday."

It was Thursday.

Nurse: "What's today's date?"

Mom: "The fourteenth."

It was the second.

Nurse: "What season is it?"

Mom: "Winter."

Technically it was still fall, but there was snow on the ground, so the nurse gave her a pass on that one.

Nurse: "What month is it?"

Mom: "August."

Nurse: "Can you give me the three words I gave you at the beginning?"

Mom: "Hmmm…no."

The nurse was getting a piece of paper out of her folder.

"Don't bother," I said to her. "You want her to draw the clock and a time you give her, right?"

"Yes."

"Don't bother. She can't do it. She has had a certain amount of cognitive issues her whole life. She may not have been able to do it when she was well. You'll just frustrate her and stress her out. Don't bother."

"Got it," the nurse replied as she began packing her things. "She's all set! You'll be hearing from the head of our Home Care division. She'll assign a caseworker, if you don't have one already, and put her on the medication schedule."

It took a couple more weeks to get her on the schedule, but at least there was some light at the end of the tunnel. Three months of being at the house to make sure she took her pills twice a day was tiring. Family helped on occasion, but it was one more thing that was added to my growing list of responsibilities. Rise and Shine required several trips to their facility for evaluations from doctors, physical therapy, recreational therapy, and respiratory therapy, just to name a few. But they were available 24/7/365 and made house calls.

***

I met the aides at the house for the first couple of visits. The aides were nice, but their presence angered Mom. She complained that they came at nine o'clock at night and got her out of bed and they came at six a.m. before she was dressed. Of course, neither was true, and I tried to calm her down and told her I'd call to find out what was going on.

From there, she went on her next tirade about them sitting in her driveway reading the paper. When I nicely explained that they were filling out paperwork, she informed me they didn't have the right to do that in her driveway. Finally, she settled into the routine with the aides and ended up liking them very much. I still stopped daily, but at least I knew she was also getting checked on a minimum of twice a day by someone other than me.

Mid-February arrived, and I was now part-time again at Sapphire. One of the reasons I enrolled Mom in the program was to get some services for her so I could get a break, but the dementia brain has no reasoning ability and thinks nothing is wrong. So she refused to let them do anything else for her. I wanted them to come in and clean the house and strip her bed once a week. She refused. I wanted them to take her grocery shopping. She refused.

I wanted her to try the day center for two hours, one day a week. She refused. It finally ended in an argument.

"Mom, part of the reason I put you in this program was to help me. You told me I was doing too much and there is only so much I can do. I need help, and this helps you stay in your home. Do you want to stay here, or do you want to move?"

"I want to stay," she said.

"Okay, then you are going to have to let some of these people help."

"I don't need any help. They will just steal everything!"

"It'll be okay. They are screened, and we can pick the person."

"NO! I don't need help! You can take me when I need to go somewhere!"

Now I was tired of her and her attitude, and my exhaustion got the better of me.

"No, Mom," I said with a nastiness that was building from having to take way too much responsibility for someone who couldn't think for herself. "I CAN'T take you everywhere! I can't do everything! Your refrigerator needs cleaning; you have two-week-old food in it. *You are making this so hard*! I have a JOB that I've had to cut back on; I have a house that needs to be cleaned, clothes that need to be washed, and groceries that need to be bought! All I'm asking from you is to let someone help me! BUT NO! YOU can't DO THAT! You just expect ME to do it ALL. And then you complain about it!" I could see her anger starting to fade and knew the tears were next. I felt bad, but at the same time, I also didn't think I was asking her to do much. "I just can't take it anymore," I said quietly as I turned and left.

Chapter 24

I stepped out the door and onto her wet driveway in the softly falling snow. I zig-zagged out of her neighborhood and drove aimlessly for ten minutes, thinking about Mom. The flickering candle of her mind didn't get very bright these days, and it was heartbreaking. She required more and more time from us.

More than once, I got home from work, changed, and sat on the couch, only to have Mom call with a "problem." Once I had to go over to "fix" the TV. I arrived to find the TV unplugged from the power strip; the power strip unplugged from the wall and plugged into itself, along with cables all over the place. The entire time I straightened out the spaghetti of cords, Mom was over my shoulder, telling me how she already tried that, and that's not the problem, and she needs a new TV, and she needs a new remote, blah, blah, blah. I'd get it all set and turn it back on. The only problem was Mom. She forgot how to turn it on, and knowing it couldn't possibly be her, she would pull all the plugs and cables apart.

Then there was the time the furnace "didn't work." Somewhere between the changing seasons, she decided she was cold.

In the winter, she turned the heat down to sixty-three at night and up during the day. I arrived to find her in layers of clothes and the thermostat set at sixty-three. I shut off the air conditioner and told her we'd open the door; it was nice out. Nope. Wasn't happening. She didn't want the door open because dust would get in the house. I tried to explain that winter was over, and she didn't need to turn the thermostat down to sixty-three at night. I finally managed to get her to understand that.

Then the opposite happened. She was sweating. Jim stopped to "fix" this problem and told me she was dressed in flannels and her air conditioner wasn't working. It was in the nineties that day, but three days earlier, it was only sixty-five out, so she decided to cover the air conditioner. When the temperature went up, the A/C kicked on, and the capacitor puked. I made a call and went to wait for the repairman and to attempt to get Mom out of her flannel shirt. I couldn't convince her, and she didn't understand that it was making her hotter.

"No, I'll get cold," she said to me with beads of sweat on her forehead.

"When you cool down, you can put it back on," I answered.

She still refused.

Then there was last fall when Jeff visited. He snuck out on the back deck to call while Mom was busy with other things.

"Hey Jeff," I answered.

"Abby, I just had to call you for a second," he said, chuckling. "You know where the dip in the backyard is? You know, where the old shed was? Well, Mom thinks that the water sitting there is being piped in from a construction site three miles away! Never mind the thunderstorm that went through yesterday! Where does she get that from?"

"I know, she told me she called the town and the police and everything else. Of course, she didn't. We know it stays wet after the rains, but Mom saw the news where neighbors were complaining about drainage issues from a construction site. Somehow her brain decided that was the issue."

"Okay, how 'bout this one," Jeff continued, "the guy next door with the satellite keeps her up nights because he is projecting the TV into her head!" He couldn't contain his laughter on that one.

"Yup! I've heard that one too! My problem is, I'm afraid Mom's going to go over and say something to him!"

"Oh no! I never thought of that!" Jeff said through laughter. "I don't know why she thinks that."

"I finally figured that one out too. Has she asked you if you hear voices?"

"Yeah! She did that a couple days ago!"

"So, Mom has tinnitus, which causes some type of ringing in her ears or something. One day the refrigerator kicked on, and she asked me if I heard someone talking. Then the heat kicked on, and she asked me the same thing. Must be a combination of tinnitus and other quiet noises, like the furnace. Her brain is shrinking. Who knows what cells go missing and in what order? I think it sounds like human voices to her, but she doesn't understand what's going on. What's left of her brain fills in the gaps."

"Hmmm...weird."

"How many people has she 'seen on TV'?" I asked him.

"Oh my God! Everyone! She thinks she's seen everyone on TV!" He was trying not to laugh too loud.

"I know! She got new neighbors and told me he was a news anchor! And she's said that to every nurse and caseworker she's met! Along with cashiers and anyone else! Not sure what's going on. People must look familiar to her or something. I have no idea!"

"It's crazy!" Jeff said. He was quiet for a second, and then reality began to take hold. "Abby, I miss Mom. Even from a year ago when I visited, and she made her lasagna and meatballs…I would never have guessed it was the last time I would have it…" he trailed off.

"I know. It's a miserable, heartbreaking, soul-crushing disease. There'll come a point where we'll suffer more than she will. We're kind of there now. Enjoy your visit as much as you can. As bad as she is, she'll never be this good again."

I had to stop myself from telling him that at least he wouldn't have to witness it firsthand every day, and that Jim and I were fast approaching our breaking point. It must be nice to have a life. We wouldn't know.

***

My aimless driving brought me to the village of Avion. I pulled into a diagonal parking space along Main Street next to Crystal Spring Pond. I got out and stepped up to the black railing and rested my forearms across it. The fountain was running, and I watched as the water sprayed into the air and landed on the layers of ice that formed beneath it. There would be no rainbow today.

I watched the mallards gathered along the shoreline. Some were sitting with their bills tucked under their wings while others were waddling around the shoreline. I watched through the giant falling snowflakes as some ducks gently paddled through the frigid waters at the end of the pond. The air was still, and the flakes looked more like white feathers swinging back and forth than they did snowflakes. It was just warm enough to create wet snow. The kind that snowmen and snowball fights are made of.

I glanced across the pond to see Freddie and Frieda Swan casually paddling along. They moved like Olympic ice skating dancers. Side by side, graceful, and completely in sync. Freddie would glide to the left, and Frieda would go with him. He'd switch to the right, and she'd go with him. They never missed a beat.

I looked past the pond to the hills beyond. Although the skies were flat and gray, the mid-winter landscape was beautiful. Leafless trees caught the flakes, snuggling around each individual branch like a fuzzy fleece blanket. The pines and spruce that cropped up along the hillside held the snow like a bird's nest full of downy feathers. Houses of red, yellow, blue, green, black, and gray colors dotted the landscape like the individual brushstrokes that make up an Impressionist painting.

The only things interrupting the beauty were the sounds of cars whizzing by on the wet road and my thoughts of Mom. *Sunrise is here*, I thought to myself, *and there is nothing I can do to stop it.*

Just as I was about to leave, I looked down into the water below. A giant rainbow trout floated in his stationary position. His tail was wagging back and forth along with his pectoral fins, and in some sort of syncopated rhythm, he managed to be in perpetual motion while remaining stationary at the same time. He seemed to be waiting for me. I looked over at the feed machines, and sure enough, there was one for the trout. I didn't notice it last time I was here. I fished around in my pocket, pulled out a quarter, and popped it in the machine, hoping what little food was left wasn't frozen. I turned the handle, and the machine released the last of the food into my hand.

The rainbow was still in position. I pinched the pellets with my fingers and dropped a few into the pond. The fish came up to the surface, grabbed them, and returned to his position. I repeated the process a couple more times until the pellets were gone.

"Sorry, fish. Show's over," I said to him as I dusted off my hands and left.

***

Jim and I had a discussion about Mom over dinner that night. I told him I lost it with Mom and how I thought the time had finally come.

"You yelled at your mom? Wow. She is the sweetest person…and you yelled at her. Tsk, tsk, Abby. What shall be your punishment for that? Hmmm…let me think about it."

"Not funny, James Preston. I feel bad, but honestly, I'm starting to feel bad about you and me. I can't take it anymore, and we need to get our lives back. I need to go back to work full time. I just hate that place and all that it is, I guess."

"Yeah. Ten years of this is enough…I think your mom is finally ready for Sunrise."

"I read an article about the signs and symptoms of caregiver burnout. Pretty sure I'm there in several ways: irritability, feeling run-down, neglecting responsibilities, lacking leisure activities, and I'm becoming increasingly resentful."

"I'm not so sure that's what's going on with you, Abby," Jim said as he gathered his dirty dishes.

"Huh?" I said, scooping my last bit of mashed potatoes onto my fork.

"Let's be realistic about this. Like I've said before, you're mean, and I don't see where irritability, neglecting responsibilities, or being resentful is new for you."

"Uh-huh, uh-huh, I see," I said, nodding my head as I turned my fork full of mashed potatoes into a catapult.

In his smugness, Jim had looked down to pick up his napkin, and with perfect timing, he looked up to see the mashed potatoes as they hit his face.

"What the? Oh, you are SO dead!"

"Only if you can catch me!" I said as I took off through the house.

Jim was wiping the potatoes off his face, and I managed to trap myself near the front door. Not to be outdone, I ran out into the snow with Jim on my heels. He grabbed me by the back of my sweater, and we both fell into the snow laughing.

I asked Jim, "Think the neighbors are calling the police right now? Maybe a domestic violence charge?"

"Probably. Everyone on the road knows how mean you are to me."

"Oh, I doubt it. Who's making the angel?" I said as my arms and legs performed horizontal jumping jacks in the snow. "Plus, I don't draw blood or leave marks!"

"Unfortunately, I lack evidence. But what I'm not lacking is a wet, cold butt crack and a starchy face," he said as he got up. He extended his hand to pull me up. "What are you going to do about Mom?"

"Call Molly tomorrow. It's time."

Chapter 25

G ood morning, Sunrise intake. Molly speaking."

"Hey, Molly. It's Abby Preston," I said, unable to hide the melancholy in my voice.

"Abby! Oh my God! How are you? And how's Barb?"

"Barb's still holding her own. I'm calling about having my mom admitted. How long's the waitlist?"

"Geez, Abby, I'm sorry to hear that. Let's see…" I could hear her rifling through papers. "I believe we will have an opening for her on March first. I'm not one-hundred percent sure yet, but that's the direction the resident is headed. I'll call Rise and Shine to have all her paperwork sent, and I'll get back to you when I know for sure. She'll need a screening and a tuberculosis test, but don't do anything yet. It has to be within thirty days of the move—you know the drill."

"I do, but I'm glad it's a short wait for once. Joe and Barb took forever."

I was stunned that the wait was only two weeks out. I think I was secretly hoping for longer in some ways. A week later, my phone rang just as I was headed into Mom's house. I looked at the caller ID. It was Molly, and I just couldn't make myself pick it up. Almost immediately, it rang again, but this time, it was Sunset.

"Hello."

"Is this Abby?"

"It is."

"Hi, this is Dr. Nader at Sunrise. I just wanted to call and let you know that Barb's eating is slowing considerably. That is the telltale sign the end is near."

"Really? I didn't know that."

"Yes. Somehow the brain and body just decide they've had enough. We aren't exactly sure how it works, but we see it constantly. I just wanted to give you a call in case there's any out-of-town family who would like to visit with her."

"Thanks, Doc. I appreciate the call."

I sent a group text to the boys and went into the house where there had been a nasty smell for a week or more. Mom didn't notice it, but everyone else did. I thought it was a dead mouse in a furnace duct in the kitchen. I'd already looked through the cupboards near the vent, thinking a ham sandwich was stored there but found nothing. I scoured the refrigerator, and still nothing. On a previous visit, Jim thought it smelled like cabbage. I began wondering if something fell on the floor and made its way under the refrigerator. Jim distracted Mom while I looked. Nothing. The smell persisted. I walked in, and Mom was in the bathroom fixing her hair.

I yelled to her, and she told me she'd be out in five minutes. Five minutes was enough time to check the kitchen *again* and throw out her trash collection.

A few weeks ago, Mom was insistent that the garbage man never picked up her trash. As usual, it was untrue, so I tried to gently tell her I'd make sure the garbage got picked up. Then she was adamant that she'd got a call from the trash company that they were no longer collecting and had gone out of business.

I have never understood this part of dementia. I watched Barb do the same thing. I don't know if they somehow realize they have a problem, so they make up the next untruth in an attempt to prove they are competent. But when I tried to help, there was always the "phone call" she made or received telling her there was no trash pick-up, the mail doesn't get delivered anymore, the town was coming to fix things...and the list goes on and on. They have an outrageous answer for everything.

When I tried to put the trash out for her, she insisted she didn't have very much and not to bother. It was true, she didn't accumulate much, but it was still trash. I found myself being the "trash thief" on more than one occasion. I would wait until Mom went into the bathroom and grab the bag out of the kitchen garbage can and run to the car with it. If she was in the bathroom long enough, I would steal a few recyclables as well. She never realized it was empty, but God forbid she catch you mid-robbery!

Now that she was in the bathroom, I began my garbage hunt. I opened a kitchen cupboard to find washed and neatly stored trash mixed in with her plates. I found pieces of paper towels that had been used countless times that were left drying on the window sills in the kitchen. I went to the garage to grab a trash bag.

In the garage, I found more washed trash—meat trays, cardboard boxes from frozen dinners, empty soda bottles, plastic bags, potato chip bags, and plastic trays that once held cookies. I collected the recyclables from the garage shelves and put them in the bin. I opened a tool drawer and found a dinner plate. Why was the dinner plate out here in the tool drawer? Not a clue, but I did notice they had been slowly going missing from the cupboard and being replaced with paper plates.

I managed to get most of the garage picked up but thought my time was running short, so I went back into the stench of kitchen. I washed the plate and was putting it in the drying rack as Mom entered.

"Did you get that plate out of the drawer in the garage?" Mom asked.

"Yeah, I did," I was stunned that she knew that.

"Put it back there for me, will you?"

"Sure, Mom…why do you have it out there?"

"There's no room in the cupboard for it."

"Oh. Okay."

And I put the plate back in the garage. When I did, I noticed a few pots and pans were also stored out there. I decided to check the cupboard where she kept her pots and pans to see if anything odd had taken their place. I pulled the door open and was immediately slapped in the face with the nasty odor I hadn't been able to find. Fighting my gag reflex, I looked down to find a bag that once held dinner rolls was now holding some type of rotting meat.

"AH!" I yelled as I grabbed the corner of the bag between my thumb and forefinger, touching as little as possible.

"What's that?" Mom asked with no sense of alarm and apparently no sense of smell.

"I don't know! It's meatloaf or something!" I said as I went out the door.

"Why did you put it in there?"

I didn't bother to answer and set the nastiness next to my car. I tried to identify it, but the forensics proved inconclusive. I couldn't decide if it was raw burger or raw meatloaf she made and never cooked, or cooked meatloaf. The slimy white stuff covering it made it hard to tell. My best guess was that she made a meatloaf with the intent of cooking it later. Instead of storing it in the fridge, she put it in the cupboard. Thankfully, Mom was a bit of a neat freak. The mystery meat was sitting on some type of tray and tightly wrapped. At least it didn't leak into the wood of the cupboards.

I returned to the kitchen, where she had already forgotten what happened. We visited for a while, and then Francesca showed up with their brother Dominick. They all decided they were headed out for lunch, so I left. I put the foul-smelling science experiment in the back of my SUV. It was a disgusting fifteen-minute drive to my garbage can. At that point, I decided I should listen to the voicemail Molly left me.

The bed would definitely be available on March first, and I would need to get Mom's paperwork in order. It was still hard to think of her living at Sunrise.

***

It was late on a Friday, and I was getting everything in motion for Mom when the next call from Sunset came; this time, it was a nurse.

"Hello."

"Abby?"

"Yes," I said, no doubt sounding weary.

"This is Rachel. I'm a nurse on Barb's floor. I just wanted you to know that Barb is now refusing to eat. She pushed the plate away last night and this morning."

"Is she drinking?"

"No."

I knew that meant she wouldn't last long.

"I'm not holding you to this, but could you guess how long she has? I'm thinking maybe a day?"

"It is hard to tell sometimes, but I'd give her no more than forty-eight hours."

***

The Preston gang all met Saturday on the fourteenth floor. Jim and I were the first to arrive. I walked into her room with Jim on my heels, stunned to see her in the state she was in. The nurse made it sound like she was awake when in fact, she was in her bed semi-comatose. One eye was closed while the other was open in a small slit. Her mouth was agape, and her breathing sounded like snoring.

"Yikes!" I said loudly as I walked in.

"Geez!" Jim said, "Was it just me, or did you think she was awake?"

"The nurse said she refused food and water. I thought she was awake doing those things." We were both quiet for a minute, "Jim, she's in the same state my father was in right before he died. When her breathing slows, she'll be in a coma, and then it won't be long."

Jim pulled up a chair next to his mom's bed and took her hand. In a quiet voice, he said, "Mom. It's Jimmy." I saw Barb grip his hand. "I love you, Mom. Thanks for everything. I wouldn't be where I am today if it wasn't for you and Dad." He waited before saying, "Drew and Sean and their families will be here in a few minutes…after that, it's okay to go."

I hunted down some tissues and handed them to Jim. Just then, I heard voices coming down the hall and went out to meet Sean and company. I explained Barb's state, so they wouldn't be as surprised as we were. Five minutes later, Drew showed up with his family, and I gave them the same speech.

Each of us went in, one by one, to say our goodbyes. And then we waited. We all gathered around her and talked amongst ourselves while keeping an eye on Barb. Every once in a while, she would exhale and stop breathing for about ten seconds. All our conversations ceased at once as we turned to Barb and then to each other. Suddenly, she would begin breathing again, and we restarted our conversations. After a few hours, hunger took over, so we all left. The boys returned the next day, spending a good part of Sunday with Barb.

Jim and I climbed into bed at ten o'clock Sunday night and immediately fell asleep. The phone rang at 1:32 a.m. Jim didn't stir until the combination of the phone and me poking him in the back while saying, "It's the call, Jim," woke him.

"Hello."

"Abby?" a quiet voice said, "This is Regina at Sunset."

"Hi Regina," I replied, waiting to see if she was actually going to tell me Barb died or if it was going to be like Joe, being "unresponsive." I was met with silence, which really annoyed me. People who constantly deal with death can't tell the family that someone died? It's not like it was a surprise.

Finally, I said, "Let me guess. You're calling to tell me Barb passed."

"Yeah…she did."

"Do we need to do anything?"

"No. All the paperwork has been filled out. I'll call the funeral home when I get off the phone with you."

"Okay. Thank you," I said as I hung up.

Jim rolled over onto his back.

"You've GOT to be kidding me," he said. "You really had to ask if Mom died? The nurse couldn't spit those words out of her mouth?"

"Nope. Amazing. How are you doing?"

"Fine. Just like Dad, I'm glad it's over. She was almost ninety. Can't believe she lasted this long."

"True. Wanna hear a story?" I asked him.

"I dunno. Are you going to be stupid? It's 1:45 in the morning, so I'm sure it'll be stupid."

"Stupid and *true*!" I answered. "So when my grandmother died, I was the one who happened to answer the phone."

"Let me guess. They wouldn't tell you she was dead."

"Not quite. It was a little like your dad. I was told she 'expired.'"

"Wha? What was she? A giant cheese wheel?"

"That was my thought *exactly*! Cheese, milk, meat. What does that mean? When I was a kid, I worked in a grocery store. When dairy products expired, the vendor gave credit and took them back...so, were we getting some sort of credit for Gram? How were they going to do that? By the pound? By the number of years on earth? Do people even think when they say stuff?"

Jim finally said, "I gotta get up and text my brothers."

***

Of course, Barb's death and funeral coincided with my mother's move date. When we found out Barb only had a few days, I called Molly. Molly told me that Mom could switch places with the next person in line. She didn't think it would be a long wait, likely April, but you never can tell. I decided to suck it up for another three weeks and get through Barb's death first.

Father John, who was now pushing eighty, officiated Barb's service. He still had a full head of gray hair and a warm smile. Just like Joe's service, he made the Mass a time of remembrance and storytelling.

He asked the grandkids to stand and then asked their names, ages, and favorite memories of Barb. More than one answered with their love for Ukrainian eggs along with card games and trips. Father John asked the boys their favorite memories as well. Stories of holidays, soup when they were sick, travels to the nurseries to pick out plants, and Ukrainian eggs filled the high ceilings of the church. Her three daughters-in-law shared stories of the struggles and triumphs of marrying her boys.

As storytime ended and Father John went back into the funeral Mass, I leaned over and whispered in Jim's ear, "She's really been gone a long time."

"I know. What a miserable disease. In some ways, people are gone long before they're dead."

I turned to look behind us in the church. It was packed. I spotted Steve, Vicki, Jay, and his wife Kimber sitting together; several staff members from Sunrise had showed up, along with countless friends of the family and even a few former acquaintances of Barb. It took us close to two hours to greet everyone before we headed to the cemetery. From there, we had a family lunch. We were all in agreement. We were glad it was over.

Chapter 26

A week after Barb died, I got a call from Mom's afternoon aide. She was an hour early, but she was calling to tell me Mom wasn't home. It was a cold and sunny mid-March day, and I assumed she had gone on her usual afternoon walk. I explained that to the aide, who then informed me a neighbor said she was "wandering" the neighborhood. Mom doesn't wander, so I thanked the aide and gave it fifteen minutes, as that is about all Mom's walks last. I called and got no answer, so I put my sneakers on and grabbed my coat before making one last phone attempt.

"Hello," Mom said.

"Hi, Mom, how's it going?"

"Oh, what?" there was a voice in the background. "Wait a minute...here, Abby, talk to him." I could hear her tell someone that it was her daughter on the phone.

"Hello, this is Officer Reilly with the Fremont Police Department. I just brought your mom home."

"Oh boy," I said, "I just got a call saying she had wandered off. Where did you find her?"

"Up by the school."

The school was about half a mile away, but it was on a very busy road. I knew what happened. She took her usual walk up the street, but instead of taking a left onto the return loop, she went straight and ended up at the main road. From there, she turned right and kept going, having no idea how to get home in an area she has lived in for seventy years.

"How did you end up finding her? I queried.

"A neighbor saw her and thought she was out of place and called us."

"Got it."

"Do you understand what just happened here?" Officer Reilly asked me.

"Am I on speakerphone?"

"No."

"Okay. I am well aware of her dementia. She is slated to go into assisted living April first, and I'm on my way over."

"Okay. Have a good day."

"You as well, and thank you for your help."

***

I got to Mom's and found her sitting in her chair.

"Hi, Mom. What's going on this afternoon?"

"Well, I got brought home."

"So I heard. Who brought you home?"

"The police."

"What'd you do? Knock over a candy store?"

"Not yet!"

I started cracking up.

"Not yet? Did you rob somebody?"

"Not yet!"

"Do you want to rob someone of candy?"

"No!" she said through laughter.

"What did you do?" I continued.

"I walked, and they stopped, and I told them I couldn't get home. Some of those streets are twisty, you know. So they brought me home."

"Were they good looking?"

"Oh yeah! Tall and handsome...men in uniform!"

"Don't know what to say, Mom. Eighty-four years old, and you get brought home by the police!"

We were laughing, but it really was no laughing matter. I visited, got dinner for her, and made sure she had her pills.

I called Molly on the way home to find out there wouldn't be a bed in April. Now what?

***

I dropped into my chair at Sapphire the next morning. Steve, Vicki, and Jay came in and pulled up chairs around my desk.

Steve started. "How's it going, Abby?" he asked with his bifocals resting on the top of his head. His long, blond surfer hair was a distant memory. It was now a blond-and-gray mix that was buzzed short to his ears and spiked with gel on the top. He'd put on a few pounds over the years, but he still had his rugged good looks and his earring.

"It's going, I guess. Mom got brought home by the po-po yesterday."

"Are you kidding? Did she get lost?" Vicki inquired as she straightened her dyed brown hair.

"Yup. I talked to her neighbor. Thankfully, they all keep an eye on her. He saw her go out, but after twenty minutes, he got nervous. He and his wife drove around the neighborhood looking for her. When they didn't see her, they called the police."

"God, Abby," Jay said, "how much longer can this crap continue? You and Jim have had your hands full for what seems like forever."

"Tell me about it. And just to add insult to injury, Sunrise doesn't have a bed for April and they have no idea when the next opening will be." I leaned back in my black leather office chair with my fingers laced across the top of my head.

"Look," Steve said, "we've all been talking about it. We think you need to take a leave until you get your mom settled."

"What if I don't want to? I'm already part-time; it's March, and you know we'll be in high gear very shortly."

"Abby," Jay said, "the three of us have already worked it out to cover you."

I felt a mutiny coming on, so I tried staring Jay down. Jay had become a partner in the business shortly after me.

"Wow, that's the best you can do? No snappy comeback? Your attempt at a dirty look isn't very intimidating anymore," Jay said as he sipped his coffee.

"Sure sign of burnout," Vicki said with a smile and a wink.

I let out a sigh, "You know why I don't want to take a leave? You abnormal people are the only normal things in my life outside of Jim right now. It's a sense of routine and a place in the world where I don't have to answer the same question over, and over, and over, and over—"

"We know," said Jay, "but it's too much for you right now. Besides, you're almost there. An apartment at Sunrise will open soon, even if it isn't until after April. And now that your mom got lost, you are really gonna need more time to keep a close eye on her until then."

I knew they were right, but the thought of doing nothing but caretaking tired me even more.

"You know what I hate?"

"I don't know what you hate, but I'm sure you'll tell us," answered Steve.

"I hate when Jay is right. He hit fifty and took up weightlifting. Now he's totally shredded, he shaved his thinning hair and waxes his head. Looks like an MMA fighter...*Never* forget how much you annoy me, Jay!" I said as I got up for coffee. I kissed the top of his waxed noggin. "Thanks, Jay," I said in true appreciation of his concern.

"Who knew Abby had a soft side?" he said back to me.

"Don't tell Jim. He thinks I'm mean."

***

What I was hoping would be three weeks turned into three months. It was a long three months. Mom's behavior continued to degrade. She told stories that made no sense and were hard to follow.

I showed up one afternoon, and she informed me that her nephew had come to the door, but she didn't let him in because she didn't recognize him. When I asked which nephew, she told me "Alan." But there are no Alans in our family. I asked what "Alan" wanted, and all she told me was that he wanted to come into the house, but she refused to let him in. First, she said he was a nephew; then he was a grandson, and then she didn't know him. We never did figure out what or who she was talking about. It could have been an aide; it could have been a dream she had that got mixed into reality; it could have been anything.

Then there was the morning she told me she was talking to "Louie." Again, no idea. First, he lived just up the street, which would make sense because there are neighbors who check on her, but then he lived in the next village over. Then he was "Cousin Louie," and then he was "Uncle Louie," and she insisted that I knew him.

"Honey, you know him; he's a midget."

"Wha? Louie's a midget?"

"Yeah! Little Louie!"

A small local company cut her grass, and the owner had a son who was around twelve. They had been there the day before, so I thought maybe she was talking about him.

"Is it the kid who runs the weedeater for the mowing crew?"

"No, he's an adult who's really short…you know, Cousin Louie the midget."

"Cousin Louie the midget...hmmm," I pondered as I was caught between bewilderment and amusement.

"Oh yes," Mom said in all seriousness, "and he's smart as a pancake!"

"A pancake..." I said, raising my eyebrows. I couldn't contain my laughter anymore, and Mom laughed along with me.

Uncle Dom stopped by and took Mom to lunch, which was my cue to run some errands and return in a couple hours. About an hour later, Dom called.

"Abby, um, yeah, so your mom was telling me about someone who stopped at her house..."

"Oh, you mean Uncle-Cousin Louie?" I said, trying not to laugh.

"Yeah. You heard this then?"

"Did she tell you he's a midget?"

"Uh-huh. What is she talking about?"

"No idea. You guys didn't have an Uncle Luigi in the Old Country, did you?"

"No."

"My guess is she saw something on TV. Her brain can't differentiate between dreams, TV, and reality. It's all a jumbled mess. Who knows what she's talking about?"

"It'd be funny if it weren't so sad," Uncle Dom said.

"I know. But, you might as well laugh; it only gets worse."

***

La Belle Communauté

I returned to Mom's a little while later. I'm not sure what my uncle said to her, but now she was telling me she was only kidding about "Little Louie," and no one could take a joke. I told her not to worry about it and changed the subject.

Then came the usual request: groceries. She drove me up the wall with her constant obsession with getting groceries. She had just been two days ago and needed nothing, so the battle began. I tried to talk her out of it and finally decided we'd make a list. We went into the kitchen.

"Okay, Mom, what do you need?"

"Well, everything…bread for one."

I opened the refrigerator. "There's bread right here."

"Those things I eat for breakfast."

I pointed to the bagels on the shelf next to the bread.

"I don't have anything for dinner."

I opened the freezer full of microwave meals. "Mom, there's fifteen meals in here."

"But that's not enough. I'll eat them, and then I won't have any."

"I'll take you back to the store when you eat some of them."

"There isn't enough in one of those for me."

"It's okay to eat two if you're still hungry. Plus, you have sausage in the sauce we made yesterday that's in the refrigerator along with lunchmeat, milk, and juice."

"I need cheese."

I opened the deli drawer and showed her the three bricks of cheese.

"I don't have any sweets."

I opened cupboards and showed her a bag of gingersnaps, oatmeal cookies, lemon cookies, potato chips, soda, and snack crackers. And before she could ask, I showed her the soups and tea on a separate shelf.

"Mom, you need to eat some of this first."

"I can't, there's not much there, and then I won't have any."

I was reaching my breaking point. She was steadily losing weight, tipping the scale at only ninety pounds fully clothed. She wouldn't let me fix her dinner, and she wouldn't eat. Sometimes she would just forget; other times, I think it was fear of running out of food. I don't know why she thinks like this. My guess was perhaps it came from being a child in WWII Italy.

***

Mom had a strong mechanical aptitude when she was well. My parents had built a camp when Jeff and I were twelve and ten. They bought a prefab kit, and we all worked on it together. My father enlisted friends for the big stuff, like raising the walls, but we did the rest. Although Jeff and I were young, the four of us mixed cement, learned how to put windows in, put the roof on, swung hammers, and painted.

I had a dentist appointment, so Jim stopped at Mom's on his way through to visit. He found her in the basement with the furnace partly in pieces. She had no clue how to use the wall thermostat, so it was obviously "broken." Thankfully, Jim caught her before she got too far, "fixed" the faulty switch, and put it back together.

I've often heard it said that dementia patients become children. I don't think that's accurate. Children understand simple commands even before they can talk. Dementia patients get to the point where they cannot understand, even when things are broken down to the lowest common denominator. I speak slowly and use the simplest vocabulary I can think of, but there comes a point when it just doesn't register anymore. They are not reverting to childhood—they are being ruled by a dying brain, as are those involved in their care.

***

Memorial Day came and went. It was June fifth when my phone rang.

"YES!" I said out loud as I answered, "Molly, tell me something I want to hear!"

"I'm good, Abby, thanks for asking!" she said with a laugh. "This morning, a resident left. Their family will clean out the apartment this weekend...how's Wednesday work?"

"You name the day, and we will be there!"

"I have to get Sue out for the nurse eval. Let me see...how's Tuesday morning at ten?"

"Perfect!"

"I also made a doctor appointment for nine a.m. Wednesday morning for the once over. They will give you the final paperwork, and then you can bring her here. There is one fly in the ointment, though. We have the flu going around, along with a GI bug. That means you can't see the apartment ahead of time, and we will only allow you in with her. Once you get her set, you won't be allowed back until this blows over."

"Wow! The flu and stomach bug in June? That seems odd."

"It is a little weird, but it seems to be winding down. We even pushed the annual picnic back. We're thinking late July. I'm guessing it might be two to three weeks until you see her."

"That's okay. At least I know she'll be taken care of, and honestly, Molly, I'm exhausted and need a break!"

"I hear ya. We'll see you Wednesday, assuming all goes well!"

I broke the news to her that same day. She insisted she wasn't moving; I gently told her she was. I told her it was a thirty-day trial; if she didn't like it at the end of thirty days, we'd look elsewhere. All of which was a complete lie. We learned a lot about how to handle things with Barb. Jim would tell Barb the same thing, "We can't move you until the end of the month." The end of the month never comes, but they have no concept of time or the fact that you've been telling them that for months. As Jim says, "Dealing with dementia becomes the fine art of lying." It was a true statement.

***

I asked Jim to take her for a haircut on Saturday while I packed up her clothes. I knew it would be impossible to do that with her on moving day. Between the stress of moving and being unable to make a decision, it would take forever. I packed up clothes and shoes and put everything in my vehicle. Jim decided to grab a pizza and wings after the haircut, which gave me the time I needed to finish up.

I knew she had already forgotten that she was moving, so I didn't bother to bring it up. I figured it could wait a few more days. Although I was glad she was headed to assisted living, I was also sad as I ate what I knew would be the last pizza at her house. When it came to food, glimpses of the "old Mom" came through.

"What do you want to drink?" she asked us as she got glasses out of the cupboard.

"Just water is fine," Jim answered for both of us.

"More pizza, Jim?" she asked him.

It was just typical Mom stuff that I knew I would never see it again.

***

On Tuesday I got to the house before ten o'clock to meet Sue. I called Mom earlier that morning to tell her a nurse was coming. I walked in to find her gathering her jacket and purse.

"Okay, I'm ready," she said to me.

"For what?" I asked.

"Don't I have to go to the doctor's?"

"Just a nurse coming to the house."

"Oh, here," she said to me as she pulled a bag out of her purse, "the office called and told me they needed a stool sample."

I was mortified as she held up the plastic sandwich bag that contained her sample along with a medical glove she obviously used in the collection process. All were stuffed into the bag.

"MOM! What the hell? That's disgusting!" I yelled as I carefully snatched the bag out of her hand. Holding it between my finger and thumb, I burst out the family room door onto the driveway.

I could hear her in the background saying, "I know. I don't know why they wanted it, but they called this morning..."

Just as I flung it across the driveway toward my vehicle, my phone rang.

"Hello!" I half yelled in a frantic tone.

"Geez, Abby, what's wrong?" Jim asked.

"What's wrong? Mom just handed me a bag of shit! If there was ANY doubt about moving her, it was just dispelled!"

"That is gross!" Jim said through his laughter.

"Oh, yeah! She informed me the doctor called this morning and told her to bring one." We both knew she didn't get any such call. Where did she come up with this stuff?

***

Sue showed up and went through the motions. After she left, I once again told Mom she was moving.

"I'm not moving!" she said angrily.

"Mom," I said, maintaining a calm, steady voice, "you are moving. You asked me to find a place for you, and the apartment is ready."

She said nothing for a minute, looking down at her lap.

"When?" she asked, barely audible.

"Tomorrow morning."

"I'll never see you again," she said through tears.

"Mom. That's not true. You'll see me."

"But not every day."

There wasn't much I could say to that. It was true.

"I live right by you and Dom and Francesca…I'll never see anyone." Tears were streaming down her face. "It won't be the same."

"I'm sorry, Mom. I really am, but there just isn't anything else I can do for you. I wish it was different. I wish I could change things, but I can't."

Chapter 27

Sadly, Wednesday morning came, and I awoke to find a message on our answering machine. I hit the caller ID time stamp to see Mom called at 1:15 a.m.

"Hi, Jim. It's Mom. Just wanted to ask you a question," she said, sounding nasally from crying.

I took off for Mom's house, fearing she had it torn apart, trying to figure out what to bring. I arrived, unlocked the door, and found her standing in front of her bedroom closet. She was such a pitiful sight; completely disheveled and still wearing a white turtleneck under her gray sweatshirt. Her flowered long-underwear was covered by the knee-high socks pulled up over them. It was June, and she couldn't comprehend it. Her hair was a mess, and it was apparent she hadn't slept much—if at all. Her bed was neatly made, and pajamas hung in their usual spot on a hook on the side of her closet.

"Hi, Mom. What are you doing?" I said, looking at the mess on the floor from items that had been pulled from the bottom of her closet.

"Just trying to decide what shoes to take."

On the floor was an array of items: shoes, slippers, sneakers, Depends, yarn, and quilting scraps.

"Mom, I packed some shoes, sneakers, and slippers yesterday," I said, not mentioning how she had helped pick out everything, as it was a fact long since forgotten.

"Mom," I said, trying to move her from the shoes, "did you eat yet?"

"No." She was still fiddling with shoes and sneakers.

"I'll get you breakfast while you get dressed. Why don't you take the long johns off and get a pair of pants?"

There was no getting the thermal underwear, turtleneck, or sweatshirt off. She owned one pair of long underwear and had been wearing them since last fall. I explained several times that it was going to be very hot. In fact, the forecast called for a record-breaking day with temps in the nineties and high humidity.

I popped a bagel in the toaster and made her a cup of tea while she dressed. I opened the refrigerator and was met with the smell of something rotting. I quickly grabbed a garbage bag, threw out the perishable contents, and finally found the one item that stunk. Thankfully, Jim arrived and sat with Mom while she ate. Mom always loved Jim, so he was a good distraction. It also allowed me to go around the house and pack up pictures, TV equipment, toiletries, and other random items that needed to be boxed up for the movers.

Mom finished breakfast, looked at me, and said, "I'm ready. Let's go." She grabbed a red winter scarf and winter hat that I managed to talk her out of as we headed for the door.

"Do you think they will let me have this at my new place?" she asked me.

I looked to see her cradling a coffee mug with aurora borealis lights swirling around the word *Alaska*. Jim and I had brought it back from a vacation we had taken there.

"Yeah, Mom. It's your apartment; you can take what you want."

She stared at the mug for a moment before quietly saying, "It's pretty...I always liked the colors..."

I took it from her and wrapped it in a piece of newspaper, and put it in the back seat with her other items.

We were too early for her doctor's appointment but wanting to make sure we were out of the house before the movers came, I decided to kill time by taking her to my house. I used the guise of having to pick something up. Along the way, Mom got quiet.

Finally, she spoke, "Thanks."

"For what?" I asked.

"For everything you've done for me."

"You're my mom. Look at all you did for me growing up."

"I know. But that's what mommas do. You're my sweetie."

I wanted to tell her what a great mom she was. How much I appreciated all she'd done for me and all she taught me, and the great memories she created. But once she said I was her sweetie, it was a struggle to hold back the tears hidden behind my sunglasses. I knew if I opened my mouth to tell her all those things, I would be crying through it all, and I didn't want to upset her. As the disease progressed, I became the parent, and my focus became her day-to-day safety and living. Sometimes I would forget who she really was. Mostly because it fades away. I found that the cruelest part of the disease for me being the caretaker was times like these. The flashes when the mom you so desperately want back decides to show up. It's as simple as her calling me her sweetie. Those are the times you realize how much has been lost and how much you miss them.

Although she didn't come into the house, our dog knew she was here and went ballistic, barking with excitement. Mom was known for always showing up with dog treats in hand. I had her sit on the porch and filled her hands with biscuits, and then let the dog out. The two of them were lost in a snuggle-struggle of a dog-treat shakedown. They were caught in a game of wills. Mom wanted the dog to sit; the dog was sticking her muzzle in Mom's pockets and hands, looking for the goodies. Mom was laughing and loving every minute of it, like always.

I put the dog inside, and Mom wandered over to our garden.

"Berries, tomatoes, garlic, and onions," she mused.

"Yup, and peas as well as cucumber seeds that haven't come up yet."

***

We got back in the car and headed for the doctor's office, where they drew blood and checked her over. Unsurprisingly, she had dropped five more pounds.

As the doctor went down the checklist, she turned to me and said, "She's wearing long underwear and overdressed for the weather."

I simply shrugged at her with a "Nothing-I-can-do-about-it" attitude.

I was pretty cranked at that point. What I wanted to do was muster up one of my snotty tones and say, "REALLY? YOU'RE IN GERIATRICS, AND YOU HAVE NO IDEA WHAT DEMENTIA LOOKS LIKE? Like I didn't repeatedly try to coax her out of her winter clothes? Like I had no clue Mom was dressed for the wrong season? You have no idea that I stopped her from putting on her red winter scarf and winter hat before we left the house. It's more like you, Doctor, have very little understanding of Alzheimer's. You're the one who doesn't realize that dementia patients will wear the same clothes multiple days in a row; they have no idea whether the clothes are dirty or clean, no clue how long the food has been in the refrigerator, no idea that four p.m. is not bedtime, no idea they can't lick a steak knife, no idea they can't stand in the middle of the road they've lived on for decades and read the newspaper, no idea used toilet paper goes in the toilet and not the sink, no idea raw meat goes in the refrigerator and not the cupboard. They lose track of time; they lose track of seasons, THEY LOSE TRACK OF EVERYTHING! It's you, dear doctor, who's totally clueless. What the hell? Do you think that all that happens is they lose their car keys, forget to take their meds, and eventually forget who people are? It's just not that simple."

***

With paperwork in hand, we left there and headed to Sunrise, almost a year to the day when Barb moved out. Mom just couldn't fathom it. She was sure she was moving into the building Francesca was headed to. My aunt was going to senior housing, and Mom was sure that was where she was going even though I explained otherwise multiple times. We pulled up to the building and backed the car into a space directly across from the front door. She looked at the four-story brick building with its stately pillars and massive double doors.

"What are we picking up here?" she asked.

"We're not," I replied, "this is where your apartment is."

"OH NO!" she yelled, "It's too far!"

"It's not that far away," I said, trying to reassure her, "it's fifteen minutes from my house."

We crossed the parking lot and rang the front bell. The receptionist answered, welcomed us in, and told us Molly would be here momentarily to take us to the apartment.

As we waited for Molly, a resident was trying to get out the front door. As soon as the women hit the door, the alarms went off, startling Mom. She watched as an aide came and shut the alarm off and redirected the woman.

"Pam. Why don't you come with me, and we'll go see what's on TV?" the aide asked the irate woman.

"I'M GOING HOME! YOU CAN'T MAKE ME STAY! I'M A TAXPAYER!" Pam yelled through the lobby.

Myself and the aide were trying to hide our smiles as she escorted the woman back to the rec area. Mom, however, was completely mortified by the scene.

Thankfully, Molly showed up and led us to the elevator. Mom was silent.

"How do you like the new elevator?" Molly asked me.

"Better than the old one that had that funk when Barb was here."

"We got central air, and the apartment flooring is slowly being changed over to vinyl planks."

Things have moved along in the last year. The hallways and common areas were probably hovering around seventy-five degrees—a nice change from the place's usual sweltering heat. Of course, the residents didn't care that it was hot. It was probably the right temperature for most of them.

As we got off on the second floor, I watched Mom take in her new environment. We made our way through the common area. As we walked the hall to her room, she informed us that she was not staying and wanted me to find a place to transfer her immediately, if not sooner.

We entered her apartment. I wasn't able to visit before, so I was forced to guess at what would fit. The maintenance crew had already brought in her couch, end tables, lamps, bed, nightstand, and other boxes of snacks and clothes I had dropped off earlier in the week. It was obvious that not all of her belongings would fit. The recliner hadn't made its way up yet, and the living room was so much smaller than Barb and Joe's.

There was a kitchenette that consisted of a two-door cabinet and a small sink with a dorm-sized refrigerator underneath. Unfortunately, it was immovable and took up a good two feet in an already-small space. A wall radiator that showed the building's age shrunk the ten-by-twelve space to about eight-by-eleven. Thankfully, the TV and its stand fit alongside the radiator. The couch was sent back downstairs, as was a lamp and end table. The lone chair and table barely fit the space between the door and the wall, and I decided to return with another small chair that I guessed would fit between the kitchenette and the radiator. Mom looked around at everything wondering whose furniture it was.

She didn't recognize her thirty-year-old couch when it was out of its context in front of her picture window.

I turned my attention to getting stuff put away to make a little space to move around. The guys had finished putting the bed, box spring, and mattress together and took the couch out. I found sheets in the bottom of a box, and Mom began making the bed. I left her to do that while I unpacked various toiletries, clothes, and drinks.

The room was sweltering in the ninety-degree heat, and I was trying to make my way to the window air conditioning unit.

Mike made his way to greet us.

"Abby!" he said as he gave me a hug. "It's great to see you, although I know the circumstances could be better."

"You got that right! This is my mom," I said as she came out of the bedroom to see who was there.

Mike made small talk with her for a few minutes before leaving with Mom's empty cardboard boxes. I opened the last box that contained pictures and began to hang them. That's when the magnitude of the move hit her.

"What are you doing?" she asked after I had the first three pictures hung.

"Hanging some pictures."

"NO! I don't want any pictures!"

Her anger was rising.

"What? Why don't you want pictures up? You just want to stare at white walls?"

"Yes!" she answered harshly, "Take them down NOW!" She slumped down into her chair and continued through tears, "They make me sad. I don't want to look at everybody."

In some ways, I understood. I looked at the pictures I had put out. Me and my brother with Mom and Dad on our respective wedding days, my father with an old golf buddy, my parents visiting my brothers' family, grandchildren, and great-grandchildren—all were a stark reminder of better days with those she loved the most. Things will never be the same, and I could understand her pain.

She recovered and decided she was going to explore the place. She wasn't supposed to leave her room due to quarantine. The flu swab had been taken, but now the waiting game began. I knew Sunrise was getting ready for lunch, so the halls were empty. Aides were busy hustling the residents down to the dining area and serving lunch. So I let her walk down the hall toward the sunroom. As she explored, I furiously hung more pictures while peeking out the door to see where she was. I didn't want to get my hand caught in the cookie jar!

I stuck my head out long enough to see my mom and one of the aides chatting. The aide took her to lunch. Mom was sure she knew the aide, as she's sure she knows everyone from either TV or the neighborhood. I heard the aide introduce herself as Tia, and Mom introduced herself along with the usual "I know you" tagline that she says to everyone. She was sure Tia was an aide that came to her house to give her meds each morning. Both aides were African American women, and dementia told her they were the same young ladies.

I knew it wouldn't be long before they brought her back, so I quickly hung a few more pictures! Within a few minutes, Mom was escorted back by Tia and a more experienced aide named Chya, who informed me that Mom was sweet.

Chya assured me she'd be back shortly. Mom sat in the chair, looking at the pictures. One was a collage.

"Do you know who that man looks like?" she asked me.

I knew exactly who she was talking about and what she was going to say, but answered, "No, Mom, who?"

"He looks just like my father!"

"That is Grandpa!" I said, keeping the conversation upbeat.

She stared at the old black and white picture of her father as a young man in a dark pin-striped suit, tie, black hair slicked back, and a sort of Mona Lisa grin on his face. I couldn't help but notice how much my uncle looked like him and, in some ways, my brother as well.

"How did that get here?" she was completely perplexed.

I ignored her, not wanting to get into another picture argument.

***

I had a few meetings to attend before I left. I returned from the first one to find Mom trying to get a picture of my brother put together. It was in a frame that I stood up and placed on the heat register. She couldn't figure out how the picture frame worked and had managed to break the stand off the back.

I finally had to leave. I was exhausted, hungry, and ready to go home. I had a second short meeting with her caseworker and then returned to say goodbye. I opened the door to find her sitting in her lone chair, crying.

"You okay, Mom?" I asked, knowing it was a dumb question.

"No," she said through sobs. "I can't stay here. My chest hurts, and I can't breathe, and I just can't do it."

"Mom," I said crouching down next to her, "I know it's hard. I don't like it any more than you do, but your brain just doesn't work like it used to." I put my arms around her and rested my chin on her shoulder, and waited a minute.

"Remember all those years I hated middle school, and you had to make me go?"

She nodded her head while wiping her tears away.

"This is kind of the same," I continued, "but this time, I have to make *you* do something you don't want. I wish things were different."

She pulled herself together while I put new batteries in her TV remote and quickly programmed the channels.

"All set, Mom."

"Thanks, Honey," she paused and said, "where are you coming from? Did you work today?" She had no idea all that had gone on in the last eight hours.

I hugged her, told her I loved her, and promised I'd be there to visit. Thankfully the TV diverted her attention and calmed her down as I left.

Chapter 28

The next day I decided to head to Mom's house to clean out her refrigerator and cupboards. It was a cool and cloudy mid-June day, which fit my mood at the moment. I took a walk through the house, assessing the mess I had left from yesterday. Books and magazines from her end tables were stacked on the dining room table and living room floor. Shoes and clothes were strewn across her bedroom floor. I let it go and decided the refrigerator was the best place to start. I grabbed garbage bags and recycling bins and opened the fridge.

The top shelf held outdated juices and sour milk that made its way down the drain. Ancient condiments followed after, along with various food items she cooked at least two weeks ago. She no longer knew to cover things with plastic wrap or put lids on bowls.

Let's see...petrified sausage, petrified cheese...petrified meatballs...and half a roll that I'm pretty sure would take a chainsaw to cut through, I said to myself. I opened the deli drawer and threw out old lunchmeat and kielbasa and half an unwrapped sandwich. I found Chinese in the back that Francesca brought her at some point. I didn't dare open it.

The fruit and vegetable drawers were full of long-outdated loaves of bread, bagels, uncovered cookies, and packages of croutons. I emptied them and opened the freezer.

The freezer was stuffed with frozen meals I bought six weeks ago. Although I was fairly sure they were okay for human consumption, I decided to toss them. Mom had a habit of taking meals from the freezer and thawing them on the counter. Often they were returned to the freezer or the refrigerator and then back to the freezer. Out they went, along with popsicles and opened cookies that had become freezer-burnt.

Since I was on a roll, I decided to work on some of the cupboards. I opened up her spice drawer and realized there was still washed trash lurking about, so I changed directions again. I took a garbage bag and started pulling old napkins, bread bags, and meat trays out of cupboards and drawers. From there, I headed to the bathroom and pulled the trash out of the vanity. I decided to check out the family room and scored an empty egg carton in an end table cupboard.

Last stop was the garage, where a combination of clean trash, recyclables, a hairbrush, and dinnerware awaited me. If nothing else, I did manage to find Mom's missing dishes along the way. Some were in the garage, but most had been shoved into the small kitchen cupboards above the refrigerator.

I returned to the spice cupboards. After going through multiples of vanilla extract, lemon extract, salt, and tins of spices from companies that don't exist anymore, I called it a day. I separated out some of her spices and put them in the bag to go with me, while the rest made the trash and recycle bins.

***

I was busy making dinner when Jim got home.

"Mmmm…smells good!" He said as he entered the door, "What is it?"

"A little something out of Mom's house," I replied.

"Really? What could you possibly salvage from there?"

"Chicken."

"Oh, *please* tell me you're kidding. God knows we didn't trust anything at my parents. Seriously, Abby. What's for dinner?"

"A little Sam 'N Ella's Chicken Surprise! It'll surprise you in a few hours."

"Good God, woman. Can you ever just answer a question?"

"Fine, Mr. Killjoy. It's lemon and thyme roasted chicken and vegetables, and it's almost done."

"Nice!" he hesitated a minute before cautiously asking, "The chicken really isn't from your mom's, is it?"

"My chicken isn't, but yours is. If only you knew which side of the pan was which," I said as I pulled it from the oven and set it on the stove.

Jim came and stood over the roasting pan. He grabbed some oven mitts and began carefully twirling the dish.

"Round an' round she goes! Where she stops, no one knows!" he said, laughing. "Who's getting the salmonella chicken now, Fun Girl?"

I laughed, "Of course I wouldn't bring anything perishable from Mom's! Even if it was for you. Then I'd have to listen to you whine when you didn't feel good. Get changed, and I'll set the table."

He returned and asked what my plans for Mom's house were. We kicked around rental and bed and breakfast ideas.

***

I checked with her lawyer and our insurance guy. Both ideas were very feasible, but after a few days of deliberation, the two of us and Jeff decided to sell it.

I had two weeks off from Mom's care after running for two years, and I really liked it. I didn't have to be anywhere at a specific time, I didn't have to run her anywhere, and I didn't have to worry about her. After my short respite, the last thing I felt like doing was being a landlord and getting calls for repairs or a bed-and-breakfast hostess that had to run back and forth.

***

Mom adjusted as well as I would've expected. Her second day there, she called me in the midst of a complete meltdown. Through sobs, she told me that she couldn't breathe, she was in pain, it was too hot, she was going to die there, and then began begging me to come to get her. I managed to calm her down and called Karen. In their attempt to contain the flu, they needed to wait for her test results. Until then, she remained quarantined in her room with an aide stationed outside her door. Karen was expecting results the following day.

I got a similar call the next day and asked Karen if she could make sure her air conditioner was running. Karen's quarantine frustrations came through as well.

"Let me see if her results are in yet...yup, she's negative. I'll go see her now and find her something to do!"

I didn't hear from Mom for days after that. I tried calling her room but got no answer. Francesca and Dom tried calling as well. When they couldn't get ahold of her, they began calling me. I assured them it was a good thing. Her not answering meant she was socializing and getting involved in activities. I think it saddened them a bit not seeing or hearing from her, but it didn't bother me. I was glad she was getting acclimated.

When she finally called me well over a week later, she was all excited. She had won two stuffed animals. Bingo!

"How'd you win them, Mom?" I asked, already knowing the answer.

"I won at bingo!"

"Wow! Good for you!"

"I'm saving them for you to take home when you come to visit me. When are you coming?"

"I'm not sure yet. They're still trying to stop the flu. Probably three weeks. Are the people nice?" I asked, changing the subject before missing me could set in.

"Yes! They are so good to me! We are like mothers and daughters here. The food is good, and the people are nice. A man visits me every day. He says he knows you."

"Mike?"

"Yes! That's him. I see him every day. We dance!"

"That's great, Mom!"

***

The honeymoon phase ended, which I expected. I received several calls from Mom telling me she wanted to move closer to me. Somehow she got it in her head that she lived in another city. No matter how hard I tried, I couldn't get her to comprehend she was only fifteen minutes from me. She missed seeing family on a daily basis, and even though she didn't understand time, somehow she knew we weren't around the way we used to be.

She called me on a particularly bad day.

"Hello."

"Hi, Honey. Listen, I've been thinking about it, and I'm going to sell."

"Okay, Mom. I can sell your house; it's not a big deal."

"You didn't sell it yet? I thought it was gone."

It had only been two weeks since she moved.

"Not yet, Mom."

"I want to sell my apartment. Maybe I can auction it off."

I swear, they come up with the craziest stuff.

Thinking on my feet, I answered, "Um, okay. I'll get a realtor. Why do you want to sell your apartment, Mom?"

Jim heard the conversation and gave me a chuckle. I shrugged my shoulders at him.

"I want to move to a place closer to you."

"You're only fifteen minutes from me."

"I know, I want to move closer. I never see you anymore."

I could hear her fighting back the tears. The flu hadn't lifted, and visitation was still off-limits, but in her mind, she lived at a distance that was too far for us to visit. I told her she was on a waiting list at the "new place" and she couldn't move until then. That seemed to calm her down, and I hung up.

The recreation staff set up FaceTime calls for me, thinking it would help. I was met with sad Mom, who would fight back the tears every time she saw me. She was afraid she would die there and never see me again. I would do my best to redirect her to another subject, but I couldn't get the tears to lift. She would end the calls by kissing the tablet screen.

After several tearful phone calls, I called Karen, who assured me that Mom was doing great. The crying phone calls I was receiving was not what they were seeing. She was involved in activities, rarely in her room, and well-liked by the staff and the residents.

"You know how this goes, Abby. Guilt trip."

"Oh, please. Guilt trip was Barb's middle name. I'm getting the calls after dinner. I would guess that it is her twenty minutes of downtime when she starts missing me. She's like a kid at summer camp. All is good when activities are going on, but when bedtime comes, they want to go home."

"Good analogy," Karen said, "never thought of it that way, but you're probably right. On another note, I was going to give you a call. There was an incident."

"Oh, good Lord. What did Mom do?"

"Well, you know those fake trees in the common area?"

"Yeah. What did she do to them?"

"She didn't do anything, but another resident was trying to pick the fake apples off them."

I interrupted, "Let me guess. Mom was trying to be a little helper and tell the woman they were fake?"

"You got it!"

"Were they rolling on the floor fighting?" I asked, laughing.

Karen stopped giggling for a minute, "No, it didn't get that bad. When the woman wouldn't stop picking the apples, your mom tried to pull her away. The woman was having none of that, and it turned into a tug of war. You know how old people's skin is, Abby. They bruise easily."

"And my mother left a mark on the other woman's arm, and you now have to file an incident report."

"You know the drill! I'm filling out the paperwork now and notifying the family."

"Eighty-four years old, and now she becomes a hoodlum! Wanna hear a funny call from last week?"

"Sure," Karen responded, "I'm always up for that."

"I answered Mom's call the other day, and she very quietly asks if Jim was around. He wasn't, so I asked what she needed. She wondered if he was available for surgery."

Karen burst out laughing, "God, Abby, warn me before you say something like that! I was drinking!"

"I asked Mom what she needed surgery on, and she told me it was her bladder. Needless to say, I brushed that off. I texted Jim and told him Mom wanted to know if he could do surgery on her. He didn't miss a beat and texted back: 'What's she need done? Spleen removal, bypass, kidney transplant? You name it; I'm on it. Could you bring me a set of vice grips and a utility knife? That should do it.'"

La Belle Communauté

Karen was now in a fit of laughter, "I swear, Abby, you guys are hysterical!"

"You just gotta roll with it sometimes! Any word on visitation or the picnic?"

"We'll know more by the end of the week. Shouldn't be too much longer."

"Sounds good. Thanks for the update on her raucous behavior."

"Anytime! We'll see you guys soon!"

Chapter 29

I talked to Steve and asked if I could come back around August first. My goal was to get the house cleaned out by the end of July and on the market by August, especially since it was a buyers' market. Steve told me to take as much time as I needed.

I started by going through her bedroom dresser drawers, concerned she had money hidden somewhere. Of course, there was, but it wasn't very much. I looked through the Dutch Master's cigar boxes that were about as old as me. My father took up cigar smoking for a while, and the boxes were used to hold various treasures for decades to come.

"What do we have in this one," I said as I lifted the first one out of her top dresser drawer. "Her driver's license that she swore she threw out, some cedar balls for the drawers, social security card, and a piece of paper with extended families wedding anniversaries."

On to box number two. This one held a hundred dollars cash, probably the emergency money she stowed away. Under that were newspaper clippings she had saved. I couldn't help but smile, looking through the old wedding announcements of friends and family. A few odd pictures of my future sisters-in-law and me at my wedding shower, along with the 1" x 4" strip of four photos taken at the old photo booth in the mall. Our point was to pack as many of us as possible into the tiny booth. I laughed, looking at my high school friends and me with our faces half cut off.

I had organized and placed the family photos into albums when I was in high school; the new ones that had accumulated were in their envelopes and tucked in the bottom drawer. I pulled them out one by one and found vacation pictures from Mom and Dad's cross-country train trip. They loved the picture of the train wrapping itself around the snow-covered Rockies.

I found my grandmother's ninetieth birthday pictures, college graduations, along with our weddings and grandkid's school pictures.

I pulled the photo albums from the top shelf of the closet. *Where has the time gone?* I thought to myself as I flipped through pictures of Dad. There were images of him captured with Jeff and me when we were babies, in our sports uniforms, building the camp, and holding up the fish we caught. Dad died nine years ago, but it feels like a lifetime. I hated that the memories of his sickness overshadowed the ones I saw in the pictures. The final memories almost become the defining moments of a life together.

Then there was Mom in her wedding dress. Their first Christmas together and family Christmases. I smiled at the picture of Mom readying the ingredients for lasagna while I had my head tipped backward with a giant, saucy noodle hovering over my mouth.

It's so hard to watch her slip away.

***

Over the course of a week, I managed to get her personal belongings cleaned out. Clothes and shoes were separated into three piles: one to keep, one to donate, and one to throw out. Her everyday dishes and china were packed into boxes along with glasses. I took a few kitchen gadgets home and replaced a couple of my beat-up cookie sheets with hers.

I opened the small cupboard where she kept paper plates and found the first set of multiples: six boxes of wax paper, four boxes of parchment paper, ten boxes of cling wrap, eight boxes of aluminum foil, and at least fifteen boxes of plastic bags of various sizes. Several were opened but never finished, so I threw them into a box that was headed to my house.

I cleaned out the hall closet. Forty-two boxes of bandages, twelve bottles of antacid, eight bottles of stool softeners, six bottles of anti-diarrheal, five bottles of vitamin D, seven bottles of nasal spray, two dozen trial-size bottles of hair products, bars of soap, and bottles of shampoo were scattered throughout the shelves.

With the exception of the soap and shampoo, most everything had been opened. Some bottles only had a few pills left. She never finished them and opened the next one. I looked at the expiration dates as I disposed of things. Several items were long since out of date, with some going as far back as 2010. Much like with Barb, I couldn't help but wonder, how long had she really struggled? And how did I not notice?

***

I moved on to the family room. VHS tapes of travel videos left from Dad were still there. The DVDs consisted of The Three

Stooges, Hee Haw, The Tonight Show, and old TV shows from the sixties.

His old vinyl records sat on the shelf. Mostly classical and operas. Music was the battle of the ages between my father and me, and both of us liked our music loud!

I remember an evening before Thanksgiving when I was in high school. I barely heard his knock on my bedroom door.

"Hey! Come with me," he said in a stern voice as he motioned with his hand.

I knew better than to question him, so I put my magazine on the bed and went to turn down the volume.

"Oh no! Don't you touch that volume. Leave it right where it is!"

I turned it back up before following him to his bedroom.

"See that?" He asked, pointing to books on the floor.

Dad's nightly ritual consisted of three things upon getting in bed: first, he did the local crossword puzzle. Second, he did the NY Times crossword puzzle. Third, he picked up whatever book he was reading at the time and spent an hour or so reading. Him pointing to his books on the floor meant nothing to me.

I gave him a puzzled look and shrugged my shoulders as I said, "And?"

He bent over to move the books. I didn't realize they were covering the cold air return grate. As soon as he moved the books, Lynyrd Skynyrd's "Gimme Three Steps" came blaring out. I erupted with laughter.

"Think it's funny, do you?" Dad said, trying to be annoyed when he was, in fact, quite amused.

"Oh yeah! It's definitely funny!"

"Turn it down!" he called after me in a loud voice as I returned to my room.

A few years later, I came home from work to find Dad listening to my Tracy Chapman album. Of course, I had to abuse him. The abuse was returned the day he came home and found me listening to his "Best of the Overtures" CD. I would have heard him come in if I didn't have Mozart's Marriage of Figaro so darn loud.

***

The last part of my clean-up was going through books. In Mom's case, it was cookbooks that were mostly from the '50s and '60s. I would browse through them, looking at the pictures when I was young. As I flipped through the pages, I found paperclips fastening her favorite recipes to the front cover of her cookbooks. I smiled, looking at all the ones I remember her making, along with her holiday favorites. She loved to cook for everyone, and scanning the newspaper for new recipes was a weekly ritual.

Some of Dad's books were still around, but most of what he read came from the library. Every book I picked up had a paper bookmark from the library that had their hours printed on it. I was busy pulling the bookmarks out when I was stopped in my tracks by one in particular. The library had printed its hours above Salvador Dali's famous painting, "The Persistence of Memory." Or, as most people know it, the melting clocks. I stood staring at the gold pocket watch draped over a dead tree branch along with the ants sitting atop the back of a watch. "I wish Mom's memory would persist," I said before I threw it out.

La Belle Communauté

***

Within a week, I had their personal effects cleaned out, which put me two weeks ahead of my clean-out schedule. All that was left was furniture, wall hangings, the basement, some tools, and the contents of her shed. Thankfully, Mom had slowly gotten rid of a lot of things over the years. Even the basement was almost empty.

Drew and Sean offered to come in on a Saturday to give us a hand, which we gladly accepted. The boys removed the furniture and emptied the basement, shed, and garage. I pulled up the old carpeting and removed the tack strips to reveal pristine hardwoods that had been hidden for over forty years.

I was sitting on the living room floor removing the last of the staples when Jeff called.

"Hey Jeff, how's it going?"

"Okay. How's it going with you guys?"

"They are just finishing. All that's left is a cleaning."

"Wish I could be there…remember the first night we spent there?" his voice changed from sadness to nostalgia.

We moved into the house when I was in fourth grade, and Jeff was in sixth. When we were too little to remember, Dad took a transfer to Selkirk, which is a couple hours away. Then he accepted a transfer back, and Jeff and I returned to the city of our birth. All our family lived here, but it wasn't home to us.

We weren't supposed to leave until Saturday morning, but we got home from school on Friday to find our house empty and the moving truck packed. Jeff and I had plans to say goodbye to our friends after school, and that was cut short. On top of that, it was

294

one week before Christmas. We left after a dinner with friends and arrived at our new house in the dark.

"Remember when we got out of the car with the dog?" I continued. "And she ran next door and started barking at the deer?"

"Yes!" Jeff responded with laughter. "And the deer was fake! What a dumb dog she was!"

"Then we had to wait for Dad and Uncle Ron in the moving truck. It seemed like it took forever for them to get there since the truck went so slow, and I had to pee!" I said.

Jeff shot back, "Mom and Dad packed the sleeper sofa on the tail of the truck. How convenient. They slept on that, and we slept in sleeping bags on the hardwood with all of us in the living room."

"I barely slept that night. Even kids don't sleep well on floors. I remember the living room curtains didn't close all the way, and I spent most of the night looking through the crack at the street light and watching the falling snow."

"That's right! We unloaded the truck in the snow! Aunts, uncles, and cousins were all there! Ever wish we were still in the Albany area?" Jeff asked.

"Nah! I hated moving and being the new kid, but I liked being around family, and I made great friends. Plus, I *loved* the snow! I used to wonder what it would have been like to stay there and graduate, and sometimes I wonder what happened to our childhood friends, but I don't wish we were still there."

"Yeah, you're right. Moving sucked, but we were related to half the school!" Jeff said with a laugh. "Benefits of a big family, I guess."

"True. I'll call you next week; the natives are restless and looking at dinner options."

***

"All set except for one thing," Sean said, "your Dad's clubs are in the garage."

I followed Sean to the garage. I just didn't know what to do with his clubs. They were expensive but also custom fit. It was the only thing that was tugging on me from a sentimental point but completely useless to me at the same time.

Jim and Drew were in the garage talking when I stepped in. I stared at the golf bag sitting in the corner. The clubs were hidden under a rain cover that was neatly snapped over the top. They had remained untouched for almost ten years.

I let out a sigh, unsnapped the cover, and began rifling through the pockets. There were still several golf balls as well as a huge bag of tees. I smiled as I pulled out a nine iron, grabbed a ball, and headed to the big backyard. The boys were on my heels and seated themselves on the deck rails.

I dropped the ball onto the grass and took a few practice swings. I hadn't golfed in at least three years.

I could picture myself as a twelve-year-old with my father facing me, "Remember, Abby, keep your left arm straight and aim for the shed." The shed was about two-hundred feet from me, and Dad used it as a way to work on my short game. "As they say, drive for show, putt for dough. Now, let's see you hit that shed."

I took another practice swing and stepped up to the ball. The boys were now quiet. I hit the ball and knew it was a perfect shot to the shed. As the ball descended, I gasped, "Oh NO!" The boys started hooting and hollering as the ball went right through the window on the small entry door.

I tilted my head toward the sky and shook my head through my laughter. The boys were all laughing as well.

Jim taunted me, "Guess you'll be calling the glass guy come Monday."

***

I returned to the house on Monday and managed to find a glass company to come out the same day. I washed the windows, vacuumed, and swept the house before my afternoon appointment with the Realtor. I signed the paperwork; the house would officially list on Friday. After the Realtor left, I took a final walk through to make sure we had gotten everything out.

The house was an L-shaped ranch. I headed down the hall, took a left, and started at Jeff's bedroom in the back. Each step I took thundered in the empty house. I checked the closet, stopped on the threshold, and turned to look back at his room. I remembered us shooting darts and aggravating Mom as we hit the wall more than the board. Jeff would stare at his old Farrah Fawcett swimsuit poster that hung on the wall as we hatched our childhood plans to outsmart Mom and Dad, looking to get our way. I grinned and headed to my old room.

The closet was empty. I stood in the middle of the room, imaging where my old posters once hung. The Who, Springsteen, Clapton, along with an old Bartles and Jaymes Ed's Red wine cooler banner, left no empty space. The walls were plaster, and every time I hung a new poster, the plaster crumbled and left a small hole. I could still hear Mom yelling at me to use tape.

My parents' room was the last part of the L. I found a lonely sweater hanging in the closet that I missed. Their bedroom set was put in place the day we moved in, and the furniture never moved. I remember the summer nights when Jeff and I were in middle school. We would lay on the bed with our father as he read the crossword puzzle clues, and we would try to guess the answers.

I turned and headed out, stopping in the dining room. Memories of holiday tables full of family flooded my mind. I stared out the window at our giant backyard where the neighborhood gathered for summer kickball games that turned the grass into dirt baselines.

I pivoted one hundred eighty degrees and stared at the living room. I had left glass cleaner on the picture window sill, so I retrieved it and peered out the front window. The same group of kickball kids would paint bases on the street. Wiffle ball games ensued during the spring while the yards were still waiting for the snow to leave and lawns to dry. Frisbee would follow.

I was leaning on the living room archway, contemplating the way life used to be and how it is now. Once a place of fun, friends, and food, our home was now just an empty house with creaking floors and echoing footsteps. I figured it would sell quickly, and soon it would go from being just a house to being someone else's home.

Before gloom could overtake me, I gave myself a pep talk. "It's the ever-changing cycle of life. It does suck that those days are gone, and family has died, BUT I had great parents who created a warm, loving home and great memories. They also kicked my butt to college, which has given me a pretty good life.

Be grateful for what you have, Abby. Not everyone is as fortunate as you."

I checked the kitchen and family room before leaving. I locked the door.

"Thanks, Mom and Dad," I said as I pulled the door shut behind me and left.

Chapter 30

I was just pulling out of Mom's neighborhood when my phone rang. It was Karen. I held my breath as I answered, fearing it would be bad news.

"Hi, Abby. I just wanted to let you know we are kicking off visitation with the annual picnic on the fifteenth! The flu and creeping crud have all passed."

"Great!" I answered, "I'm sure Mom will be happy."

***

We arrived at Sunrise at 3:45 on July fifteenth, ready for the annual picnic. Jim backed the truck in across from the entrance. He put it in Park, shut the engine off, and sat staring at the building for a moment.

"I just can't believe we're back here again," he finally said.

I pushed open the door and answered, "Tell me about it."

"Think Jean-Pierre will be at the door today?" Jim asked as we walked to the entryway.

"Hard to say. It's been a year. And a year in the life of a person with dementia?"

We could have put the code in and let ourselves in, but we decided to ring the bell and see.

Mike pushed the door open and greeted us. "Jim!" he said as he shook his hand and gave him a hug. "Hi, Abby darling!" he said as he put his arm around my shoulders.

"No Jean-Pierre?" Jim asked.

"No. He's still here, but he doesn't do door duty anymore."

"That's too bad," I said. "I loved being greeted by the 'maître d'."

Honestly, it just made me sad. I knew it meant Pete was losing the battle. Not that it's one that's winnable.

"Your mom's doing well. She is so sweet. I check on her daily. She loves to dance!"

"She is sweet, always has been," I said.

Jim stepped in with, "Obviously, Abby doesn't take after her mother."

I gave him a look, "You're a funny guy, James Preston. A real funny guy."

***

We crossed the lobby and got on the elevator.

"Hey," Jim said, "no more elevator funk."

"I know. It's brand new. You'll also see they don't put carpet in the apartments anymore. Nice vinyl flooring. It takes a little of the warm feeling out, but no doubt it cleans easier."

The elevator stopped on Mom's floor, and we stepped into the short hall. The aides were busy hustling from room to room, getting residents ready for the picnic. We spotted Mom outside her apartment chatting with an aide. She looked up and saw the two of us.

"Jim!" she exclaimed. She turned to the aide and said, "That's my favorite son-in-law!"

She made her way down the hall, heading directly for Jim.

"What is this?" I said to Jim, "She's headed to you?"

"Of course, she's headed to me. Your own mom knows you're mean, Abby."

I gave him a sharp poke in his side. Mom was just about to hug Jim when she suddenly stopped.

"Abby Marie! Don't you be mean to my favorite son-in-law!" She then turned to Jim and said, "I missed you so much!" and hugged him.

I was now standing behind Mom during their hug.

Jim stuck his tongue out at me, "I told you she knows you're mean."

Finally, Mom hugged me. "I've missed you so much!" she said through tears.

"I know, Mom. I missed you too! But we're all here now, so let's go to the picnic."

"There's a picnic?" she asked, although I'm sure she'd been told more than once.

"Yes, it's outside on the patio," I answered.

"Oh…that sounds nice!"

***

We made our way down the hall to find Sheriff headed in our direction. He had traded in his cane for a walker but was still fairly mobile.

"This man is nice," Mom informed us. "But I think he's looking for something. Maybe he's lost."

"Hi Sheriff," I said to him.

"Oh. Hi." He hesitated a minute and then said, "Have you seen my badge?"

I stuck my hand in my pocket and pulled out another "Sheriff" badge. "Is this it?"

His eyes got wide, "That's it! That's it!" he said excitedly.

"Can I pin it on you?"

"Yes! Yes!" he said.

I pinned it to his shirt pocket, "There you go! All set! C'mon, let's go to the picnic."

"Uh, okay," he answered.

I know he had no idea what I was talking about but he walked with us anyway, proudly showing his badge to everyone we met.

***

"I wonder who's left?" I said to Jim as we waited for the elevator.

The elevator doors opened, and there was just enough room for Mom and Sheriff, so we put them on it and took the stairs. As we stepped out of the stairwell, we saw Randy, Val, and Pete. Val looked at us and then did a double-take.

"Oh, my God!" Val said as she ran to give me a hug. "What are you doing here?"

"I moved my mom here in June," I answered.

"Are you kidding me?"

"I wish. She's about to get off the elevator."

Randy came over and greeted us with handshakes and hugs.

I heard the elevator "ding" announce that it had arrived with its cargo.

"Let me get Mom, and we'll meet you in the courtyard," I said, making my way to the elevator.

***

We walked out the back door and were met by the smell of hotdogs, hamburgers, and sausage. Smoke was rising from the grills, and staff was busy moving the food to the buffet table.

"That smells good!" Mom said.

"I know! Are you hungry?" I responded.

"Yes," she said but then suddenly stopped, and a sad look began to form.

"What'sa matter, Mom?"

"I can't stay out here…it's too hot, and you know my skin."

She was still well aware that due to her lupus, the sun and heat could make her miserable in an instant.

"You know what?" I asked her without expecting a response, "See the big white tents?"

"Yeah," she said.

"Well, those tents are for us. We are going to sit under them so you won't be in the sun."

"Ohhh... I think that will work."

"I think so too. Let's go find our seats."

***

We slowly moved toward the tent. Teddy, the Music Man, was setting up in his usual spot. I was scanning the crowd looking for familiar faces and wondering who was no longer here. Suddenly I heard a voice from somewhere in the crowd scream our names. I looked around, trying to find the source, when I saw Shirley making her way toward us.

"I'm so glad to see you! What are you guys doing here!" she said as she gave us her "Momma-Bear Hug."

"Shirley, this is my mom."

Mom looked at Shirley and said, "Oh, hi!" and gave her a hug, "Do I know you from TV?"

"She's so sweet!" Shirley said to me.

"She is. Look at you! You look *amazing!* What have you been doing to yourself?"

Just then, Will came up behind her, gave me a quick hug, and shook hands with Jim. The two of them chatted away, and I noticed Will no longer had his cane or limp.

"It was so stressful dealing with Josiah. Between taking care of him and the depression that came from watching my son slip away, I ended up gaining thirty pounds. Last fall, I finally came to a place where I realized all the tears in the world wouldn't make Josiah better, but all those tears were taking a toll on me. Not that his disease isn't saddening, but they do more for him here than we could do for him. I try to live in the moment with Josiah and consider each day a gift. So, I joined a gym and changed my diet!" she said with her hands in the air as she did a 360-degree twirl showing me the new Shirley. "And, that motivated Will to get his hip replaced just before last winter. We walk three miles together most days."

"That's great! I'm so happy for you guys! How did the wedding dance go?"

I was interrupted by Kelly making the announcement for everyone to take their seats.

"C'mon, Silver Foxy," Will said to Shirley, "we'll all catch up after dinner."

"Silver Foxy?" I said.

Shirley rolled her eyes but was clearly loving it when Will said, "Oh, yeaahhh!"

***

We were looking for our table when Maggie saw us.

"Hi, Sweetie," she said to Mom.

306

"Hi," Mom said back as she hugged her.

"Your mom is doing great here! We love her, and your seats are right there," she said, pointing to a table just to our right. "Hope you don't mind, I put Sheriff with you."

"No problem at all," I said.

"Look, look," Sheriff said to Maggie as he pointed to his badge.

Maggie inspected the badge, "That's great! So glad you found it!"

***

We sat down at the end of our empty table. I had Jim lean over to read the name tag.

"Shelley's crew," he said.

"Must be they're running late," I answered.

I was facing the door that entered the courtyard when Shelley appeared. When I saw them, I winced, which Jim noticed.

"What's the matter?" he asked me.

"Shelley and Kathleen are on the way. Look for yourself."

Jim turned to see Shelley holding Kathleen's hand as they came down the walkway. Kathleen's other hand held "the baby." Usually, she had the baby cuddled up, but now she had the doll by one hand and swung it as she shuffled along. She had that "vacant" look dementia patients get. To me, it always looked like the person was totally lost and afraid and needed someone to guide them. I've seen that look when a person with dementia is out of their familiar element. They clench their caregiver's hand tightly while their eyes try to connect to their mind and process everything. They no longer understand the world and become fearful. The caregiver is their lifeline.

"Oh, geez," Jim said as he turned back. "She's got "the look." Where's Bob, I wonder?"

I stood up and waved, trying to get Shelley's attention. When she finally saw me, her mouth dropped, and she put her free hand over it. I smiled and pointed to the empty chairs signaling to her that these were their seats. When they got to the table, she hugged Jim and me.

"I can't believe it. What are you doing here?"

I looked down at Mom, who was chatting with Sheriff. "Meet my mom."

"Oh, no. You've got to be kidding. One was enough; I can't imagine three. I'm so sorry, you guys."

"Yeah, well, there's nothing we can do about it," I said as we all took our seats.

"Lotta empty seats at our table," I said.

"My siblings will be here after they get out of work."

With a low voice, I said, "Should I ask about Dad?"

"His heart finally gave out in February."

"We're sorry to hear that, Shelley," Jim said, offering our condolences.

"I know he had a bad heart, but I wonder how much heart-break played into it with Mom…I guess we'll never know. We took Mom to the funeral, but she didn't really understand. She's getting worse. Sunset can't be far. I'm praying the good Lord takes her before then."

"I hear you. I've prayed that prayer many times myself."

***

Our table got called for the buffet line, and I watched as Mom worked the crowd. She was always a people person, and she was definitely in her element. One resident saw her and yelled to her. Mom turned to wave back and blow kisses. Jim and I laughed and shook our heads.

"Maybe I should have put her in sooner," I said to Jim.

"I dunno. It's always so hard to tell."

We got our food, and on the way back to the table, Mom was still saying hello to people and offering to get them drinks. Maggie intervened, telling Mom it was time for her to sit and enjoy her family.

"But she has a cane. I can get her a soda," Mom protested.

I jumped in, "Mom, it's okay. See that person in the red shirt?" I said, pointing to some random guy in the food line.

"Uh-huh."

"That's her son. He's taking care of her."

"Ohhh...okay."

Maggie looked at me with a huge smile and shook her head.

"Three times through this crap," I said. "Learn from the master!"

We both laughed as I directed Mom back to the table.

Dinner finished, and the Music Man was now taking requests. Shelley's family showed up, so Jim, Shelley, and I decided to chat with the Morrises, Randy, and Val.

"What about Mom?" Jim asked me.

"You're kidding, right? Look at her."

The Music Man started by getting the crowd to clap as he was playing John Denver's "Thank God I'm a Country Boy." Mom was clapping along, and Mike just happened to be passing out ice cream sandwiches.

"My favorite dance partner!" Mom exclaimed, and the two were in the middle of the tent dancing while everyone clapped.

We sat down at the table with the gang.

"Your mom's a trip!" Randy said to us. "She seems like she's doing alright here."

"They tell me she's doing great, but that doesn't mean I still don't get the crying 'take-me-home' calls. But at least I know that by the time she hangs up the phone, she's moved onto the next activity and forgotten about home."

Josiah got up and cut in on Mike. We were all laughing.

Mike turned to all of us and said, "I've been dissed!"

The crowd laughed as he continued on his ice cream route.

***

"So, catch us up!" I said to everyone. "Obviously, you're all still here. How's Pete doing? Sad he wasn't at the door today."

Val answered, "He's slowing down. He doesn't talk as much as he used to, and he stays in his room more and participates in activities less."

I looked at Pete and noticed our impeccably groomed and dressed maître d' was unshaven and sporting a sweatshirt. No more ties with matching pocket squares. He was becoming distant.

I turned to the Morris family. "When we left last year, Josiah was practicing for the father-daughter wedding dance. How'd it go?"

Will laughed, "Now you've done it," he said, his slight Alabama accent sneaking in. "Now you're gonna have to watch the video. See? Miss Foxy is already scrolling through her phone for it."

"Oh, Will, you hush! I've got momma and grandmomma privileges right now!"

Jim and I watched as Josiah and Trinity danced to "The Sound of Philadelphia."

"He did great!" I said.

"It didn't go exactly as we practiced, but I knew it wouldn't. He's such a good dancer that he just went with what moved him, and Trinity had no problems keeping up. He's had that girl movin' to the beat since she could sit up!"

"How are the newlyweds?" Jim asked.

"They'll be here shortly," Shirley answered.

I asked how Josiah was doing overall. Will said he seemed to be holding his own since he came here. I asked Will how he was doing with Josiah's diagnosis.

"Well, you know. Never in a million years would I ever have thought I would be taking care of one of my own children with dementia." He said, shaking his head, "But what can I do? There's no cure. I was angry for a while, but it subsided. You hear the horror stories about places like this, and you don't want to put a loved one in. Honestly, it's worked out, though. He seems happy now, and the staff does a great job."

"They do," I answered.

"Look at this picture!" Shirley said excitedly as she handed me her phone.

"You both hiked this?"

"Yup," Will said with a proud grin. "Shirley convinced me to get my hip takin' care of, and the doctor gave me the okay to go."

I was looking at a picture of Will and Shirley and several grandkids at the summit of Castle Rock that overlooks Blue Mountain Lake in the Adirondacks. It's a moderate hike with a beautiful view.

"Wow! You guys are crushing it!" Jim said.

"And he joined the gym with me," Shirley said excitedly.

Will did an Arnold Schwarzenegger pose, and we all laughed when he told us, "Gotta keep an eye on Miss Silver Foxy ya know!"

"Is this everyone? Are we missing anybody?" I asked.

"Jenny," said Val.

"Oh, that's right! Did Rose Marie die?"

"Not really sure. Jenny moved Rose Marie to Sunset around early March. That's the last we saw of them."

"We must have just missed her," Jim responded.

"What's that mean?" Shelley asked.

"Barb died at the end of February," I said.

No one had realized she passed, and they all offered their condolences to Jim as I hunted Karen down and asked for Jenny's number. She broke away and ran to her office, sure she still had it.

I returned to the table and announced that I had Jenny's number. I called and told her it was annual picnic day and invited her to come down.

"Be there in ten! I can't stay long, though," she told me as I hung up.

* * *

Jenny came through the back door, and once she found us, she ran over and hugged everyone. She told us that her mom wasn't expected to live much longer.

"Where's your dad?" Shelley asked.

"I finally convinced him to spend some of his money and go into one of those ritzy retirement facilities. You know, the ones that have all the amenities, including transportation and trips. He's headed to Casino Niagara in September and is looking at a Caribbean cruise next January."

"Good for him!" Randy said, "How's he doing without your mom?"

"Better than he was. I know he's sad that she doesn't have much time left, but I think he's relieved as well. Plus, I think he likes a woman he dines with but would never disrespect my mother by asking her on a date. We'll see, I guess."

I looked up and saw Trinity and Daryl headed in our direction with a baby in tow.

"Shirley, did they have a baby already?" I asked, completely stunned.

"Sure did! I think she was pregnant shortly after their honeymoon. He's only three weeks old."

"Abby!" Trinity said, surprised to see us.

"Before you ask, that's my mom chatting with your dad."

"Oh, no. I'm sorry."

"There's nothing anybody can do about it. Let's see your little bundle of joy before Great-Grandma scoops him up! What's his name?"

"Daryl Josiah."

"He is adorable! Look at those cheeks and curly black hair!" I said.

Josiah spotted Trinity and made his way over.

"Congratulations, Grandpa!" Jim said to him.

Josiah was beaming as he cradled his infant grandson in his arms. Mom made her way over as well and began fawning over baby Daryl.

***

I sat back and took in the sights for a few minutes. The staff was just about done feeding the latecomers. They were all smiles as they chatted with families and residents. Mike was making his way around the last set of tables with ice cream, and the aides were bussing tables.

I looked down the table at everyone. All the caretakers were laughing and conversing. Val and Randy were like Jim and me;

they had been dealing with this disease for years. The four of us had long since been at a point of just enjoying the moment. We had already learned and accepted the sad reality that this day would be forgotten by tomorrow morning.

Will and Shirley had blossomed in a way I never thought was possible. Josiah was so depressed when he first arrived but had settled into a routine. Will was proud of his Adirondack hike, and Shirley was radiant. Caught in a life they didn't expect, they managed to make the most of it and reinvent themselves in the process. It will get harder as Josiah's disease progresses, but I believe they will get through it. They are a close family, which always helps.

I could tell Shelley was struggling a little. I'm not sure how much time she and her family had had to grieve Bob's death. Caretaking puts a lot of things on hold. Although she didn't believe her mother comprehended her father's death, I bet she did. Even though they forget at times, she told me her mother got considerably worse after the funeral. I noticed Shelley perked up when she saw all of us.

Jenny was also happy to see the gang again. Sunrise is a small, close-knit community with a cozy atmosphere. You don't realize this until you end up with your loved one in the nursing home of Sunset. No doubt that when Jenny saw the stark contrast of rotating aides, baby food, and the hospital-like atmosphere, she understood the caregiver camaraderie she had had here. I know she will be glad when her mom finally passes.

***

La Belle Communauté

I watched the residents as they clapped, swayed, and sang "Sweet Caroline." Neil Diamond and Paul Simon always made me think of Mom, as they were her favorites in her younger years. I watched as she helped Sheriff unwrap his ice cream while the music changed, and they both moved to "Joy to the World" by Three Dog Night. It brought a smile to my face as I remembered dancing with Mom when I was somewhere around four years old and yelling my favorite line about my friend, the bullfrog.

I observed the interactions of the staff—an amazing bunch in their own right. When Joe and Barb moved to Sunset, they visited them on their own time. The staff also attended their funeral Masses, as well as the funerals of many other former residents. I've watched them as they laughed and played with residents when they were happy and comforted them with hugs when they were sad and scared. They feed, clothe, bathe, and change diapers along with a hundred other little things every day. These are all things families can no longer do as the disease progresses. Their care allows the rest of us to enjoy the time spent with our loved ones instead of being constantly concerned with their well-being. In that moment, I realized Jean-Pierre was right. It really is The Beautiful Community. I wouldn't wish dementia on anyone, but I can honestly say I've met amazing people along the way.

"What are you smiling about?" Jim asked me.

"Just thinking…how does a bullfrog become a friend and help drink wine?"

"Drugs, Abby. Lots of 1970s drugs!"

We both laughed.

***

316

I got up and went over to the buffet line.

"Kelly, can I borrow this for a second?" I said, pointing to a cheap plastic megaphone she used to make announcements across the length of the tent.

"Help yourself."

We were seated near the front corner of the tent. I pulled a chair back, and as the Music Man ended his song, I climbed onto it and gave a loud whistle with my fingers in my mouth. The hustle, bustle, and conversations came to a dead stop.

"Hello everyone!" I yelled into the little megaphone, "I'm Abby Preston, and my mom is a resident here. I see a lot of new faces that weren't here at last year's picnic. For the past several years, we were greeted at the front door by an amazing Frenchman named Jean-Pierre. This year he was unable to fulfill his usual duty, and quite honestly, we missed him! You've probably heard Sunrise is nicknamed La Belle. It's short for La Belle Communauté, and Jean-Pierre is the one who rebranded this place!" I looked at Pete to see a faint smile begin to form. "Any chance you could welcome us, Jean-Pierre?"

He slowly stood up, and I got off my chair and held the megaphone for him. I think he surprised Val and Randy when he loudly said, "Monsieur et Madame. Bon après-midi! Bienvenue à La Belle Communauté!" as he raised his hands in the air.

He was met with clapping and shouting. He took his seat with a giant smile that filled his face.

I returned to my post on the chair and continued, "If you don't know, Jean-Pierre said, 'Sir and Madam. Good Afternoon! Welcome to The Beautiful Community!' Now I know we'd all rather be anywhere but here, and it may not seem that beautiful, but I'm gonna share some short and friendly advice. My husband's parents came here eight years ago. Both had the disease, and both have died. This year I moved my mother in. It kind of makes us the experts around here!" I heard the quiet groans of the crowd when they realized we have had three parents live here. "Make friends with other families at the family functions. It just makes life here more fun! Residents come and go. Sometimes they spend several years here; other times, it's only a few short months. I can guarantee you that some families you see here today will not be at the Christmas party. It's just the way it goes, but make new friends anyway! Let go of your guilt! It's a hard decision to move someone in here, and your loved one will lay a guilt trip on you. Check with their caseworker. They are probably having a great time but want you to feel bad. It's just like having a teenager sometimes!"

I saw faces in the crowd nodding in agreement while a lightbulb came on for others.

"Enjoy the moment and fight the urge to lament over the fact that your family member won't remember the time you are with them. YOU will remember the time, so take pictures, make videos and have fun! You'll know you did your best! Last thing, don't beat up the workers here! In the eight years we've been here, I've only made one complaint. We've all worked, and all of us have had at least one terrible coworker. This place is no different. Every once in a while, someone will suck, but don't be nasty. We all have bad days, and these guys are doing a job we could no longer do ourselves. If it were easy, our loved ones would be home with us. So let's have a round of applause for the amazing staff here at La Belle: Kelly the administrator, Maggie the head of recreation, along with her staff, Mike and his maintenance crew, the caseworkers, nurses, aides, and food service workers!"

Everyone clapped and shouted for them.

"Thank you for all you guys do! I'm getting off my soapbox now!" Everyone laughed as I jumped down.

The Music Man was taking requests when Josiah started singing TSOP again.

"That one's a little hard to play on acoustic guitar! Let me see," Music Man said as he fiddled with his phone. "Just for you, Josiah, I pulled it up on my phone, and I'm gonna see if it runs through my PA system."

It worked. As soon as the music started, Josiah turned to Trinity and said, "C'mon, baby girl! Disco dance line!"

Trinity handed little Daryl off to big Daryl and started dancing with her father. Mom was dancing by herself when Mike came alongside her and took her hand. Will and Silver Foxy found their place in line, as did Val and Randy.

'C'mon Jimmy, you cavone! Break out some chest hair, and let's get in line!" I said to him.

Making up for his lack of rhythm, Jim was pretty funny when he took the iconic John Travolta *Saturday Night Fever* pose and hopped down the aisle while holding the pose. I danced around him.

Shelley and Jenny decided to team up and disco down.

After we all took our turn, we crashed back at the table. I turned to see that Josiah had Trinity by one hand and was pulling family members up with his other hand. They obliged, but then again, it was hard to resist Josiah's charm.

As the song continued, the rest of us decided that we wanted to get together outside of La Belle with a monthly dinner or breakfast. Jenny had to leave but told me she was definitely in. So was everyone else.

We had several family members come up and begin asking us questions. We heard the familiar: guilt, depression, and the general symptoms of burnout. Shelley offered to start a "La Belle" social media page. Val thanked me for having Pete welcome everyone. Will and Shirley thanked us both for helping them get through their guilt, and the staff thanked us for recognizing them.

***

The festivities were wrapping up, and I suggested to Mom that we head back to her apartment. As she turned toward the door, the flowers caught her eye.

"Oh, Honey. I want to show you the garden."

"Okay, Mom."

We made our way over to a long cut-flower garden that was placed between the sidewalk and the building.

"Isn't it beautiful, Honey?"

"It sure is, Mom."

We walked along the garden as Mom fussed over the multi-colored zinnias with their deep orange, red, and purple heads now in full bloom. They were one of her favorites. Shades of pink and white cosmos swayed in the light evening breeze while gladiolas were emerging. Vibrant patches of dwarf sunflowers were beginning their show in cherry, yellow, and two-tone yellows with bronze. They are my personal favorite. Blue spikes of delphiniums and the bold colors of German statices were in the mix. The front of the bed along the walk was filled with Barb's favorite, gerbera daisies.

I purposefully designed the beds with a path at four-foot intervals. The path ran from the walk to the building creating continuous beds that were three by four feet. This allowed the residents to step between the beds and cut the flowers without tripping. Each bed was exactly the same, with fifteen beds total. Mom had no idea I designed and installed the soil last summer. Sapphire donated the time and materials to build the beds. We decided we would provide flowers every spring, and Maggie made it into an activity with residents. Those who were able helped with the planting while others sipped drinks and watered. Now it was harvest time, and it was a big hit.

Mom stopped us in front of a plaque.

"Joe and Barb's Place," Mom read to us, "I wonder who they were?"

"Probably a nice couple with three sons," Jim responded.

"Do you think maybe they lived here?" Mom asked.

Jim answered her, "I'm pretty sure they did."

***

We walked Mom back to her room. I watched as she said goodnight to everyone we passed. She still hadn't lost her love for people. She unlocked her apartment and insisted we wait a minute.

We took our seats in the two chairs in her tiny living area as she disappeared into the bedroom. I looked at the pictures that were looking back at me from the walls and the register. The past. A life that once was but is no longer remembered.

La Belle Communauté

Mom returned from her bedroom with a twenty-dollar bill, insisting that we take it. A losing argument ensued with me putting the bill in my pocket. I watched as she hugged Jim and said, "You know you're my favorite son-in-law. Love you, Jim." The present. A brain that shrank a little more today. Tomorrow, she will not remember today, but she is happy, and in some ways, I still see "Mom."

She hugged me, "I love you, Honey. I miss not seeing you every day."

"I know, Mom. It's hard. I love you too," I said as I hugged her.

As I embraced her, I looked out her window to see the fifteen-story nursing home that dominated the skyline two blocks away. Its ominous silhouette loomed large against the sky as it forecast the future.

Sunset was on the horizon.

Epilogue

I awoke at six the next morning. Unable to get back to sleep, I decided to head downstairs for a cup of coffee. I poured my cream and headed for the overhang that sheltered part of our patio. Rain was just starting to fall as I sat down and tucked my feet under me.

I began thinking about the last decade of our lives. Parental illnesses have ruled it, and to some extent, we are still ruled by it, but the worst is over. Mom's house sold in two days, with the closing scheduled for late September. I met with Steve and Jay and will be headed back to work full-time next week. My thoughts drifted to those who don't have the luxury of flexible work with no cut in pay. I understand I am a rarity. What happens to those who don't have those resources? Caretaking is hard enough. The stress spills into family life, and the financial burden just adds to an already difficult situation.

According to the Alzheimer's Association, in 2020 there were five million Americans living with the disease. There are more than sixteen million unpaid caregivers who provide more than 18.6 billion hours of care. The value of that care is 244 billion dollars. They project fourteen million will be living with the disease by 2050. Who will take care of everyone?

It's a brutal disease. Frustration and exhaustion for caregivers is astronomical. I have no statistics to back up that claim, I just know we've lived it, and those we've met will tell you the same story. We try not to complain too much, and we appreciate when we're asked about our loved one at a social event, but we don't want to relive the trying weeks that have just passed. We'll probably just say they're "okay," or "as well as they could be." Trust me, depending on how the week went, a social event is the last place we want to be. It's not that we don't want to have fun and socialize, but we're too mentally and physically worn-out to enjoy it as much as we could. Sometimes it's just one more item on our "to-do" list.

We won't tell you about the double duty of taking care of two houses; the amount of time we spent on the phone trying to untangle some random mess our loved one made with the cable company; or how they've lost their toothbrush for the twentieth time, only this time we can't find it, so we have to make a trip to the drugstore. Or that the trip was at nine-thirty at night when we were already dressed for bed.

We won't tell you how we cringe when the phone rings from the memory care facility, fearing Mom has to make a trip to the hospital...again. Or about when she did have to go, and all the hours that we spent there trying to understand what was wrong and correcting the incorrect information Mom gave to the staff.

We won't tell you how heartbreaking the phone calls we got this week were. You know, the ones where Mom is crying because she wants to go home. Or the others where she informed me she's in pain and wants to die and is insistent I bring her a pill so she can end it all.

We won't tell our siblings how much we resent being the primary caregiver. While their lives seem to go on, ours is in a constant state of flux. And those trips to the hospital that we made? They've interrupted dinner after a long day's work, our plans for cross-country skiing, a dinner planned with friends, the one day of relaxation we get each week, and they've sent us to work on only a couple hours sleep. We love to hear how great your weekend went after we were forced to give up ours yet again.

How about all those doctor appointments, facility tours, home visits, and the unending paperwork that needs to be done? Guess who has to use their vacation days, personal business days, and days off to take them? That's on top of trips to the grocery store, drug store, and department store, as well as paying their bills and helping with chores.

How about phone calls from loved ones when they can't work the phone, or the TV, or the furnace? Guess who had to stop what they were doing to fix that?

And then there's the people who've taken lower-paying jobs and gone part-time in order to caretake. They've given up money on a weekly, monthly, and yearly basis. What about the under-funding of *their* retirement accounts?

Whose car is racking up all the miles and taking all the wear and tear, and who's paying for all the gas?

But no one really thinks of all that—and we won't tell them.

***

The whole experience has changed me. Sometimes I don't know if the changes are good or bad, but you can't come out unchanged.

I already liked the geriatric crowd. Longevity runs in my family, and Jeff and I were around great aunts and uncles who lived into their nineties. I think it left me with more appreciation and patience for them. It's also made me realize how short life really is. Even if you live to ninety, we just aren't here that long. So quit treating each other badly. It'll be over before you know it.

I now have very little patience to answer the same question for healthy people who want to be helpless people. I've sent group texts with the time, date, and address, only to receive texts a week later asking me what time. It takes every ounce of strength I have to not rip the person's head off. I'd really like to text back and tell them to quit being helpless and scroll back through their texts! It's not that hard! Your brain works, so stop being lazy and FIGURE IT OUT! It may sound strange since you haven't been there, but your laziness is causing me to answer the same question over and over. I have spent almost ten years answering hundreds of the same questions multiple times. I have explained and re-explained things more times than I can count, trying to get a disintegrating brain to comprehend what I'm telling it—and you can't be bothered to look through your texts to see what time you're supposed to be somewhere?

A decade of Alzheimer's has created a keenness in spotting the disease in others. I can tell if someone simply forgot, as we all do on occasion, or if something else is going on. I'm not particularly fond of this newfound talent.

The back door opened, and Jim interrupted my thoughts.

"You're up early."

"Yeah. I woke up at five and couldn't get back to sleep, so I thought I'd listen to the rain."

"With all the activity yesterday, I never found out how your meeting with Steve went. Headed back to Sapphire anytime soon?"

"Next week, I think. He told me I could take another week or two off, but I think I'm ready for some routine."

"I guess I can understand that. These last couple years have been the worst."

"That's no lie."

"So," Jim continued, "I also talked to Steve yesterday."

"For what?" I asked.

"Calm down, Miss Snotty-Pants. I asked him if it was okay to surprise you."

"Well, that's always okay, but why would you need Steve's permission for that?"

"Maybe you'll need some more time off for my surprise," he said as he handed me a 9" x 11" envelope. "I'm taking you to your favorite vacation spot."

I gave him a skeptical look as I set down my coffee and took the envelope, "I have a favorite spot?" I asked as I pulled out a brochure.

Before I had a chance to read it, he answered, "Yes. The beach is your favorite spot. Not thinking you cared what beach, I picked Martha's Vineyard."

I looked down at the reservations. "This will be amazing!" I said as I hugged him.

La Belle Communauté

"I told Steve to ignore your request to come back, and I would return you in a week. I also talked to Karen at La Belle. They've agreed to deal with Mom if anything happens while we're gone."

"Deal with Mom? You mean keep her on ice if she dies while we're away?"

"Honestly, Abby. Try a little compassion."

"You know I'm kidding...sort of," I said with a smile.

"Truth be known, I told her to check your mom's 'expiration date,' and if anything happened while we were gone, we'd be sure to give La Belle credit when we returned. I also told her not to call us."

"I don't think they can do that, from a legal standpoint."

"I called Jeff and asked him to take the calls. He said he'd do one better and bring the family up for ten days. I told him they could stay here."

"You're the best!"

"That's true. I am. And the best has to finish getting ready for work."

I couldn't wait for an uninterrupted week of sun and sand. There is nothing I like more than early morning walks looking for shells along the beach before the world wakes up.

As Jim returned to the house, I thought about what I'd given up. As time went on and the disease progressed, I started to lose myself. I hadn't realized that I was no longer involved in the things I loved to do. I love my vegetable garden, which has been in disarray for a few seasons. I love to invite people for dinner at our cobblestone oasis and we haven't done that for almost two years. I've been too tired to entertain, and I really missed it.

My phone went off, and I looked down to see Silver Foxy had sent a group text with dates for a get-together.

I responded, "If u can wait 2 wks, I would luv for everyone to come here for dinner."

Within ten minutes, all the parties agreed.

"Nice," I said out loud.

I've often wondered what the point of all this was. Why? Why three out of four parents? I would see the obituaries of those who were once residents at La Belle. The disease took them fast, and sometimes it made me almost jealous. We've ridden this thing all the way to the ground with Barb and Joe both dying of dementia. Now it appears that Mom is headed for the same fate. It's so hard to watch them suffer, and the family grieves more, as they are gone long before they die.

I've spent a lot of time talking with family members at La Belle, as well as those who haven't reached the assisted living stage. I've watched as they go through the various stages of anger, sadness, depression, and guilt. I've tried to get them to the point of acceptance and joy in the moment. Maybe that is the point— to help others. I know Mom would say that; it was part of her favorite psalm and just the way she is.

Mom lived with lupus, which limited many of her activities, yet she got up every morning with a smile on her face, ready to meet the new day. She never seemed bitter about what she couldn't do but instead focused on what she could do. Lupus is a disease that waxes and wanes; some days are worse than others, and with a compromised immune system, she was sick more than average.

"Abby," she told me when I was about sixteen, "there are valleys in life. We are not meant to camp there; we are meant to pass through them."

The rain was letting up, and the sun was peeking through. A rainbow flashed its colors across the gray backdrop.

I smiled and softly said, "Sorry, Mom. I wish things were different, but they aren't. I love you, and I did the best I could."

I finished the last sip of coffee and headed inside, ready to start a new day.

Psalm 84:5-7

Blessed are those whose strength is in you,
whose hearts are set on pilgrimage.

As they pass through the Valley of Baca (Weeping),
they make it a place of springs;
the autumn rains also cover it with pools
They go from strength to strength,
till each appears before God in Zion.

About the Author

Deb Procopio, a Central New York native and first-time author, is a humorous storyteller who has spent the last ten years caring for family members with dementia. Deb has an AAS in horticulture and has worked in landscaping and perennial gardening for over twenty years.

Deb has recently embarked on developing a YouTube channel called Life Under Deborah's Palm. A portion of the video series addresses things that she and her husband wish someone told them about caring for people with dementia. Often, caregivers are left to muddle their way through a system that can be difficult, all while navigating a disease that takes unexpected twists and turns down a long road. Life Under Deborah's Palm vlog gives insight into things most people aren't told so that those who have been thrown into that role won't have to learn the hard way.

When Deb is not writing, she is busy landscaping, gardening vegetables and perennials, and blankly staring at her physics-teacher husband as he attempts to explain to her that the recent discovery of gravity waves proves Einstein's 1916 general theory of relativity was correct.

Deb and her husband also spend their time attempting to tame a unit of energy named Joule, a German shorthaired pointer/Labrador mix. Joule has chewed a riding lawn mower to pieces, pulled wiring apart, and played "chase" around the dining room table with a butcher knife. The Procopios fear that one day the dog will completely rule their house.

Deb can be contacted at lifeunderdeborahspalm@gmail.com or at www.lifeunderdeborahspalm.com.

Made in the USA
Coppell, TX
26 May 2023

17352142R00199